I0612120

The Risen Sun

Max Anderson Mysteries, Volume 4

Hayden Trenholm

Published by House of Straw Press, 2025.

THE RISEN SUN

First edition. January 20, 2025.

ISBN: 978-1927881682

Written by Hayden Trenholm.

Also by Hayden Trenholm

Max Anderson Mysteries
In the Shadow of Versailles
By Dawn's Early Light
The Glare of Truth
The Risen Sun

Standalone
Let Me Gather My Thoughts

Watch for more at https://www.haydentrenholm.com/.

This book is dedicated to Paris, city of light

Cover Illustration by Jean-Philippe Fourier

Chapter 1 Monday, April 30th, 1923

"The police put it off as a chance drowning or a drunken accident but I know Walter was murdered."

The young woman, who had burst into Max's office above Chez Jake, had started speaking as soon as he lifted his head to look at her. She was attractive in that American fresh-faced way, her hair in the now-fashionable bob, her cloche hat unabashedly clutched in both hands. Her eyes were red and skin blotchy from crying. Her lower lip trembled and Max thought she would cry again, but she held off.

"What makes you think that, Miss...?"

"Miller, Helen Miller. I just know. I feel it inside me."

Max wondered how one could be so certain about an event that they already said they hadn't witnessed, but his interest was piqued. He hadn't had a stimulating case since the murder of Count Remy de Montreux the previous year, or any case at all for the last three months.

"Perhaps you should sit down and give me the details, while we have lunch." Max lifted the receiver of his phone and called down to the kitchen. It was early yet but he had skipped breakfast and he listened better on a full stomach. She nodded her agreement and took off her jacket and hung it on the coat rack near the door. The wide-lapeled garment was new and looked expensive as did the silk blouse beneath it. Its scoop collar showed off her long slender neck and the string of dark beads around it.

He directed the young woman to take a seat at the small table Jacqui had bought him for Christmas and took the chair opposite. A few minutes later, a waiter arrived with a plate of sandwiches and a demi-liter of white wine.

Helen looked dubious but selected a ham and Gruyère on white and allowed Max to pour her a small glass of the Sauterne. Max selected a poboy with roast beef, fried shrimp, Emmental, tomatoes, pickles and hot sauce in a baguette. Jake had recently introduced the Louisiana classic to the menu and it had proved popular with the local factory workers that made up much of the lunch clientele these days.

The food seemed to do the young woman good and the threat of further tears receded. Max took the brief interval while they ate to complete his examination of his prospective client. Her hands were delicate and adorned with several rings—though none on the third finger of her left hand. Her posture was erect and there was a sense of athleticism about the way she held herself.

"Perhaps we can start with a few basic facts, Walter's last name, your relationship to him, and the circumstances of his death?"

"Walter Gladstone was from Chicago though he has been living in Paris for more than a year. He is working on a novel though I'm not sure how it is... was progressing." She hesitated for a moment, her hand to her mouth. Max refilled her glass and she took a sip before continuing. "I suppose I'll have to get used to referring to Walter in the past tense."

"Were the two of you close?'

"If you mean, were we romantically involved, no. I came to Paris a couple of months ago when my fiancé died in a car accident. I wasn't ready to move on and Walter was one of the few men I met here who understood that. He was very kind. He was also funny and entertaining to be with, very involved in the local artistic community, especially the avant-garde theatre. He was a good distraction. I suppose I did care for him and something might have come of it but..." Her eyes glistened and she took a bigger sip of the wine to steady herself.

"You say the police mentioned drowning?"

"Walter's body was found face down in the lake in Parc Montsouris. Do you know it?"

Max shook his head. Though he had heard of the place—Jacqui had mentioned it as a possible picnic destination—he had never been there. It was somewhere in the south of the city, a part of Paris he had seldom visited.

"A passerby noticed it in the rushes by the shore just after noon yesterday. The police said he had been in the water since sometime the night before. He had been seen in a bar not far from the park. Hence, the conclusion of 'drunken accident.' I tried to tell them that Walter barely touched alcohol and, in the three months I had known him, I had never seen him drunk. But the Captain in charge wouldn't listen."

"His name wasn't Fontaine, was it?" Max's opinion of Marcel Fontaine had risen over the last few years of working with him, in an "unofficial" capacity, of course, but the man was still prone to dismiss cases unlikely to lead to plaudits from above. The death of an American writer in easily explainable circumstances would qualify as unimportant in Fontaine's eyes. If he was to take on this case, the Captain was more likely to be a hinderance than a help.

"No, something like DesChamps or DuChamp. My French is not very good and he spoke quickly. He seemed very sure of himself."

Not Fontaine but someone in the same style. If the head of the homicide division saw this newcomer as a rival, Max might find him a help after all. The Prefecture would be his first stop, if only to make sure Fontaine knew he was back in the field.

"Have arrangements been made for burial?"

"No, we're still trying to track down his family—he has no-one in Paris. One of the other writers is from Chicago, he's sent a cable off to his father to see if he can help track them down. He's a doctor and well connected in the city."

The morgue would be his second stop. If the body was still on ice there, it would be worth examining it to see if the police missed anything. After a dozen or more hours in water, there wouldn't be much to see, but any clue was useful. The French had a funny attitude toward the dead; if no one had come forward to identify Gladstone, the body would have been displayed in a window in the hope someone would come forward. The viewing of the corpses was a bizarre pastime, often involving entire families.

"I..." Helen hesitated. "I told the Captain I was Walter's cousin. Not true, of course, but I maintained the fiction even after the police had shown little interest. I thought it would be helpful if I was able to engage a detective." Max nodded his appreciation. It was clever of her to do so and would certainly aid the investigation.

"What led you to me?" Max didn't particularly advertise his services. It kept away the divorce cases and business was sufficiently good based on the referrals of happy clients or, occasionally, the Prefecture itself.

"The oddest thing. I was meeting someone in Gare du Nord last evening. I must have looked distraught because this elderly porter asked me what was wrong. I blurted out my story and he suggested I come here today." Max smiled. His old friend, Henri, loved a good mystery and a damsel in distress about a dead man in a lake would be as good as it got. After his visits to the Prefecture and the morgue, he would drop by Le Coq Bleu to see what the occasional porter and full-time gossip had to say on the matter.

He agreed to take the case and explained his rates: expenses plus a fee if he closed the case. Helen handed over a wad of francs –2200 as it turned out—and left her card with a contact address and a café, La Closerie des Lilas, where the Chicago writer, a man named Hemingstein, could generally be found.

FONTAINE WASN'T AT his office when Max arrived on L'Ile de France but Ferdinand LePêcheur was. Now a senior sergeant, LePêcheur had an office of his own and was always willing to spend a few minutes with Max, no matter how heavy his own caseload was.

"Andre Duchamps just transferred here from Brittainy. Very ambitious but not what I would call rigorous. You'll be happy to know Captain Fontaine doesn't care for him, so if Duchamps gives you a problem, I think you can rely on him to smooth the way."

LePêcheur recovered the file on Gladstone's death. It was marked "CLOSED" and the contents gave little reason why it shouldn't be. The captain's report was brief, noting the location where the body was found, a dozen metres from the small Theatre Guignol, and concluding with: "an accidental drowning after a night of debauchery." It listed Helen Miller as his cousin and main contact regarding disposal of the body. It mentioned the Chicagoan, though not his name, but provided an address on Rue Jacob where he lived. *An odd coincidence*, thought Max, *it's only a few doors from our new apartment.*

He obtained Gladstone's address from the official registry and thanked LePêcheur before making his way to the nearby morgue. He showed Helen's card and a hundred franc note and was given access to Gladstone's body. The smell of disinfectant barely covered the stench of death; the body had begun its decomposition despite the cold storage.

Gladstone had been tall but slim, almost to the point of emaciation. Max wondered if he was a heroin addict but there were no marks of needle use, though he supposed he might have been an habitue of opium dens and their languorous odours. His features were fine, almost feminine, with high cheekbones and a full mouth, bleached pale now by death and his watery grave. He wore his hair long, though not excessively so. His fingers did not show the indentations left by rings but there was a lighter band of skin around his left wrist indicating a watch. Max assumed it was in his personal effects, which he would examine before he left.

The face and body were unmarked, no bruises, scrapes or cuts and the two visible scars were old, one from an appendix operation and the other, a zig-zag cut on his left breast. He might well have fallen in the lake after drinking and, if it were not for Helen's utter conviction that he had not, Max might have considered the case settled and returned her money.

His intuition told him the man had been helped to his final resting place. He reached around to the back of Gladstone's head, combing through the tangled hair until he found what he was looking for, a small puncture wound at the base of the skull, something that might have been made by a very thin blade or perhaps an icepick. Any blood would have been washed away in the lake and the wound was small enough to escape attention if the examination had been cursory. The police Captain's conclusion would have been sufficient to persuade an over-worked coroner to leave well enough alone.

Helen was right. Gladstone had been murdered and whoever had done it had made sure to leave as few traces as possible. Somewhere in Parc Montsouris, he had been attacked from behind and his body thrown into the reeds at one end of the lake. He would need to examine the area, later today or first thing in the morning, before what little evidence of the crime disappeared.

Gladstone's effects revealed few salient clues. His wallet had over a thousand francs and nearly fifty American dollars so robbery had not been a motive for his murder. Most of the papers had been washed clean by the water, though Max recognized the requisite

Prefecture identification that listed his name and local address, though the latter was illegible. Two keys on a ring likely provided access to his lodgings and Max surreptitiously pocketed them for later use. A silver cigarette case with the monogram WG contained a small lighter and a few soggy cigarettes. A few coins, a souvenir replica of the Eiffel Tower, a notebook, with only a few markings still visible, and a pencil made up the remainder of the things found on his body. Max replaced everything into the envelope provided and passed it back to the bored attendant.

Max returned briefly to the Prefecture to inform LePêcheur of his discovery. The sergeant frowned but he flipped through the case file and extracted one of several photographs of the dead man "That should help. I'll do what else I can but, honestly, I'm up for a promotion and can't afford to rock the boat too much." He promised to inform Fontaine of the turn of events. "But don't expect him to do much about it, either. He's dealing with the murder of a Senator and has bigger fish to catch. Come back when you have someone we can arrest and send to the guillotine."

MAX STOPPED FOR A COFFEE at the café Helen had mentioned but no one seemed to know a writer named Hemingstein, though a few grinned when he asked, as if it were a joke he didn't quite understand. He wrote a few notes in his journal, mostly listing people it would be worth talking to, Ginger Buchan at the USA Embassy and Pierre Delacroix, a reporter and social gadfly, who knew a lot about the local arts scene, both French and ex-patriate. He didn't approve of Delacroix's lifestyle but his years in Paris had softened his small-town moralism enough that he could see the man's worth.

The trip to Parc Montsouris proved fruitless. He found the spot where Gladstone had been discovered but the recovery of the body had obliterated any footprints or other clues. The park itself wasn't large and could be circumnavigated in less than an hour. The pathways past the open lawns were narrow but pretty with rich green foliage and the promise of later flowers. A small waterfall tinkled in the background and, in one small clearing, he interrupted a couple courting on a small stone bench. However, there was nothing of note along the few paths near the area where the body was found. Jacqui was right; it would make a nice spot for a picnic, though not until after the memory of murder had been erased.

An elevated train ran through the middle of the grounds and a restaurant stood on the south side of the lake. Close to it, a small bandstand was surrounded by several rows of folding chairs. A notice was posted announcing a series of concerts for the next day in celebration of International Labour Day. Though the poster didn't mention it, Max knew there were bound to be numerous speeches as well and he hoped this case didn't require him to return to the park before Wednesday.

Farther along the lake, near the north end of the park, a small green building with a miniature proscenium arch, a bright red curtain drawn across the stage, proclaimed itself to be the Theatre Guignol. It was, Max noted with bemusement, a stage for marionettes. Gladstone was fascinated by a puppet show? That hardly seemed avant-garde but there had to be something more to it than that. Perhaps Delacroix could shed light on the subject.

Jacqui had told him she had to work late—she had recently been hired as costuming assistant at the Grand Opera—so he decided to head for Le Coq Bleu on the other side of the city. The train took him to Gare du Nord where he switched to the Metro, disembarking at Pigalle. The climb up Rue Drevet, the street punctuated by a set of connecting stairs, left him slightly breathless. Time to return to Kid O'Brien's gym, he thought.

Le Coq Bleu had grown considerably since he had first joined Havel Barsani for a drink at one of the back tables in late 1918. Yesim had first added a row of tables along the street and then, in 1921, had persuaded Max to purchase the closed café next door so he could expand and turn the establishment from a bar that served food into a restaurant that served drinks. A reasonable crowd for a Monday night was keeping Henri and his business partner, Josette, busy serving tables both inside and outside. Henri and Josette handled the food side of the operation while Yesim was happy to stand behind the bar and glare at customers while serving drinks.

Max took his usual seat at the end of the zinc bar and nodded at Yesim when he held up a bottle of Bordeaux. A glass of deep red wine quickly appeared and Max asked for the *plat du jour* without asking what it was. Josette seldom disappointed in her selection of menu. A soupe au pistou, a creamy vegetable concoction with squash, beans, potato and white rice, was followed by lamb chops flavoured with Dijon and tarragon and served with roasted potatoes and carrots. By the time Max had finished his second glass of wine and Josette had delivered a lemon meringue flavored with orange liquor, the crowd had thinned and Henri slid onto the stool beside him.

"I suppose I owe you a finder's fee," said Max.

"That young woman from the train station came to see you, then?"

"She did. And once again, the Prefecture let down a foreigner. Her young friend was murdered."

"Fontaine?"

"Captain Fontaine has mended his ways, remember? A new bumbler has just arrived from Brittainy, Captain Andre Duchamps, come to the big city to make his name."

"I've heard that name, but nothing good attached to it." Yesim had delivered a small brandy and Henri paused to savour the aroma before taking a sip. "I only wanted to prove myself useful, Max. You haven't had any assignments for me in a while."

"Cases have been few and far between. You know I value your opinions." Max dropped two hundred francs on the bar. "That's for finding an interesting case for me. I expect I'll have some work for you soon."

Max mostly relied on Alain Laurent to do his leg work. He was clever, eager to please and filled with the energy of youth. Henri was seventy-three now and had visibly slowed in the last year. Max had hoped he was making enough from the restaurant to give up his very occasional shifts at the Gare du Nord, but apparently, he was finding it hard to make ends meet. He would find him something useful to do, something he could succeed at without putting him at risk. He and Yesim were his oldest friends in Paris—and friends didn't let friends down.

Chapter 2 Tuesday, May 1st, 1923

Getting around the city proved difficult as numerous unions had stopped work for the day. Many Metro lines were closed and hundreds of protestors, including Jacqui and some of her anarchist friends, filled the streets. Noisy protests against the French occupation of the Ruhr and the anti-labour policies of Prime Minister Poincare and his Bloc National government led to numerous clashes between demonstrators and police.

Max stuck to the back streets but, even then, his way was often blocked by marchers representing various factions of the left. Black Marias or ambulances, carrying prisoners or the wounded to their respective destinations, were also avoiding the main thoroughfares. It took Max nearly an hour and a half to walk to the American embassy on Rue De Chaillot from his apartment on Rue Jacob, a journey that normally took half that time.

The main gates were closed, guarded by several nervous looking junior aides. If they were armed, their weapons were hidden by their coats and Max wondered how effective they would be if a determined Paris mob decided, for some reason, to storm the embassy. He had been caught in several riots and knew they could turn on a sou.

Max presented his papers at the gate but it was more than ten minutes before permission to enter arrived. He was then escorted by one of the aides to Ginger Buchan's new office on the second floor of the embassy. Even after four years, Max still didn't know what Buchan's job was, but he must have been good at it. This was the third office he had occupied, each one bigger than the last.

Buchan greeted him at the heavy oak door and led him into the wood-paneled room. At one end, under a large bay window, partially covered by heavy brocaded drapes, was a large desk, its surface bare, save for a brass penholder and a neat stack of files in one corner. Buchan gestured to the other end of the room, where a sitting area surrounded a fireplace.

"To what do I owe the pleasure," Ginger asked, once they were settled in wing backed chairs with cups of steaming coffee in their hands.

"I'm looking into the death of Walter Gladstone. Know anything about him?"

"There are lots of Americans in Paris these days. I can't keep track of them all."

"This one was found dead in an artificial lake in Parc Montsouris."

Buchan sat his coffee down on an elegant side table and went to his desk and flipped through the files there. He had put on weight in the three months since Max last had seen him, his waistcoat bulging from the extra pounds. His red hair had thinned to a mere fringe but his mustache had become extravagant, perhaps in compensation for the loss. He selected one of the manila folders and flipped through it.

"The police said he drowned—perhaps assisted by alcohol. Your presence here suggests there is more to it."

"Alcohol didn't shove an icepick into the back of his head. I'm trying to find out who did."

"Any reason the Prefecture isn't investigating?" Buchan glanced up from the file, his expression blank.

Max shrugged. He had no doubt there were plenty of good policemen on the Île de la Cité, he could name a dozen, past and present who did fine work. Their methods were advanced and well-established and, according to Captain Fontaine, often studied by police officers from all over the world, including England and the United States. Yet, the organization often seemed to turn a blind eye to crimes against certain kinds of people, those they considered deviant or, often, those with darker complexions and foreign accents. Still, it was unusual for them to ignore the death of an American citizen.

"None that I've discovered so far but I'm sure something will turn up."

Buchan nodded but stayed near his desk. "There's not much in his file but I'm happy to share what I have. He *is* from Chicago; his father moved there from New York and now owns several small factories making office and household furniture. Nothing on his mother or other family members. It's like they sprang from the brow of Zeus. We don't even have an address for the father but I'm sure one will turn up soon, if the boys in Washington ever get off their duffs."

"Anything since he arrived in Paris.?"

"Not much. He registered at the embassy and I think he picked up his mail here, not uncommon when people don't expect to put down roots. I'm sure he was told to file his address with the Prefecture—you know how they are about aliens wandering about the city. Whether he did or not, you would have to check with their registrar."

"They had on address on file but it dates back over a year so it may not have been accurate. They didn't seem too put out by it," said Max. "I think they cut a little slack for Americans and Brits if they expect they are just passing through."

"So I've heard. We have him on Rue Visconti – that's not far from your new place." It was the same as the address at the Prefecture. He would check with Miller to see if it were still accurate before he dropped by to take a look.

Buchan scribbled the address down on a card and passed it to Max. He glanced at it before tucking it into his jacket pocket. Visconti was only a block over from Jacob. It appeared he might be living in the centre of a writing community without knowing it.

"Gladstone has been in town about 14 months—arriving in the city, according to this, the end of last March. We've had no reports of run-ins with the police or questionable associates but with something like thirty thousand citizens visiting or living within the 20 arrondissements, our staff, that is me and three others, are hard pressed to keep track of miscreants let alone those who stay out of trouble, which is, thankfully, the vast majority." Buchan closed the file and slipped it back into the pile on his desk.

PIERRE DELACROIX, AS usual, proved elusive. Max tried all his regular lunchtime haunts but he had either "not been in for days," "was expected tomorrow," or, in the case of Le Dôme "had only just left in the company of several young men." The latter was delivered with a knowing wink that suggested that he might not be seen again for weeks.

Still, the visits to Le Dôme, La Rotonde, Les Deux Magots and a return visit to La Closerie des Lilas in search of the equally elusive Hemingstein were not without value. Each of them was occupied by tables of young American men and women, some of whom also claimed to be in Paris to pursue a writing career. Several were polishing their craft by working for the several English language papers that published in the city or the British and American wire services. Max thought of his old friend, Erich Harvey, who, in the face of this low-cost competition, had given up his own career in journalism to return to America and live with his brother.

In any case, among their number were several who knew Walter Gladstone. Most had heard of his death but few seemed deeply moved by the loss.

"He was alright at a party," said one young man at Le Dôme, "but I don't think he had much talent. He was one of those chaps who talk a lot about writing but never seem to do any."

"That could be said about a lot of people, Charlie." One of the young women replied. "Talk and drink and gossip are a lot easier than actually making something, don't you think?"

Charlie had blushed and snapped back. "Sleeping with someone who claims to be the next great novelist is even easier, don't *you* think?"

Max wasn't surprised that Charlie got his face slapped but he was a bit shocked when everyone else at the table laughed and another round was ordered. Whatever animosity Charlie had for the young woman was soon washed away with gin.

At La Rotonde, he heard much the same. Gladstone was well known it seemed but more for the generous allowance his father provided and his success with women than for any artistic talent.

"He was a big devotee of Edgar Allen Poe, always going on about how detective stories were the true American literature and how Poe would have been recognized as the greatest writer of the age if not for his premature death."

"Like Walter himself," another piped up, "although he never wrote anything other than a few salacious love letters."

"No," responded a young redhead, whose blushing countenance suggested she had been the recipient of one of the letters. "He was working on a play."

"Yeah, Clairice, a play for a puppet show."

The table erupted in laughter and little else was forthcoming. Still, it did explain Gladstone's interest in the Theatre Guignol.

He had better luck at La Closerie des Lilas. Hemingstein was, apparently a joke name, that the writer used to bond with his friends while keeping away those he didn't care for. One young man—Max wasn't sure which category he fell into—told him Hemingway, the man's real name, could often be found at a club on Boulevard de Raspail which had a boxing ring in the basement. "If you don't find him there, you could look for him over on rue Descartes. I'm not sure of the address but he has a room in an old hotel where he goes to get away from his wife and concentrate on his writing."

"I thought all the American writers did their work in cafés."

"If by work, you mean drinking and bull shitting, you'd be right," he said. "But serious writers have a private place they go—real or imagined—to do the true thing."

It wasn't much, but it was the only lead he had.

HEMINGWAY WAS IN THE ring when Max arrived. He was a big man, a shade over six feet tall with broad shoulders, a barrel chest and muscular arms. His left arm and both of his legs were patterned with scars, similar to those that covered his own body. Hemingway had undoubtedly been wounded in the war. Despite the scarring, which included a nasty rip in his right knee, he moved well in the ring, not exactly graceful but with confidence and deliberation. The man he was sparring with was bigger still but shambled more than danced and it was clear that Hemingway could probably fell him if he had a mind to. Still, he lacked technique—a true amateur like Max but without the hard lessons Kid O'Brien had taught him over the years.

He wondered how he might do against this big American but he had come to talk, not fight, and that test, if it came at all, would have to wait. For now, he was content to observe. He was not alone; a number of men had stopped their own workouts to watch the match and surprisingly, several well-dressed women, Hemingway's wife and her friends, perhaps. One, older than the man in the ring, seemed particularly anxious, her hand rising unbidden to her mouth every time the bigger man landed a blow.

It was a strange scene and Max was reminded of some of the charismatic politicians he had known, like Andre Bucard and Denis Jourdain who drew the eye and held your attention even when you disagreed with their ideas or approach to life. Many of the young men he had spoken to in the cafés had seemed strangely in awe whenever Hemingway was mentioned—though, as far as he could tell, his only success as a writer had been as a freelance journalist for a newspaper.

The bell rang and the two boxers touched gloves to end the bout. The bigger man seemed almost grateful for the opportunity to fight the writer and leaned into him to whisper something in his ear. Hemingway laughed and clapped his gloves together before patting his opponent's shoulder and climbing out of the ring. Despite the sheen of sweat that covered his upper body, the woman, who had been an anxious witness to the fight, threw her arms around him and tilted her face up for a kiss. Hemingway obliged but there was something in the way he moved his face away and ended the embrace that suggested a tension between them. Whatever it was, her response was still tender and she brushed her fingers across an abrasion that had formed beneath his left eye.

Hemingway had stripped off his gloves and accepted a beer from one of his admirers when Max stepped forward.

"Mr. Hemingway?"

The writer turned his gaze in Max's direction, his dark eyes seeming to weigh Max's character and intent before deciding to speak. Hemingway was handsome, though not overly so, with a square visage and a full mouth, partly hidden by a thick dark mustache.

"My friends call me Hem. I won't say what my enemies call me. There are ladies present."

Everyone laughed at that and Max wondered what Ernest Heminway might have done to earn enemies at such a young age.

"My name is Max Anderson. I'm investigating the death of Walter Gladstone."

Hemingway looked puzzled as if he had never heard the name.

"The one who drowned in that park," said one of his friends, a tall older man with a thick head of hair.

"Of course, that lady friend of his—Helen, wasn't it? —asked me to help track down his parents. I sent a telegram to my father, he's a prominent figure in Chicago society, which I'm sure he'll answer soon, though we aren't exactly on speaking terms. Do you get along with your father, Max?"

It was none of his business but Max answered anyway. "My father is dead. I don't have much to do with the rest of my family. Were you acquainted with Mr. Gladstone?"

"He wasn't a friend, if that's what you mean, or an enemy either, for that matter, but I'd seen him around, and spoken to him a few times. As I recall he had asked for an introduction to Gertrude, isn't that right, Ez?"

The older man nodded. "I think you told him he'd have to have something to show her, other than his second-rate charm."

"Yeah, that sounds like me."

Max wondered who this Gertrude was and why a young writer would want to meet her. Then he recalled a meal he had shared with Joseph Asper, the first time they had eaten together, when he pointed out an older woman talking to a, as it turned out, famous artist. All that had registered at the time was the name Gertrude.

"The art collector?"

"More like an artist collector," one of the young men quipped, earning an angry glare from Hemingway.

"She has a regular salon but you only get to go if she sees something in you. Gladstone didn't qualify."

"You said he wasn't your enemy, but did he have enemies?"

"Who doesn't?"

"You remember, don't you, dear? That young man who interrupted you during your chat with Gladstone about Gertrude. He was so angry; I thought they would come to blows."

"I remember though he didn't seem like the fighting type to me. Anyway, Libion stormed out of the kitchen and threw him right out of La Rotonde." Hemingway laughed. "What did we call him, Allie Mincer?"

"You called him that," said Ez, almost reprovingly "but I think his name was Alex or Alec Minter or Miner."

"Well, there you have it. You should talk to him. Now I have to get cleaned up for dinner at the Murphy's. It was nice meeting you, Max. We should have a drink sometime. You can tell me all about the detective business."

Max watched Hemingway leave followed by his entourage. There was something oddly cruel about the man's manner. Max doubted he would ever follow up the invitation.

Hemingway stopped at the door. "You might try talking to Lewis Galantière. That son of a bitch pretty much knows everyone."

GALANTIÈRE WAS SURPRISINGLY easy to find; if he knew everyone, apparently everyone knew him as well. He worked for the International Chamber of Commerce, located on Avenue du President Wilson, and was at his desk when Max arrived mid-afternoon.

"Hemingway sent you, did he? How is that son of a bitch?"
Galantière was smiling when he said it so Max supposed the
imprecation was now a common reference among the new
Americans in Paris.

"He seemed fine if a little sweaty."

Galantière raised an eyebrow at that and peered at Max through
rimless eyeglasses. He looked the part of a commissioner's assistant,
which is what the nameplate on the door had said. Short and thin,
with a neatly trimmed square mustache, he was impeccably but
conservatively dressed. His mannerisms were precise, almost
deliberately so, and his voice had the same flat intonations as
Hemingway. Perhaps they were both from Chicago.

"I did meet Walter Gladstone several times. He dropped by
about a year ago, maybe less, and then again about five or six weeks
ago." Galantière didn't need to consult his diary, and Max wondered
if Gladstone had made a particular impression on him or if the
man simply had a prodigious power of recall. "He had a letter of
introduction from Ben Hecht, whom I knew because we both wrote
for The Little Review. Hecht is a journalist in Chicago but really
should devote his life to fiction. His first novel was a masterpiece.
Erik Dorn – do you know it?"

Max shook his head. His own reading consisted mostly of Paris
newspapers and the occasional novel Henri gave him "to improve his
mind and his French."

"No matter. You came to ask about Gladstone, not rising stars of
American literature."

"Which Gladstone was not."

"Quite. I thought the first time I met him that he had potential.
He'd had a few poems and one short story published in small but
respected journals. And he showed me another short story he was
working on—not to my taste but not badly written either. I
suggested he meet Sylvia Beach and even took him down to

Shakespeare and Company on Rue de l'Odéon. I don't know if they hit it off—she hasn't mentioned him to me since."

"Not Gertrude Stein?"

"No. Gertrude makes her own choices. Besides Sylvia is much kinder to novitiates."

"You met him again not long ago."

"Yes, I ran into him one evening at Le Dôme. We chatted briefly—he was the only sober one at his table so conversation was possible. He seemed to have fallen in with a group of actors from the Theatre Guingol."

"The marionette troupes?"

"That's what they do in the daytime—entertain the children. But before the turn of the century, they did their performances in the Catacombs and it was definitely adult fare. The censors shut them down and, well, even artists have to eat, so some set up their little stages in various parks; others gravitated to the Grand Guignol, a theatre in Pigalle on cité Chaptal, where they do a toned-down version of what took place in the Catacombs. But it is rumoured they still get together and do private performances as well that are not only horrifying but disgusting."

"Have you seen one?"

"No," said Galantière. "I have not had—nor do I want—that pleasure, either in public or in private. I heard that Walter had drowned."

"Something like that."

"It's a pity. Another young life wasted. I had hoped we had seen the last of that when the war ended. I suppose human nature never really changes, does it?"

Chapter 3 Wednesday, May 2nd, 1923

Although May Day had been relatively quiet by Paris standards, more than sixty people had been injured, including one police officer whose life still hung in the balance, when a riot had broken out in the communist controlled area of Bobigny. The police claimed that a mob had formed and was marching on Paris; representatives of the French Communist Party claimed the police started the trouble by trying to illegally arrest several of its leaders. In any case, Max was thankful Jacqui and her friends had been far from the main action, marching and singing labour songs in the area around the old Bastille. No violence reported and no arrests made. The demonstration and subsequent party had carried on well into the early hours and Jacqui was still asleep when he left.

At least the travel disruptions had abated and he was able to make his way to his office above Chez Jake. Jake himself was away—he had gone to London to scout new talent for the bar—but a sleepy-eyed Smitty let him in and roused one of the sous chefs to make him some breakfast. Several of the kitchen staff lived in a small staff dormitory in the back, a recent addition Jake had made to keep employees in the increasingly competitive Paris restaurant industry. The low franc and American prohibition had driven many Americans to visit or even take up residence in Paris and finding and keeping staff had become an issue in recent months, especially with so many young men still invalided by the war.

It is often said that in Paris, you might wait thirty minutes for a bus only to have three arrive all at once. It appeared the same joke might be applied to detective work for Max's letter box was filled with correspondence from potential clients. Many, of course, involved issues of suspicious spouses, mostly men worried about their wives. Despite claims of sexual tolerance, the French were as prone to jealousy as any others. These Max relegated immediately to the basket below his desk, having given up on replying to them years before.

The rest he examined more closely. Several were missing persons cases—an area where Max was selective in what he took on. Whenever a soldier was involved, which even nearly five years after the end of the war, still cropped up with depressing regularity, Max would make an effort to find the man, usually for less than his expenses. Most grieving families could not afford much but Max had learned that charging even a token amount assured them their son still mattered to someone besides themselves.

A middle-aged couple from Saint-Denis-le-Thiboult had written to request his services. They had heard of him from a cousin in Paris who Max had helped the previous summer. Their son had returned from the war and seemed to have recovered but recently disappeared without a trace. As it happened, he and Jacqui had visited the pretty farming village with its small castle in the autumn, as part of her efforts to get him to know the "real" France, so he was doubly inclined to help them. He wrote a note accepting the case, asking for as many details as they could provide and quoting a modest retainer fee. Once they replied, he would set Henri to work to see what he could uncover.

He also took a second missing person case—this one involving a missing heiress—but only because the request came from Blaise Cleroux, a lawyer that Max had frequently dealt with when he or one of his friends ran into trouble with the law. He would make an appointment to see him as soon as possible to get the details in person. The other three he declined with a respectful letter, claiming he was already too busy (which wasn't far from the truth) and recommending one or other of his colleagues for the work. They sometimes reciprocated when their own caseloads were too heavy or they wanted a vacation away from the city.

Finally, the manager of a car manufacturing plant—there were now half a dozen in the city—reported a series of thefts that looked like an inside job. They were reluctant to call in the police "because of the delicate circumstances," but had heard from other factory owners that he was "the soul of discretion." Max wasn't sure about that but they were offering a fat fee so he called the manager at the number provided and arranged to visit the plant that afternoon.

AFTER SENDING A MESSAGE to Alain about the thefts, another arranging to see Cleroux the first thing the next morning and a third to ask Helen Miller to confirm Gladstone's address, Max returned to Parc Montsouris to catch the early presentation at the puppet theatre. The factory wasn't far from the park and he would leave after the show to meet Alain there. He arrived early and bought a sandwich and a glass of white wine from La Pavilion du Lac, the restaurant which overlooked the lake.

About two dozen children were seated on the benches waiting for the curtain to rise, with a cluster of adults standing behind them, talking in low voices. Several of the young mothers eyed Max curiously as the only unaccompanied man in the crowd. He took out his notebooks and scrawled a few lines with a pencil. Perhaps they will think I'm a critic come to explore the nuances of children's entertainment. The last thing he needed was to answer questions from an outraged swallow.

A chime rang, inducing a momentary silence. The curtain snapped open to reveal a round-faced puppet, presumably Guignol, the star of the show. He was arm in arm with a female marionette. The background of a city street was on some sort of roller so the two puppets seemed to be strolling along while remaining at the center of the small stage.

"What should I do today?" asked the round-faced puppet, looking out at the eager audience.

"Steal a sandwich! Rob a bank! Trick the gendarmes!" The children's quick responses, mixed with laughter from both young and old made Max smile. He suddenly thought of his brother, who always returned to the same tattered story books, even though he knew the tales within by heart. He felt a pang at the memory, he had not written Ben for over a year, having given up on ever receiving a response.

"Ah!" said Guignol, slapping his head as if taken with a sudden thought. "I do feel the pangs of hunger. Stealing a sandwich is a very good idea.!"

"Oh, Guignol, stealing is wrong!" exclaimed the female puppet, which according to the article Max had read on his way to the park, must be Guignol's wife.

"But, Madelon, my dear, the rich have more food than they can eat." Turning to the audience, he asked: "Isn't it also wrong to waste food when so many are going hungry?"

"Yes! Steal from the rich to feed the poor," one of the older children yelled. Some of the parents murmured among themselves, though whether in approval or disapprobation Max couldn't tell.

The plot quickly unfolded over the next few minutes. Guignol, teamed up with his friend, the wine-loving cobbler, Gnafron, identified his target and crafted his approach. The repartee between the two was quick and sharp, filled with puns and double meanings that made both children and adults howl with laughter.

"This sandwich is fine, but it would be better with wine," said Gnafron.

"You think everything is better with wine," answered Guignol. "And it would be hard to prove you wrong."

"Not hard at all." Madelon looked pointedly at Guignol's pants.

"A bottle of wine in the night will make for a hard morning, my dear."

"Not if you have another bottle for breakfast!" declared Gnafron.

"Drink will kill you!"

"My dear, a little death never hurt you."

The story concluded with appearance of Flageolet, the pompous police officer, who might well have been modelled after Captain Fontaine in his arrogance and ineptitude. Cries of "Watchout, Guignol!" and "The Gendarme!" showed whose side the children were on.

Flageolet immediately began striking both Guignol and his companion with his baton but was quickly foiled when Guignol produced an even bigger stick, seemingly out of nowhere and beat the hapless copper into submission, while yelling insults and quick asides to the audience. "A swallow might have wings but a silk maker has the shears to clip them!"

The play's end was met with raucous applause and cries of encore. Guignol peeked out from beneath the curtain. "Encores are for opera singers and 'les blareaux.' Remember, always stand up for right, even if they tell you it is wrong."

With that the show ended and the audience slowly dispersed, most in the direction of a small cart that sold flavored ices and fruit drinks.

Max waited until the performers appeared, exiting the small building through a narrow door on one side. The company consisted of two men and a woman. The men were similar enough that Max thought they might be brothers or close cousins—portly men in their middle years with dark thinning hair and brown eyes. The woman, on the other hand, was young, slim with light brown hair and strikingly blue eyes. They busied themselves with cleaning up the grounds of wrappers and discarded bottles and straightening the chairs for the next performance, which would begin in about an hour.

The older of the two men appeared to be in charge and, as they finished their tasks, Max approached him, introducing himself and asking if they had known Walter Gladstone.

"Poor Walter," said the man, who identified himself as Eduard Mourget. "We saw him half a dozen times, though he was less interested in the puppets than one of the puppeteers. He nodded at the young woman. "Ilsa could probably tell you more."

"You knew Gladstone?"

"Knew him, yes, but not well. He was more interested in my cousin, Yelena Semenova." Ilsa spoke French with a slight Russian accent. "She sometimes worked here or at the stage in Buttes-Chaumont Park. Only when she wasn't performing at the theatre on cite Chaptal. Walter would drop by and flirt with her between shows."

"She was his girlfriend?"

"Maybe. I don't know. She liked the attention and the gifts he gave her but whether she liked him is hard to say. He seemed to think so but she *is* an actress."

"Did he see her outside the park. At the Grand Guignol, perhaps."

"If he did, he was taking his life in his hands. Oh, I... don't think Carlos would have..." Her voice trailed away.

"Carlos?" Max asked but Ilsa just shook her head.

Mourget filled in the details. "Carlos Herrea is Yelena's fiancé or at least he says he is. Jealous type, you know, he works as a stage hand at the theatre. He always swore he would kill anyone who touched Yelena but I never took him seriously. Spaniards, you know."

Max had gone to Spain in 1919 but he didn't think Spaniards were any more or less likely to kill their rivals than Frenchmen. He would have to speak to Herrera to find out.

THE FACTORY WAS LOCATED in Ivry-sur-Seine, a small industrial commune to the southeast of Paris. No easy train connection left from the park so Max hailed a taxi which delivered him to a modest two-story building in about ten minutes. Alain was already there lounging against a wall across the street from the factory.

The boy Max had first used as an informant three years before had grown into a man, not as tall as Max but nearly as broad, his muscles and fighting skills developed by regular sessions at O'Brien's gym. He knew Alain still lived in a cold water flat on the sixth floor of a Hausmann row house but it was not for lack of income. He worked regularly for Max as an investigator and, during slow periods, took shifts at Le Coq Bleu, where his cousin, Josette, worked with Henri in the kitchen.

Alain, it seemed, preferred to spend his earnings on the latest fashions. He was currently wearing a grey double-breasted suit over a matching vest, a pale, yellow shirt with a silk tie in red and blue. He had a dark blue trench coat slung over one arm and his shoes were two-toned patent leather. Alain's light brown hair was cut short and slicked back, most of it covered by a grey fedora with a dark blue band. Max's own clothing was less fashionable—despite Jacqui's best efforts—and almost looked shabby in comparison.

Alain raised his hand in greeting and stepped away from the wall to meet Max on the path leading to the front door.

Inside the main entrance, signs directed visitors left to the factory proper and right and up a flight of stairs to the offices. A young man seated behind desk at the top of the stairs, asked their names and business. Max gave him the former but not the latter.

"Ah, Mr. Anderson. M. Duvalier has been expecting you."

He led them through a door behind the desk, down a short hallway to a large corner office. Banks of windows covered three sides, two looking out into the street, the third down onto the factory floor. A heavy-set man in his mid-forties, Charles Duvalier, was looking at the workers below and gestured for them to join him. He waited for his assistant to close the door behind him before speaking.

"Have you seen an automobile being built before, Mr. Anderson?"

Max had been driven in motorized vehicles on numerous occasions and, recently had spent some time looking at purchasing one for himself. His thirtieth birthday was less than a month away and he had thought of making himself, and Jacqui, a present of one. His few trips out of Paris had been by train and he thought of how much more they could do with their own vehicle. Jacqui had brought the latest edition of the Michelin Guide home a few weeks before and they had spent several pleasant hours exploring the possibilities of "road trips," an expression recently imported from America, ever since. Still, he had given little thought to how an automobile was actually made.

"It looks complicated."

About thirty workers were stationed at benches on one side of the open workshop. The majority were men but there were a number of women as well. France had suffered terrible losses during the war, nearly six million killed or wounded, and, unlike in some less afflicted nations, women continued to fill jobs that had previously been thought of as the sole purview of men. Some of the workers were assembling engines while others were putting together other components. On the other side of the plant, a number of partly assembled vehicles were sitting on a kind of moving track, with workers at several stations using winches and power drills to attach specific pieces to the automobile as it moved along. As he watched, a completed vehicle rolled off the track and was pushed through a set of large double doors to join others in a separate warehouse.

"It is," said Duvalier, "and has been since we started building cars in France in the 1890s. In most plants, each car is assembled completely by hand before another is started. Some designers have become attached to these old-fashioned processes and risk being over taken by more progressive firms."

"Like your own?"

"Yes, though a bigger risk comes from the Americans. Up until now, France has been the biggest producer of motorized vehicles, nearly half of the world's production last year. But Henry Ford will change all that. That moving track, what the Americans call an *assembly line* was installed here after my youngest brother came back from Detroit, where Ford is ramping up production of his Model-T. Unlike Citroën, Peugeot and Bugatti who build cars for the well-to-do, Ford wants to cater to the middle and working classes. We hope to do the same here."

"You mean even someone like me might someday get behind the wheel of my very own car?" asked Alain, his eyes glinting with excitement.

"That's what we hope. In addition to 'borrowing' ideas from the Americans, my second brother has been developing some innovations of his own. And that is why I have asked you to come here. Some of his prototypes have disappeared."

"You said it was a delicate matter, too much so for the Prefecture to get involved." Max had worked for factory owners before so he anticipated Duvalier's answer before it came.

"Car making is a highly competitive business. Even rumours of my brother's inventions would spur my competitors to go down the same road—so to speak—and, with more resources than we can muster, would soon leave us in the dust.

"To make matters worse, only six people have access to the laboratory where he works: myself and my two brothers, the foreman here and two engineers fresh out of the Ecole Nationale Des Ponts et Chaussees, the most prestigious school of its type in the world. One of those six, and I assure you it wasn't me, has been stealing those prototypes. I can only hope they haven't already sold them to my competitors."

Max considered the problem. Normally, he would have Alain or one of his other operatives take a job in the factory to try to determine the likely culprits. However, the existence of a separate laboratory with limited access posed a problem. None of the people who he had on his roster could pass for an engineer or even a skilled machinist. He would have to investigate each in turn, starting with the two recent graduates, though he wouldn't exclude the others from his research—sibling rivalry could lead to all sorts of trouble.

"Can you help me? Time is of the essence."

"I'll get working on it right away. I hope you understand that my approach must remain secret even from you but I do think I can have results for you within a week. Let me know if there is another disappearance as soon as you can." Max handed Duvalier a card with his contact information, including the phone number of his office at Chez Jake. "Do you have photographs or descriptions of all those who have access to the lab?"

"I anticipated your request." Duvalier went to his desk and extracted a large envelope from the top drawer. He handed it, plus 10,000 francs as a retainer, to Max.

"In the meantime, I suggest you install a second lock on the laboratory door, to which only you have the key. It may occasionally prove inconvenient but will ensure no one can enter the room when you are not present at the factory. A book where individuals are required to sign in and out could also prove useful. Any of the five found in the lab without signing in should be questioned closely or searched. I know this will be awkward, especially if it is one of your brothers, but the measure should only be required until we identify the culprit."

With handshakes and un bise to seal the deal, Max and Alain left the factory, stopping at a café in the Latin Quarter to examine the documents Duvalier had given them over cafés au lait and brioche.

The first sheet was a list of five names: Leo and Andre Duvalier, the younger and middle brothers; Jordain Lefebre, the foreman and the two engineering graduates, Pierre Caron and Jean Dupont. There were photographs of the first four but only a description of the last. The lack of photograph and the name—Jean Dupont was a common enough name but was sometimes used in the same way "John Doe" was in English—immediately made Max suspicious.

"I want to you to follow Dupont and find out as much about him as you can, from the official files but also neighbours' gossip and the like. Be discrete, if he's our man, we don't want him to run off. Duvalier will want to know who he is spying for and what he's handed over." He handed Alain a thousand francs to cover expenses—including bribes to encourage the aforementioned gossip.

Max doubted he had time to follow the other engineer but he knew someone who would and would be happy of the work. Pierre Roget was a former military police officer and gangland enforcer who had dabbled in politics from left to right. He had eventually settled on being a detective—a kind of back-handed compliment to Max—doing mostly divorce work. Max had used him a few times when Alain was too busy or otherwise unavailable. He wasn't brilliant but he was workmanlike and surprisingly reliable, given his chequered past.

He had a room, that served as both accommodation and office, in the 18th arrondissement not far from Le Coq Bleu. Max could drop by on his way to Chez Jake to see if he was available and interested, though as it turned out, the man wasn't in residence and the concierge didn't know when he would return.

JACQUI WAS WAITING for him at their usual table. She had found time to change out of her work clothes and was wearing a bright blue calf length dress with a matching shawl. Even her high-heeled shoes were blue and she had tied up her shoulder length dark hair with a blue ribbon decorated with rhinestones. She smiled up at him, her eyes twinkling in her heart-shaped face.

On stage, a swing combo was playing a foxtrot and half a dozen couples filled the small dance floor. He and Jacqui would dance later but first he wanted to catch up with her day.

Since she had started work at the Opera House, making costumes, they had less time together. Although he knew the work made her happy, he sometimes wished she would give it up and let him support them both. There was little chance of that, of course; Jacqui craved her independence and the freedom her own money gave her. It was one of the things that had drawn them together and he certainly wouldn't ask her to change. He would have to make the time they did spend together as special as possible.

Over soup – a light vegetable broth with shreds of early spring lamb– he told her about the recent influx of cases, finishing with the apparent murder of Walter Gladstone.

"Shouldn't the Prefecture be dealing with it?"

"They should but police politics has gotten in the way; a new Captain has declared the case closed and Fontaine is too busy with bigger matters to intervene. Until that changes, it's up to me."

"Up to us. I want to help."

Jacqui was smart and brave and beautiful and if he didn't love her so much, she would be the perfect addition to his growing team. She had contacts who would never speak to him and, undoubtedly, would be an asset when it came to interviewing women. But his work was sometimes dangerous. He himself had been shot at numerous times, though only hit once, and he would not put her at risk. But he said: "Of course, I value your opinions and insights."

"But not my direct involvement."

Max shrugged and looked away. Jacqui put her hand on his arm until he looked back. "I know you worry about me but I had a life – sometimes a dangerous life – before I met you. I worry about you, too. And I love you and won't press the point. But if you ever need my help…"

"You'll be the first to know."

The waiter – someone new that Max hadn't seen before – delivered the main course, a filet of sole with lemon and white wine sauce served with thinly sliced potatoes and fresh asparagus. A bottle of white Burgandy was a perfect match.

"This Gladstone was interested in the theatre?"

"Of a certain type. At first, I thought it was the puppet shows they do for kids in some of the parks but it turns out his interest was in one of the puppeteers who also acts at Le Grand Guignol here in Montmartre."

Jacqui made a face. "I've heard of them. They only consider a show a success if half a dozen people faint or vomit during the performance. Some of the women who sew costumes for the Opera sometimes work for them as well. These days, women have to take work where they can get it."

"Maybe I could interview some of them to see what they know about this actress—" Max checked his notebook "—Yelena, before I go to talk to her myself. It always helps to know a little gossip about the people you are interviewing."

"Maybe I could get a job there myself—be your woman on the inside."

"Ah, maybe..."

Jacqui laughed. "If you could see your face! It's okay, Max, I don't think I want to have anything to do with them if what some of the girls say is true. Now, let's talk about something important. And let's do it in English; I need the practice. What do you want to do for your thirtieth birthday? It's only 25 days away and I need to make plans."

Chapter 4 Thursday, May 3rd, 2023

Helen Miller had sent a messenger confirming Gladstone's address and Max added a visit to the house on Visconti, which he could do on his way home. A package from the couple in Saint-Denis-le-Thiboult was waiting for him when he arrived at his office at Chez Jake. It detailed the history of their missing son, René Voisin. He had served in the French infantry, surviving the first battle of the Marne as a private, and the even bloodier fighting around Verdun where the French army suffered over half a million casualties. By the end of the war, he had risen to the rank of Captain and had won several commendations during the final great battle of the war at Amiens, where Max had also fought and been severely wounded.

Voisin had been more fortunate, suffering only a few minor wounds which had healed quickly in the loving care of his parents. However, as they wrote in the accompanying letter, "René was never quite the same and we often caught him sitting by himself, staring into space with an indescribable blankness to his expression." The photo they enclosed showed a young man of about thirty-five with the haunted expression of one whose years have been too filled with pain to forget. He had gone out, he had said, "to clear my head and see some old friends." Yet, when evening came and he had not returned, none of his few surviving friends in the town had seen him. The Voisins had had no word from him in the month since he disappeared and had little idea where he might have gone, though he had often spoken happily of his occasional leaves in Paris, though inquiries with cousins and the authorities in the city had turned up nothing.

Max sat staring at the photograph for nearly half an hour, his own memories fleeing back to the horrors he had experienced at Passchendaele, which had nearly broken him. While the wounds he had received in the final months of the war had now mostly healed, his leg still ached whenever his thoughts were drawn back to his time in the war and tended to bother him for hours afterward.

He held out little hope that Voisin had actually left his little town and come to Paris—more likely he had found some quiet place in the surrounding woods to end his misery. Still, Max had promised himself that he would never give up on a fellow soldier or his family. If René Voisin could be found, he would find him.

This was a job he could ask Henri to take on. He would send him to Saint-Denis-le-Thiboult to interview the parents and the young man's friends and acquaintances. Henri was skilled at lending a sympathetic ear and was particularly attuned to gossip, able to sift the few kernels of truth from the chaff of idle chatter. If there was even a rumour that Voisin had fled to Paris or taken another escape from under the burden of the war, Henri would sniff it out. If the man had come to Paris, he and Henri had avenues they could pursue to track him down.

He put the documents in a small valise along with a few thousand francs to cover Henri's expenses and fees. Depending on how long Henri thought he might be away, he could use the small suitcase for his personal effects as well. He would try to catch Henri at Le Coq Bleu or would leave the case along with a short note with Yesim.

On his way, he stopped at Roget's rooming house to see if he had returned.

"He's back alright," said the woman sweeping the front step. "Stumbled in at three in the morning, waking half the clients with his noise. I'm not sure he's accepting visitors this morning," She finished with a laugh before stepping aside to let Max see for himself.

Roget's room was on the fourth floor and Max's leg complained at every landing. A polite knock elicited no response so Max pounded it with the flat of his hand. Roget jerked the door open a few moments later and glared at Max for several moments before recognition dawned in his bleary eyes.

"Oh, it's you. I was expecting..." Roget didn't say who but it was clearly no friend, if the thin blade clutched in one fist was any indication. He waved Max into the small room but took a wary glance up and down the hall before pushing the door closed and sliding the bolt shut.

"Expecting trouble"

"Nothing I can't handle."

Max had no doubt that was true. Roget had made a living with his fists and, occasionally, more dangerous weapons, though he had always drawn the line at murder. He had more lines in his face than when Max had first met him nearly five years before but his body, revealed now in shorts and undershirt, retained a lithe muscularity and a sense of coiled readiness.

"I have a job if you're interested."

Roget nodded his agreement. "Details."

Max had rehearsed a story that would get the job done without revealing much about why it was necessary. Duvalier had stressed the need for confidentiality and, while Roget had recently shown he was reliable, Max knew he couldn't be trusted with details that had a commercial value to the auto-maker's rivals. He gave him the photograph of Pierre Caron and some background of where he might be found. Max's instincts told him that Caron wasn't his man but he had to be thorough.

"I want to know whatever you can find out about his background and where he goes and what he does when he's not at work. If he has any special friends, well, you know the drill."

Roget nodded again and gave Max a salacious wink. If he thought this involved a love triangle, he was hardly likely to look into Duvalier's business. If Caron was involved, Roget would see enough for Max to put together the clues.

MAX STOPPED FOR A QUICK lunch of potato and leek soup and a slab of dark bread slathered in butter at Le Coq Bleu, where he was able to describe the assignment to Henri in person. Henri had been thrilled at the idea of a trip out of the city and promised to be on the next train to Saint-Denis-le-Thiboult.

"I am on the case, Max! I won't let you down." Henri didn't even finish his small beer before heading for home to fill up the valise Max had given him. "Don't worry Yesim," he said as he headed out the door, "Josette can handle the kitchen. I trained her myself."

Yesim snorted but the smile on his face was broad. "You're a good man Max. I was starting to worry about Henri. Despite what he says, Josette does better without him hanging over her. Now you've given him a new lease on life, something useful to do that will strain neither his body nor his patience."

Max smiled as well and carried on to see the lawyer, Cleroux, barely noticing that his leg no longer ached.

Cleroux's office was its usual disordered mess, his desk piled high with over-stuffed files and unopened correspondence. The only clear space was now occupied with the remains of the lawyer's lunch; a well-chewed baguette stuffed with ham, cheese, fried eggplant and slices of tomato competed for space with a sliver of chocolate cake and an empty coffee cup. He waved Max to the sideboard with his cup; a carafe kept warm by a small candle and several more cups were scattered between stacks of legal tomes. Max poured himself some and refilled Cleroux's drink before settling into the one uncluttered chair.

"What can I do for you, Max?" Cleroux asked after he had emptied half of his cup in a single gulp.

"You sent for me."

"I did?"

"Something about a missing heiress, I think your note said."

"Yes, yes, of course. You see how busy I am—one thing pushes out another." Cleroux thrust his hand into a stack of paper. It emerged with a thin manila file, testament to the efficiency of the lawyer's unique filing system. "Here it is."

The folder was stained with coffee and at least two types of sauces but the documents inside were pristine. Max found himself looking at a photograph of an exceedingly attractive young woman, not more than twenty or so years of age. Her face was slightly in profile, showing off her delicate features, a long attractive neck, and a pile of thick dark hair piled artfully atop her head.

"The Lady Evelyn Wentworth, eldest child and only daughter of Robert Wentworth, 6th Earl of Deal, went missing during her coming-of-age tour of the Continent. She was last seen in Paris. The Prefecture did a cursory investigation but dismissed it as 'another dissolute Englander gone astray.'"

"How did this wind up on your desk?" Cleroux was more likely to have petty criminals, anarchists, journalists and the impoverished bourgeoisie as clients. British nobility hardly fit into any of those categories.

"Robert spent a year abroad in 1898, attending the law school at the newly created University of Paris. He helped me with my English and I helped him with his French and we helped each other consume copious quantities of cheap food and good wine. The following year his father died unexpectedly and he returned to England to take up his duties. However, we stayed in touch over the years and, when I heard of his distress over his missing daughter, I sent him a telegram. I assured him I had just the man to help him. I trust that is true."

"I think you may have overstated my credentials but I'm more than happy to help you out. Afterall, you've bailed me and my clients out on enough occasions."

"Yes, I think on balance you are in my debt but solve this case and our fortunes will certainly be reversed." Cleroux named a sum that widened Max's eyes. He didn't need the money but he could certainly think of things he could use it for.

Max glanced through the remaining documents in the file; the information was sparse. Lady Wentworth had been staying at The Meurice, not the most luxurious hotel in Paris but certainly in the top ten, but had not been seen there for nearly ten days. Her traveling companions, Lady Janet Kellog, her best friend and Dame Edith de Gant, their chaperone, were in the dark about her whereabouts. However, Evelyn had been particularly taken with the many art museums that the city boasted, having returned several times to the Galerie Barbazanges, where a display of young French artists had captured her attention. Inquiries at the gallery had led nowhere.

Lady Wentworth had taken few of her clothes but all of her jewelry with her as well as several books she had purchased while in Paris, including one that her chaperone called scandalous. She had forgotten the title but remembered it had been obtained from "a curiously named bookstore on Rue de l'Odeon." Max wondered if it was the same Galantiere had mentioned.

When he asked Cleroux about it, he smirked. "The book is probably called Ulysses, written by some Irish writer. It was apparently refused by all kinds of publishers and has been banned in the United States. Sylvia Beach at Shakespeare and Company took it on and published it in installments. I tried reading it—you know, to practice my English—but couldn't make head nor tail of it."

Max briefly described the murder of Walter Gladstone and his connection to the American writing community as well as other less reputable parts of the Paris arts community. He showed Cleroux the photograph but he shook his head. "I suppose the connection is purely coincidental but it seems odd in any case."

"I wouldn't be so sure," said Cleroux, leaning back in his chair with his coffee cup perched precariously on his expansive waistcoat. "Young people come to Paris from all over the world and get swept up in the excitement and mystery of Lutèce. Anything is possible. Maybe Lady Wentworth, like your poor murder victim, has been caught up in the world of the surrealists. If she has, heaven help her."

"That sounds like bitter experience," said Max.

"Bitter no, but definitely an experience. I had one of them as a client briefly. He was suing his gallery, of which he was part owner, for its misuse of his work to advance the cause of 'colonial aggression' in Morocco. It never came to court but it almost came to blows. When he came to settle his account, he gave me a small painting, of which I could also not make head nor tail. I hung it in my bathroom—though I'm not sure if it is the right way up—to remind myself every morning to be more careful who I let into my office."

The file held several copies of the photograph and a list of cafes, galleries and shops that Lady Wentworth had visited in the week before her disappearance. Max accepted ten percent of the promised fee as a retainer and promised to report back to Cleroux after the weekend.

MAX SPENT PART OF THE afternoon visiting some of the establishments on the Wentworth list with little to show for his efforts. He finally gave up and headed for the address on Rue Visconti. The narrow street was lined with dark brown row houses, mostly two stories but a few three and four. No windows were at street level and those on the upper floors had bars across them. A café, currently empty of custom, was on the corner of the block containing Gladstone's flat and a small shop, marked by small signs advertising the products it stocked, stood next to the 3-story building containing the apartment.

The large key on the ring he had taken from the morgue opened the front door so Max didn't have to deal with the concierge, if one was present. He climbed the stairs to the third floor. Gladstone's rooms were on the left side of the landing, overlooking Visconti. The second key gained him access and he closed the door softly behind him.

The two windows in the first room had no curtains so the flat was dimly lit from the outside. An electric light hung from the ceiling but Max decided to leave it off, so as not to draw attention to himself. An overcoat hung from a coat rack by the entrance; its pockets were empty. The room was fairly spacious. At one end, was a small kitchen, with a sink, a modern icebox and a small gas stove.

He had heard that Gladstone was well-off and the presence of both gas and electricity in the flat provided evidence of that. He and Jacqui paid a premium for the same amenities. A quick inspection of the cupboards revealed a small stock of canned and dry goods, but no alcohol, and carefully arranged dishes and cutlery. He did not bother with the icebox as its contents would have begun to spoil by now. A small table for dining was stationed near the kitchen with three chairs arranged around it.

At the other end of the room was a sitting area, including a large couch and several well-padded chairs around a large low table. The room was as tidy as the kitchen cupboards and Max wondered if he had a housekeeper or was simply fastidious. Miller might know and he made a note to ask her.

Two doors were at that end of the flat. One led to a small but well-equipped bathroom which included a toilet and bidet and a modest-sized tub with a shower attachment. The vanity included shaving gear, a comb, a brush, nail scissors, a bottle of men's cologne and a small bottle of pain killers.

The second led to a spacious bedroom, also lit by two windows, although these had drawn curtains so Max turned on a table lamp on the bedside table. The bed was carefully made; it was a matrimonial but only held one pillow. The bedside tables contained half a dozen books, all in English, including the complete works of Edgar Allen Poe.

The closet held several suits, a dozen shirts, pants carefully hung to prevent wrinkles. At one end was an ironing board and iron and, on the floor, three pairs of polished shoes as well as white ones, probably used for tennis, given the racquet leaning against one wall. A quick examination of the clothing revealed nothing but a few dinner receipts, plus in each of the suit jackets, a notebook and pencil. The notebooks mostly contained brief descriptions of buildings or people, such as Max imagined a writer might make.

Under one window, was a small desk with a typewriter and a table lamp. The desk drawers contained paper and pens and some type-written pages. There were several poems and what appeared to be two short stories and something resembling part of a play but nothing long enough to be the novel Gladstone was purportedly working on. He folded the half dozen pages of script and put them in his jacket.

A small drawer held a passport and a small bundle of francs. Max checked the underside of the desk drawers for hidden papers but nothing came to light. Nor could he find other hiding places elsewhere in either the bedroom or the main room.

He was about to leave when, on a whim or by instinct, he opened the icebox. The little food inside had indeed spoiled and the smell was unpleasant but not overwhelming. In the back of a second, colder compartment, behind a packet of still frozen meat, was a small handgun. What, he wondered, was Gladstone doing with a gun and why was it hidden here? Yet, another mystery on top of the pile of questions he was beginning to form about the dead writer.

He returned briefly to his apartment a few blocks away on Rue Jacob for a light meal of cheese and bread with Jacqui before heading back to Parc Montsouris.

He wanted to get a sense of what the place might have looked like on the night Gladstone was murdered. If he were lucky, he might run into someone who had been there and would be able to provide some clue as to what had happened. As well, he hoped the fresh air and relative calm of a park well away from the centre of the city might help him clear his head and get some perspective on the many cases he had now, perhaps foolishly, taken on. After months of relative quiet, the clues ratcheted around his head like ball bearings in a steel bowl.

As Max descended from the elevated train station, shouts and curses from within the park quickened his step. He had expected peace and quiet; this sounded like a full-blown riot. The area around the bandstand was filled with more than two dozen men and half as many women. Most were content to stand on opposite sides of the pagoda, yelling at each other, waving their hands in the air or pointing at the structure's contents. A few were grappling with their opponents and some clumsy punches were thrown though with little effect.

The object or, rather, objects, of their anger appeared to be a makeshift art show, pieces of sculpture crowding the floor of the pavilion while paintings of various sizes hung from pillars or were propped upon easels. A few had been knocked to the ground and several of the men were preoccupied with restoring them to the exhibit. The scene was played out in shadows with no moon in the sky and only a scattering of lamps lighting the pathway and the entrance to the nearby restaurant.

Max stopped on the edge of the clearing, uncertain if he should intervene and, of so, on whose side. He recognized the two brothers who had been working the puppet show the previous day but they seemed more observers than participants, standing and laughing with a swarthy man in a leather coat. They were not alone in that; several women stood in a group near the entrance to La Pavilion du Lac that overlooked both the bandstand and the artificial lake. They were clearly bemused by the spectacle of struggling artists and Max suspected they were more likely American tourists than members of the local art scene. Perhaps one of them knew the Lady Wentworth.

On the other side of the impromptu art display—it had the look of something that had been thrown up in a hurry—one man stood apart, leaning against a street lamp. He held a sketch pad in one hand and was glancing from it to the melee in front of him, drawing with quick deft strokes. He was small, almost insubstantial, though with a peculiar immediacy that drew the eye. His dark hair framed a pale oval face. A monocle covered his right eye and his neck was swathed in a multi-colored cravat. If Max had been asked to describe an artist, this would be it.

Although the man was standing apart for the fray, it seemed to Max he might be at its very centre. From time to time, one of the combatants lunged in his direction only to be blocked by one or two on the other side. The sketcher took no notice of this and continued his work. Max slowly made his way around the yelling, pushing crowd until he was standing next to the man by the lamp.

"Any idea what this is all about?"

The man lifted his head and studied Max as if examining a specimen in a jar.

"It is the last gasp of a dying idea," he said. "It was neither new nor old, but necessary, and now it is finished." Max must have looked confused so the man continued. "Some of these cretins say Dada is dead, and of course they are right though not in the manner they think. This last exhibit and my soon to be published manifesto will show them the error of their ways."

The explanation did nothing to dispel Max's confusion. "This dispute, if that's what it is, is worth fighting over?"

"Your French is very good but I take it you are not from France." The abrupt change of subject puzzled Max further. "Not American but something like it."

"I'm a Canadian. Max Anderson." He stuck out his hand but the artist looked at his own full hands and shrugged.

"Tristan Tzara." He smiled gently, as if at a joke only he understood. "What brings you here, Max Anderson?"

"To Paris? The war—"

"No. Here, right here, in this ineffable moment. There must be a peculiar reason or no reason at all."

Max hesitated. Maybe it was the absurdity of it, men fighting over abstractions when the hard reality of the war was still visible on the horizon, but a moment of clarity descended.

"Peculiar enough, I suppose. A man died here—was murdered here—not long ago. His body was left in the shallows of that lake." He gestured at the still water, black except for the glimmering reflection of the few street lamps and the emerging stars. "I've been engaged to discover who did it and why. I thought I might find a witness or discover some clue I'd missed; instead, I discover this chaos."

Tzara laughed. "I could not have created a better scenario. You came here to try to make order out of the madness of violence and instead witness a pantomime put on by men who were either too young or too old to have participated in the great chaos. This, this, this—"Tzara pointed with his pencil at the mix of light, darkness and frantic action—"it is how the world is now. We tear it down so we can build it up into something different—not better perhaps but different. But I suppose that does little to help you with your quest."

"You're not wrong." The fight appeared to be over. Most of the combatants had disappeared into the dark paths that led away from the lake toward the train station. The women outside the restaurant had also left—an opportunity lost—though the two brothers from the puppet theatre were still watching the remaining artists tidy away the exhibit. "I don't suppose you met Walter Gladstone, the murder victim. I was told he had an interest in the avantgarde, especially the theatre. He was a writer, though not, I understand, a particular successful one."

Tzara cocked his head to one side. "The name is not familiar to me. Perhaps he went by another name; it is not an uncommon thing in Paris these days. Do you have a picture of the man?"

Max had left it in his other coat but was embarrassed to admit it. He shook his head and made a mental note to keep it handy hereafter.

"I will ask around. After all, we can't have people running around murdering artists, even minor ones." Tzara produced a calling card, with his name in small black letters against a garish wash of color. "I'm easy to find. Check in with me in a few days and I'll let you know if I've discovered anything."

Max watched the small man walk away until he faded into the night. Perhaps the Mourget brothers could shed some further light, though Max had his doubts.

"We haven't heard anything else about it," said Eduard, "And we haven't seen anything of Yelena either."

"What does he want with Yelena?" The man in the leather coat took a sudden step forward. His flashing eyes and thick Spanish accent identified him as Carlos Herrea, the supposed fiancé of the actress Gladstone was reputed to be interested in.

"I'm investigating the murder of Walter Gladstone."

"Murder? You say it was murder?"

"Yes. And you were heard threatening him. Over Yelena."

Herrea blanched and took a step back raising both his palms in a gesture of denial. "I don't know who told you that." He glanced angrily at Eduard Mourget. "Yelena is my girl and of course I didn't like this American sniffing around, with his clever words and cheap presents. I guess I got angry with him but it wasn't serious. I didn't kill him."

Max shrugged. Maybe Carlos Herrea was innocent, just another hothead in love, but he wasn't about to rule him out as the prime suspect. "I didn't say you did. But maybe you could answer a few questions."

"Sure, sure, but not now. Meet me tomorrow for lunch at Au Petit Riche on Peletier. It's nice walk from the theatre where I work so I'll be sure to have an appetite. And if you see Yelena, tell her... tell her I miss her."

Chapter 5 Friday, May 4th 1923

Alain was waiting for him when Max arrived at his office at Chez Jake. Jacqui had worked late the night before and wanted to sleep in so Max had slipped out without pausing for breakfast. Alain hadn't eaten either so Max ordered a couple of tartines—baguettes sliced in half, toasted and slathered in butter and strawberry jam—orange juice and two large café au lait. He waited until both hungers were sated before asking Alain to report. The orange juice, with a few slivers of ice, was particularly welcome give the unseasonably warm temperatures of the last few days and Max ordered two more.

"Dupont seems to lead a quiet life according to his neighbours, no guests let alone parties or other social affairs. He lives near the river on rue Malar in a small flat on the second floor and is often seen on his balcony drinking copious amounts of coffee with his nose buried in a book. The official records don't say much either. He graduated last year from the Ecole Nationale Des Ponts et Chaussees as Duvalier told us. He was a good student though not outstanding and his specialty, not surprisingly, was in mechanical engineering. He started with the company a little over six months ago."

"Not right out of university?"

"Apparently not. It took a bit of encouragement—" Alain rubbed his finger and thumb together "—but I was able to discover that Dupont spent almost six months out of the country, travelling in and out of France to Spain, Italy and Switzerland, spending four to six weeks in each."

"They might not have been his final destination."

"I thought of trying to search his place while he was at the factory to see if his passport was lying around but decided that wasn't what you would call discrete."

Max laughed and nodded for Alain to continue. He took a glance at his notebook before doing so.

"I followed him from the factory both Wednesday and, again, last night. I can confirm he does spend time on his balcony reading but not on Thursday. He arrived home at a little after six, having stopped to pick up a light supper at one of the neighbour hood cafés, but he didn't pause to eat it. Ten minutes later he was out and walking briskly toward the river. He crossed into the 8th on Pont de l'Alma. Thirty minutes later he entered a restaurant across from the—" Alain checked his notes again. "—Alexander Nevsky Cathedral."

"The Petrograd." Max had eaten there a few times, usually in the company of Joseph Asper, though not within the last year.

"That's the one. I glanced through the windows while walking past and saw him at a table with two other people. The light was dim and they were quite far back but I'm sure it was a man and a woman. The man was heavy-set and wore a beard; the woman was in the shadows but her gestures were feminine. I found a place to wait where I could see the main entrance without being too obvious. The sun had set and I was about to give up when Dupont came out alone. I followed him to the nearest Metro which he took to Invalides before strolling through the park and on to home. I watched the place until after nine but there was no further sign of him. Should I have stayed at the restaurant to see who he had met?"

Max shook his head. It might have been useful to know who Dupont met and why but that could wait for another day. The

Petrograd was a favorite haunt of a number of White Russians, where they met to drink and plot the overthrow of the Bolshevik regime in Moscow. It was hard to imagine what their connection to Dupont might be but he would check with his contacts to see what they knew, starting with Asper, who was now an established lecturer at the Sorbonne.

"Good work, Alain. Keep after Dupont to see if his weekend activities shed further light. Do you need any more money?"

"Maybe. The immigration clerk was easy but he wasn't cheap. Another five hundred?"

Max took the money from petty cash and asked Alain to report back as soon as he had something, along with a detailed account of expenditures, including "unofficial" ones. Duvalier was a business man and would want a careful accounting; Max hoped he was experienced enough to understand the necessity of bribes.

Before Alain left, Max remembered the file Cleroux had provided him. The list it contained was long—the woman must have been indefatigable to have visited them all in a week—and Max had barely put a dent in it. He could hire one of his regulars, but there was no certainty any would be available and, besides, the work wasn't hard and their fees were high.

"Do you have a friend who could make some inquiries for me, nothing too difficult." He showed Alain the Wentworth picture. "I'm trying to find this woman and I have a long list of places she is known to frequent. I need someone to show the picture around and ask if she's been there in the last ten days."

"What about Josette? She's always after me about doing 'police' work."

Josette would be good at it, too. She was intelligent with a pleasant demeanor. The customers at Le Coq Bleu loved to chat with her, telling her things Max was sure they would never mention to him. But if he hired Josette for the job, Jacqui would become all the more insistent on being a part of his "team," too.

"With Henri out of town and the current heat wave expected to last through the weekend, Yesim will need all the help he can get. Any other candidates?"

Alain looked slightly reluctant but finally said.

"Well, I have another cousin..."

The young man seemed to have no end of cousins, all looking for work. "Go on."

"Gaston recently arrived from Lyon and is working moving cargo on and off boats on the Seine when he's not helping the local fishermen with their nets. He's not a very big fellow and the work doesn't really suit him, though you'll never hear him complain. He's solid, Max, and very polite. He's not a snappy dresser like me but his clothing is always clean and tidy. No would take offence to him asking questions. And he finished le lycée last year so he reads and writes and can handle money."

Max agreed to give him a try and Alain promised that he would come by as soon as his shift ended at 4 that afternoon.

"Have him meet me at Le Coq Bleu. I'm having drinks with Jacqui there before we go to a new restaurant in the Latin Quarter."

In case Gaston didn't work out, Max sent a note to his friend Hugo Pomeroy to also join him at Le Coq Bleu. Hugo was still working as an orderly at the Invalides hospital but Max knew his hours had been cut as many of the long-term patients died, were released or sent to smaller hospitals in Paris or in the regions of their origins. The recent government move to cut budgets in the wake of dwindling revenues (which had also contributed to their seizure of the Ruhr earlier that year) was likely making matters even worse. If Max could give Hugo a bit of extra work, he was happy to do so.

BY THE TIME HE HAD dealt with the morning mail and signed a few cheques for Chez Jake, Max was running late for his lunch with Carlos Herrea, so he took a taxi instead of walking. He spotted Herrea at one of the few outside tables enjoying the late morning sun. He didn't seem to mind the heat; perhaps it reminded him of home. At least, a light breeze stirred the humid air. Max doubted the fans inside would do a better job.

As he neared the table, a waiter placed a lentil salad in front of the Spaniard, along with a glass of wine, a pinot gris by its pale-yellow colour. Max ordered the same while perusing the menu for a main course.

"I'm having the sole," said Herrera. "But the chicken stew is also good if you want something heartier."

Max's breakfast was a distant memory, but he knew he had to save some appetite for the evening's excursion, so he chose the sole as well.

Herrera got right to the point. "Have you seen Yelena?

"No, I'm planning on going to the theatre tomorrow. Won't I see her there?"

"I thought you were a detective. If she was still coming to Le Grand Guignol, I wouldn't be missing her."

"I thought she was one of the stars of the show."

Herrera smiled, his eyes flickering away as if he were somewhere else altogether. He looked down at his food and pushed the salad away before downing the remainder of his wine in a single gulp. He signalled the waiter for another and sat, unspeaking, until it was in front of him. He reached for it but then drew his hand back without drinking.

Max let the silence linger. Herrera wanted to tell him something but, at the same time, didn't want say it out loud. Max took several bites of his salad, enjoying the mild earthy taste of the lentils, sharpened by the sweet taste of small tomatoes and the bite of red onion. The mint and lemon dressing brought it all together; the ripe sweet taste of the French wine was a delightful counter point. He had almost finished both before the Spaniard spoke again.

"All right, all right, Yelena hasn't been at the theatre for nearly a week, since the day the American was found in the lake. I thought she was grieving but now you tell me it was murder, I'm not so sure."

"You think Yelena had something to do with it?"

"No, no, nothing like that!" Herrera gulped a quarter of his wine. "Yelena is a sweet kid. People don't realize that, given the monstrous shows she preforms in. It's all fake, you know, despite the rumours. I think Camille Choisy, the director, deliberately spreads those rumours to attract a wider audience. Yelena was never the star; that honour goes to Paula Maxa. But Yelena was a regular. De Lorde, the chief playwright, liked her youth and innocence." Herera's voice turned bitter. "The audiences particularly like to see sweetness defiled, mutilated, killed. It made them feel something. Given what I sometimes heard from the private boxes, I think it excited them, you know, sexually."

Max recoiled at the description. Hadn't the world had enough horror in the trenches of eastern France? He certainly had, but he also understood the numbness that the war had caused for so many people, not merely soldiers but those who loved them, who had to deal with their deaths, or worse, the half-lives so many continued to live. He had felt something the same himself; Jacqui had saved him from that. He reminded himself to tell her so.

"Why do you think she has been away?"

"I don't know. Maybe she saw something? Maybe she's afraid and went into hiding. Maybe she's—" Herrera's voice broke and Max reached across the table and gripped his forearm. Herrera nodded and managed a small smile before pulling away.

Another missing woman. It seemed Paris was full of them these days. A lot of people seemed lost in Paris now.

"I'll check with my contacts in the Prefecture. If I hear anything, I'll let you know."

"Thanks. I... I appreciate that."

"Maybe you can tell me a little about the events leading up to her disappearance, who her friends were, where she lived, any conflicts you witnessed. Maybe start with a description so I'll know her if I see her."

"She is beautiful," said Hererra, as if that was all Max needed to know.

"Perhaps specifics would help."

"Sure, quite tall—I mean for a girl—with a dancer's body. You know, lean and strong. Long brown hair, dark eyes, dark brown but almost black in certain lights. Oval face, pale complexion." He paused, as if trying to call her image into his mind's eye. "She had dimples when she smiled. She hated them and always tried to look serious, but I liked them and did everything I could to bring them out."

"Good, what can you tell me about the rest?"

The waiter arrived with the plates of sole and Max gave Herrera a few minutes to gather his thoughts while they ate. The sole was simple, served with lemons and slivered almonds and accompanied by a small serving of potatoes au gratin. The pinot gris served as an appropriate counterpoint to it as well.

"I'm the assistant stage manager, at least, that's what they call me, but really, I'm the dogsbody, doing all the boring work no one else wants to do. I paint and assemble the sets but don't design them. I make sure the props are in place, the machines are working, the buckets of blood are close to hand. I put out the programs before the show and clean the stalls after. I'd like to do more but they tell me I lack imagination, though I think they think my French is not good enough."

Herrera's French was fine, though he spoke it with a heavy accent. Max had worked hard to sound like a Parisian but was still sneered at from time to time for his "Americanisms."

"As a result, I go everywhere, see and hear things that weren't meant for my eyes and ears. Nobody notices the servants; we're just part of the furniture." Herrera sounded more amused than bitter.

"Each night, we present five or six short plays. It's all horror, you know that right?"

"I'd heard. Ghosts, goblins, creatures of the night, that sort of thing."

"You need to go and see for yourself. They call it naturalistic theatre—ordinary people doing extraordinarily evil things. Rapes, murders, acts of torture, insanity, depravity, all of that with plenty of special effects and more gore than you can imagine. People faint, you know, or vomit, yet we pack them in every night."

Max took a deep breath. He knew he had to go to the theatre, witness it for himself and question those who may have known Walter Gladstone. He only hoped he wouldn't be one of the ones who fainted.

"Yelena used to appear in one play every few days but she's become a crowd favorite, featured in at least one play, every night, sometimes two or three. You might think Maxa would be jealous but I never heard her say a mean word either to Yelena or behind her back. I asked her once why she was so nice. She said she had experienced a lot of nastiness when she first appeared on the scene in 1917 and didn't want to pass it on. 'Besides' she said, 'starlets come and go, I am the most assassinated woman in the world. That makes me immortal.'"

"Is that what happened? Yelena got tired of the theatre or fell out of favour."

"I always thought she loved the limelight—it was something she was born to do—and Choisy and De Lorde ask me about her every night. I think they suspect I have something to do with her disappearance. But I don't, you have to believe me."

Max did believe that Herrera thought of himself as innocent but something had caused Yelena to avoid the theatre. She had disappeared the day Gladstone had died. Had she seen something or did she suspect Herrera had killed her new suitor? Or both?

"Tell me about Yelena and Gladstone."

"I already told you. He would show up at the theatre, or sometimes at one of the bars where the actors hung out. A lot of fancy words—he spoke Russian, you know—and presents. Nothing expensive, flowers, sweets, cheap jewelry, but she seemed to like it. I tried to match him but they don't pay me well and the only words of Russian I know are 'da,' 'nyet,' and 'ya tebya lyublyu.' A friend told me that means 'I love you,' but she only laughed when I said it to her. But I did love her and I know she loved me back.

"Anyway, a few days before he... died, I confronted him at one of the bars along Pigalle. It started out quiet enough but he got insulting. I pushed him and he took a swing at me. I knocked him to the ground and told him to get out. He did and I never saw him again."

"How did Yelena react to that."

"She laughed and said she liked it when I got 'Spanish' like that. Whatever that means. Then she said something funny. 'Poor Walter, he should know that getting involved with Russians will always lead to trouble.'"

"What was funny about that?"

"Well, she liked it when he spoke Russian to her—I could tell by the way she smiled and looked at him when he did—but other than her cousin, Ilsa, she didn't associate with any of the other Russians in the city, either white or red. They all live in the 8th but she lived in the 14th, about as far from there as you could get and still be in Paris."

Parc Montsouris was in the 14th. Did she live there to be close to the puppet theatre? Could she have been in the park the night Gladstone was murdered? Finding Yelena Semenova had risen to the top of his list of urgent tasks.

MAX RETURNED TO THEIR apartment on Rue Jacob to find Jacqui gone and a note, along with an unopened envelope on the kitchen table. The note, written in Jacqui's familiar scrawl, said: *The larder is bare. Gone shopping. Meet you at Le Coq Bleu.*

Max smiled to himself. Jacqui was shopping for more than food. He looked forward to seeing her new outfit.

The envelope was addressed to him in an unfamiliar hand. The note inside had lines that sloped down and with exaggerated loops on many of the letters. He glanced at the signature. It simply said: Hem.

> I heard back from my father at last. Gladstone's patriarch is unconcerned about both the death and the body. Suggests you deal with it as you see fit. Intriguing but not atypical for Chicago. Everyone there is as cold as the wind off the lake. Come to lunch at the Murphy's tomorrow. It should be a fine affair. Bring a guest. They are moving to the Riviera next month and everyone will be there. You might pick up some clues. Address below. 1 o'clock would be fine.

The address was on Gît-le-Coeur, only a ten-minute walk from their own place. Although he had taken a dislike to Hemingway on their first meeting, he still appreciated the invitation. Clues to Gladstone's death were few and far between. In any case, it might be fun and it would give Jacqui a chance to improve her English.

JACQUI'S OUTFIT DID not disappoint. She was sitting at the table that Yesim kept reserved for them Friday's and Saturdays until 8. Her new dress was a brilliant blue-green, like the feathers of a Teal duck, and reached to the middle of her calf, showing off her delicate ankles. The shape of the dress accentuated her slim figure, while revealing the smooth skin of her shoulders. A short grey jacket hung over the back of her chair which matched the colour of her shoes. A pair of grey gloves and a grey felt cloche hat decorated with a few bright feathers completed the outfit.

Max watched her through the glass for a few minutes before entering the bar. She was talking to Josette who laughed at something Jacqui said. Even the sour-faced Yesim broke into a broad grin as he served her a glass of white wine. Jacqui lifted the glass to Yesim before taking a sip, her own face glowing with happiness. He joined her, leaning down to kiss her lightly on the lips, before taking the chair opposite. Yesim delivered a glass of red—his own favorite tipple—almost before he had settled in his seat.

"What a handsome couple!" declared Yesim, glancing around at the other customers. "You elevate the quality of the place." Yesim was always trying to figure out ways to attract more fashionable, that is, richer, clientele, but the majority of the regulars remained local and working class.

Max felt rather dull next to Jacqui, though he was dressed in his best suit, a fitted grey pinstripe with a double breast and matching vest. He had brought a top coat but wasn't wearing it as the afternoon remained unseasonably warm, though it was likely to cool off as the evening progressed. Still, he agreed that the two of them looked good together and he once again considered how lucky he was to have her by his side.

He quickly explained that Hugo, whom Jacqui knew and liked, and Alain's cousin, Gaston, would be joining them briefly. He told her about the missing English woman and his so-far futile search for any sign for her. "It will take a lot of boring detective work to find any trace, I'm afraid."

Jacqui frowned at him. "I'd be happy to help you out. You only have to ask."

"With your job at the Opera, I don't see you enough as it is. Besides, Hugo and Gaston need the work. The recent devaluation has hurt working people especially hard."

"Ah, the detective has become the philanthropist," said Jacqui, smiling. "As you know, I strongly believe in making the rich pay so I can't disapprove of your logic. And, as you also know, the Opera is giving us all a break before we have to prepare the costumes for a brand-new opera, called Padmavati, which opens on June 1, so I have the next week off to spend entirely with you. You'll see plenty of me before my little holiday is over." Jacqui's wink and accompanying smirk let no doubt as to her true meaning and Max felt himself blushing at the images it evoked.

Jacqui reached across the table to lay her hand on his. "Have I told you today how much I love you?"

Max's face grew even hotter and his grin broader. "You just did. I love you, too."

"Do you two need to go somewhere more private?" Hugo stood a few paces away, grinning broadly, his teeth white beneath his light brown mustache. Another young man stood beside him—Gaston, Max presumed—looking uncertainly around the bar. Gaston was as Alain described him, short and lean though his posture suggested he was wiry rather than thin and the arms beneath his short-sleeved shirt were muscular. While Hugo was wearing an inexpensive suit, Gaston was dressed only in shirt and slacks.

Max shifted his chair to make room for them at the table. As they settled, Josette appeared to take their orders, greeting her cousin, Gaston, warmly.

"Nice to see you again, Josette," said Hugo. Max noticed that Hugo's grin had grown even broader as he gazed into the young woman's face and he wondered if someplace more private might suit them as well.

Josette returned in a few minutes with two lagers and plate of olives for the table. Max quickly described the tasks he had for the young men.

"The places you need to visit are roughly divided north and south of the river, all within the 1st through 8th arrondissements. Hugo lives in the south and works at Les Invalides, so he can take that section of the city, while Gaston can take the north side if that's agreeable."

"I have a room in the 11th, so that works well for me."

"There are a lot of places to visit and, as well, if you see any similar places in the same neighbourhoods, ask there, too. If anyone has seen Lady Wentworth, find out when, what if anything she purchased, and if she gave an address, for deliveries or whatnot. Report back here on Wednesday with your findings."

"If we get an address, should we contact her?" asked Hugo.

"No, she took off once and might do so again. Go by the place to see if you can spot her but be careful not to frighten her off. I don't think she is being coerced in any way but if you see signs of it, notify me at once, either here or at Chez Jake, or, if it seems urgent at our place on Rue Jacob."

Max took out his wallet and handed a sheaf of bills to each of them. "That's 350 francs for the job and another hundred for expenses. Keep receipts of purchases and records of any 'inducements' you need to hand out."

Gaston stared at the money as if he had never seen the like before. It was a generous wage—perhaps double what they paid for a week on the docks—but Max wondered if his employer had been cheating the boy.

They shared another round of drinks before Max and Jacqui left for their dinner date at Le Select, a brassiere that had only just opened in the 6th arrondissement but was already the talk of the town, with a reputation for avant-garde art on the walls and lively conversation at the tables. After, they would make a quick visit to a recently opened club, The Jockey, not far down Montparnasse for music and dancing. If they were lucky, they might even see an impromptu performance by Kiki, the young singer and model who had taken Montparnasse by storm.

Chapter 6 Saturday, May 5th to Sunday, May 6th 1923

On reflection the next morning, The Jockey had perhaps been too fine a cap on the evening. Kiki had been there and had performed, scandalously in Max's opinion, daring and bold according to Jacqui, who had roared with laughter at the look on his face when Kiki had flipped her skirt up right in front of him and then leaned forward to show him her breasts while crooning an improvised love song in his ear.

Despite his embarrassment, it had taken little for Jacqui to persuade him to stay and to join an impromptu line of dancers that snaked its way around the club and out into the street. They had finally left before two, though the party was still in full swing. Max had told Jacqui about the luncheon invite and her cooler head insisted they needed to get to bed before the sun came up.

She had also insisted they needn't go to sleep right away. The excitement of the evening still filled their bodies and they spent another hour kissing, talking, making love and then repeating the cycle until, at last, collapsing into sleep in each other's arms.

Despite the exertions of the night before, Max drifted awake sometime before ten. He lay in bed listening to Jacqui in their small kitchen. The rattle of plates was accompanied by the aroma of coffee. Max roused himself, pausing in the bathroom to relieve himself and brush the remains of the evening from his teeth. He pulled on the flannel robe Jacqui had given him for Christmas; time enough to put on a suit when his fast had been broken.

Jacqui had gone out while he slept and picked up a selection of brioche, croissant, and fruit tartlets from the bakery across the street and had perked a fresh pot of coffee—only her third attempt since they had purchased the coffee maker at Galleries Lafayette. He hoped she had had better success this time.

The coffee wasn't as good as what he could get across the street but it was hot and dark and he didn't have to get dressed to drink it. He looked at the half-dozen or so pastries on the table.

"You do remember we are having luncheon in a couple of hours?"

"Almost three. And what is a luncheon anyway. Less than lunch? More than a plate of canapes served by waiters in white? And who's to say they will feed us anyway? You weren't invited by the hosts but by one of their guests. And what am I supposed to wear? Not too formal, surely, but not work clothes?"

Max had seen Jacqui happy, mad, sad, excited, curious, loving, bored but he had never seen her nervous before. "It's only a luncheon, a few people getting together to say good-bye to these Murphy people. If we don't like it, or if it was a mistake, we can go for lunch at Le Dôme. You like the food there—"

"It's not about food. It's about... I don't know what it's about. Your friend Hemingway said everyone will be there. Who does that include and why does it include us?"

Hemingway was now his friend? How did that happen? "He's a writer, he probably means some other writers, people who might have known this Gladstone, the one whose death I'm investigating. Or maybe he simply is looking for characters for his next book. The Detective and his Anarchist Wife."

Max wasn't sure what he had said that was so wrong but Jacqui was crying now, great heaving sobs, her fists clutched in the fabric of her robe. He put his arms around her, felt her push him away one moment and then fling her arms around him the next.

"I don't want to be a character in a book! I don't want to be an interesting attachment to your side. I don't want to be your *wife*. Aren't I more than that to you?"

It was comfortable to think of Jacqui as his wife but he knew the limits of their handfasting vows—two free people who choose to travel together but who, if love failed, could freely walk away. He knew how important it was for her to feel, no, dammit, how important to both of them for her and for him to truly be free—free to love each other with all their hearts.

"You're everything to me, Jacqui. Everything that is good about me now is because we've known each other and loved each other. I need to go to this luncheon, whatever it is, because right now I don't have a clue what is going on, how any of the things I've learned or guessed at are connected. But you don't have to go with me."

Jacqui lifted her face from his chest and smiled up at him. "I want to come. But don't you dare refer to me as a wife. Now, let's eat, just in case all they serve us are quail eggs and tiny toast. Besides I have thought of the perfect outfit to wear."

Nervous and now mercurial. Everyday was a new adventure.

"They taught me in the trenches never to turn away from food or fun. You never know when either will come along again."

ALL HINT OF NERVOUSNESS had disappeared as they approached the address on Gît-le-Coeur. Jacqui looked both elegant and casual in a lemon calf-length dress with sky-blue trim and mother of pearl buttons. She wore a fine straw white hat with a blue taffeta bow and simple silver drop earrings with tiny blue stones. At

Jacqui's insistence, Max had donned a herring-bone sports coat over a pale blue shirt with button down collar and thin dark blue tie. He wore his dark blue fedora and carried a light overcoat in case it rained, though there seemed to be no break in the hot weather. As they were leaving, he slipped the note from Hemingway into his pocket to show they weren't gate-crashers.

The Murphy's apartment occupied the top two floors of one of the four-story rowhouses that lined the narrow street. A tired looking concierge waved them up the stairs to the third-floor landing without questioning their right to be there. Max hesitated before knocking on the door, fingering the note in his pocket. Before he could decide quite what to do, the door was flung open and the broad form of the American writer filled the doorway.

"Max, I knew you were the type to always arrive right on time. Glad you could make it. Gerald, Sara, this is the guy I was telling you about. The detective, from Canada."

The couple glanced over and nodded. He was tall, over six foot, and quite slim and perhaps in his late thirties though his receding hairline suggested he was older. He had a cane in his right hand and Max wondered if he had been wounded in the war. She was the same age or perhaps a bit older with a thick head of dark hair. They were talking to a pair of men, one short and barrel chested with thick dark hair and a penetrating gaze, which lingered for a few minutes on Jacqui before turning back to the conversation. The other was the man called Ez who had been with Hemingway in the gym.

The place itself was impressive and, from the faint smell of paint and glue that lingered in the air, had been recently renovated. The furniture had been arranged to allow for both an open space for guests to mingle as well as cozy nooks where more intimate conversations could occur. Against one wall was a table loaded with trays of food, some sitting over chafing dishes to keep warm. About a quarter of the two dozen or so guests were hovering over the delicacies and loading up small plates to carry with them as they mingled with the other guests. It wasn't lunch but it was much more than quail eggs and small toasts. From time to time a white jacketed waiter would appear from a backroom to replenish the repast.

A fully stocked bar manned by a mustachioed bartender had its share of devotees as well including an attractive young woman with red hair and a form fitting red dress. She was vaguely familiar but Max couldn't place her. She was engrossed in something the bartender was saying and kept her back to the rest of the room.

Hemingway glanced appreciatively at Jacqui and, for a moment, looked like a predator assessing its prey. Then he smiled and turned to Max. "I believe that introductions are in order. You can start with this lovely young lady."

Jacqui responded before Max could gather his thoughts.

"I'm Jacquiline Grandet, Mr. Hemingway, but everyone calls me Jacqui. I work at the Opera and live with Max. That's all you need to know for now."

Hemingway's brows went up and then he laughed. It was a warm full-throated laugh and Max could see, in that moment, why so many people seemed to like him. Behind the bully's façade was something deeper and more decent.

"Well, Jacqui, I look forward to learning more about you and what you see in the mysterious Mr. Anderson. You can call me Hem, or if you like, Papa. Now, let me make some introductions."

Hemingway led them around the place as if he were the hosts instead of the Murphys. They seemed unconcerned and greeted both Max and Jacqui warmly before returning to their conversation. Ez nodded brusquely in their direction but the other man ignored them.

"That's Pablo Picasso, the Spanish painter. Whenever he's exploring one of his big ideas, it's as if he's in a world of his own."

Max was surprised that he recognized several of the other guests. Galantière was there, chatting with a short square woman whom Max recognized from his lunch with Asper as Gertrude Stein.

"A private detective, is it? Like the ones Mrs. Christie writes about?"

"You never cease to amaze me, Stein," said Hemingway. "I didn't know you were a fan of mysteries."

"I am not a fan of anything. I'm a student of everything. Speaking of which have you been keeping up with your reading."

"Every morning after writing, you'll find me with my nose in a book. Just ask Hadley—Hash says it makes me dull." He gestured to a woman seated in one of the nooks talking to several young men.

Tsara was also there, leaning in one corner of the room, sketchbook in hand. He seemed strangely unapproachable and Hemingway cut him a wide berth. Instead, he guided Max to a group of four young men gathered in one of the nooks. They were all of a type, casually dressed in sporty attire, almost as if they were about to go to a tennis club or golf course, short hair, clean shaven except for one who had an artfully waxed mustache. Americans, Max guessed, based on the volume of their conversation and their forced smiles as Hemingway approached. Two stood, thrusting out their hands, which Hemingway grasped too firmly and shook briefly. The ones who remained seated smirked at their colleagues; they were familiar with the big man's show of dominance. Hemingway introduced them in a flurry of names, too quick to be remembered.

"They were... acquaintances of Gladstone. I overheard them *gossiping* about his death at Le Dôme and asked them to come and meet you. I'll leave you to it." Hemingway touched Jacqui lightly on her shoulder, a momentary gesture meant to guide rather than possess. "I'll introduce Mme Grandet to Diaghilev, if she wishes."

"The impresario?" Jacqui's eyes had widened. She knew who he was even if Max didn't.

"The very one. I'm sure he'll take time out of trying to get money for the latest season from the Murphys to chat with a charming young woman. And, don't worry, Max, she definitely isn't his type."

Max watched as Hemingway guided her back across the room to the so-called impresario. He was a tall man of about fifty with dark hair (with a single streak of white running through it) and mustache and an imperial air. He was dressed in formal attire, a sharp contrast to the casual clothing most of the guests had chosen. He was talking animatedly to Gerald Murphy, gesturing to a younger man standing at his side, who appeared completely bored by the whole thing. When Heminway approached with Jacqui, Diaghilev's face broke into a warm, almost fatherly smile.

"You had some questions about Walter?" The man with the mustache gave up his chair and joined the others on one of the chaise lounges that formed the rest of the nook. Max's thoughts scrabbled for his name before coming up with Stephen Something-or-other-wood. Max took out his notebook and sat down.

"How did you know Mr. Gladstone?" he asked.

"Are you really a private detective?" one of the others asked.

"Do you work for the Prefecture?" asked another, looking dubious.

"I am and I don't, not directly at least, but sometimes with them."

"Why are you investigating his death?" asked the dubious one.

"His friend, Helen Miller, asked me to look into it. She wasn't satisfied with the official police version." It reminded him that he should report to his client on Monday, even though he had made little progress so far. "Now perhaps I can ask a few questions."

The dubious one raised his eyebrows then glanced at his fellows before nodding. "Again, how did you know Mr. Gladstone?

"Why don't you start Archie? You probably know him best."

"Sure." Archie glanced down at his hands, which were small and had faint ink stains on the fingers of the right one. "Walter and I came over on the same ship, the Majestic. It was the end of March last year and the weather was rough so the trip took twelve days. We met up in the lounge on the second day. He was funny and outgoing and had a way with the girls, so I hung around with him. I... guess I thought I could bask in his reflected glory or some such."

"Good line!" exclaimed the fourth of the quartet, the only one wearing glasses.

"Probably hoping to latch onto one of his cast-offs," said Mr. Dubious, whom Max was starting to dislike. Archie glared at his so-called friend before continuing.

"Anyway, he was a funny bird. He talked a lot but never seemed to say anything. Ten days later, all I knew about him was he came from Chicago, was amazingly lucky at cards, good with dames and planned to write the great American mystery novel. I asked him about that—I am trying to finish my first book myself—but he wouldn't talk about it, said it ruined his thinking to discuss his work.

"We took the same train up to Paris and even roomed together for a couple of weeks in an apartment a friend had arranged for him. One day, he politely asked me to vacate, said I was too much of a slob. I was jake with that. He wasn't easy to live with, moody, you know, and like he had these big secrets that he wanted to tell you but couldn't."

"Any idea what they were?"

Archie's brow furrowed. "Something about his family, I think. I was complaining how my father didn't really support what I was doing with my life—he wanted me to go into the family business—and Walter said something like 'well, at least he tells you what he thinks, my father lives to lie to me.' He said a couple of things later on that made me think his parents wanted him out of the country and gave him plenty of money to let him do it."

"Did Walter have any enemies?"

An awkward silence was finally broken by Stephen the mustache. "Enemies may be too strong a word but there were a couple of people who really took a dislike to him. You should track down Alec Minter when he gets back to town."

"He left Paris?"

"I think he said he was going to Berlin for a couple of weeks, to see if it was as decadent as they say. He, ah, left right around the time Walter died."

"He's definitely coming back," said Spectacles. "He kept his room on Saint-Sulpice. He asked me to go in to check on his cat while he was away, a pretty little calico that... I guess that's not important."

Max shrugged and made a note of the address. "Any thing can be important. What was Minter's beef with Gladstone?"

"He claimed that Walter was somehow interfering with his writing, bad mouthing him to magazine editors and publishers. I think Alec was jealous of Walter," said Mr. Dubious.

"Of his writing?"

"Hell, no," Dubious looked around as if concerned his blasphemy might have been over heard, though Max doubted it would matter to this crowd. "Walter had a few credits to his name but most of us do, the odd poem or short piece published in journals that we all read but, frankly, the general public has never heard of. Minter had had no success at all and had been rejected by all the places that had taken stuff from Gladstone. But the real reason was, as the Frenchies say: cherchez la femme."

"Any particular femme?"

"Helen Miller," they all said in chorus. Max scribbled a quick note. His client hadn't told him the whole story. Nothing new there.

"She was Minter's girl?"

"Hardly," said Stephen. "Minter made a play for her. She's a pretty girl, likeable, too. I made a pass myself but she wasn't interested... she had a good reason to say no but it's not my business to say so. Anyway, Minter wasn't... well, he wasn't a gentleman. He cornered her at a party and—"

"Gladstone knocked him on his ass!" Spectacles grinned as he said it, suggesting he might have liked a go at Minter himself.

"Did he ever," chimed in Dubious. "Then when she and Walter began to pal around, Minter claimed he had stolen her away from him. Pure applesauce, of course. If you saw them together, they were like brother and sister."

"I don't think Helen was his type," chimed in Archie. "Too strait-laced. I think he liked them kind of wild. There was a girl called Clarice, what was her last name?"

"Michaels," said Spectacles, his grin broader than ever. "She took it hard when he dumped her for that Russian actress. Clarice almost scratched his eyes out when he brought Yelena to La Rotonde."

Max recalled that one of the young women he had met during his initial investigations had been called Clarice. He made a note to track her down. "Anyone else?"

Archie shook his head. "A couple of fellows took a dislike to Walter but it didn't seem serious. Mostly they would high-hat him at parties, make a few smart remarks, but it never came to blows."

Max chatted with the quartet for a few more minutes but it was clear they had nothing more to add. He took down their actual names and where he could contact them if he had further questions. He left them his calling card so they could reach him if they thought of anything else.

He looked around for Jacqui and spotted her talking to the one called Picasso. Several other men and a couple of young women were listening attentively. He headed in their direction when Galantière intercepted him. "Max, Miss Stein wants to speak to you."

Gertrude Stein was holding court in another nook, talking to Heminway and two women, the slim brunette with short hair, dressed in mannish clothes and an older woman, small and slightly stooped. The former was introduced as Sylvia Beach, the patron of young writers, and the latter as Alice Toklas. Stein dismissed Beach and Hemingway—she took it with a patient smile, he, with a broad grin—and asked the other woman to get her a drink, which she left to do with a long-suffering expression.

"Hemingway has told me that you are investigating the death of a young American writer. Did you know him? Did you meet him in 1917 after the Germans were foolish enough to resume attacking passenger ships with their U-boats? Or were you a volunteer like Hemingway come to serve in the ambulance corps?"

"I'm a Canadian. I signed up as soon as the war started. I was 21 and could do as I wanted and I wanted to serve my country."

"I thought Canadians fought under British command."

"We were a separate corps commanded by British generals until General Currie took over in 1917. When you're in the trenches the only real distinction is between us and them—and sometimes you're not even sure about that. Is that what you wanted to talk to me about? My military career?"

"No. I needed some context. A man's relationship to the Great War tells one a great deal about him. I think Hemingway still suffers from his experiences. His suffering is what will make him great, mark my words."

"My suffering only made me suffer."

"Yet, I understand you have made a life for yourself and have devoted yourself to solving crimes. You make your living seeking justice. I must believe the war had something to do with that."

"Maybe. I try not to think about the war."

"And yet, I see by your expression that you do. In any case, the murder of a young writer concerns me; it should concern us all. This Gladstone had shown little talent but he was young. Some writers burst upon the scene; others require growth and maturity. It is a loss in any case."

"My generation has suffered a lot of losses. Ask any Frenchman what they lost."

Max was getting annoyed. These people stand around or lean back in soft chairs and discuss the world as if they actually lived in it. Art, music, literature, it had its place, maybe even an important place but it was only an imitation of life, not life itself.

"I see that I'm boring you. Still, I may be of some help if you'll take it. I have lived in Paris for a long time, twenty years this fall, and I have come to know the city and its inhabitants. I have seen waves of Americans make their way here, looking for fame or fun or fortune. This generation is no different except perhaps they are more lost than those who came before. In any case, I have many friends and contacts from all walks of life. Give me a week or two then come and see me and I'll tell you what I've found."

"Why would you want to help me?"

"Why not? I am a collector, of art, yes, but also of experiences. And I, too, have a sense of justice. Will you come? You can generally find me at 27 rue de Fleurus."

Max nodded. She might be a useful source of information. She certainly understood the art world in ways that he never would and there was no doubt art had something to do with this murder. He took out his notebook and noted the address as well as a telephone number he could reach her by.

He retrieved Jacqui—she seemed more than ready to leave—and thanked his hosts. Before he could exit the salon, he was stopped by Tsara, who was also making his way out, seemingly without talking to any of the other attendees.

"Pardon me, mademoiselle, I need a few words with Mr. Anderson."

"I'll wait for you downstairs. I need some fresh air. Don't be long, Max, it's been a long weekend already."

Tsara and Max stopped on the landing outside the Murphy's apartment.

"You expressed an interest in the Grand Guignol. You might want to go tonight. There is something planned you might find interesting."

Max had intended to take in a performance. Tonight was as good a time as any.

A NAP AND A SHOWER refreshed them both and, after a light supper at a local café, they set off for the theatre on cité Chaptal. The theatre itself was unimpressive, a three-story structure at the end of a narrow lane. A passing shower earlier had left the cobbles glistening and slightly slippery as they picked their way along the street. A single tree overhung the narrow lane, its branches looming over them lit only by a few lights and a waning gibbous moon. The show was scheduled to start in only a few minutes and they were the last to arrive.

The choice of seats together was limited to a pair in the front row against the outer wall or ones in the second row of balcony tier. Max debated whether a close-up view was preferable to a broader perspective. Jacqui was more practical, pointing out that the front row chairs were called the spit seats for a reason and, given the reputation of the theatre, spatters of saliva might be the least unpleasant thing they might encounter. In any case the theatre was small—fewer than three hundred seats—so even the balcony would provide a good look on the action.

They had barely settled in their chairs when the lights dropped and the blood red curtain rose to reveal a woman swathed in white sheets and strapped to a gurney. She struggled for her freedom but the straps were tight. Her moans and inchoate cries echoed through the theatre while lights flickered and sparked from arcane devices in the background. A door creaked open as a hunched figure, in a long white coat, crept onto the stage. Their head was swathed in bandages, obscuring their face and hair and it wasn't until she spoke that Max realized it was also a woman.

"The patient is ready for you, Herr Doctor," she called out and a tall handsome man strode through the open door. It was only when he reached the head of the gurney and turned to face the audience was it revealed that one side of his face was hideously scarred as if burnt by fire or acid. When he spoke his voice was guttural, as if it too had been mutilated.

"Here we see the struggles of the demented, incurable by routine treatments. See how her body lifts at my approach, as the lust of the nymphomaniac struggles with the murderous rage of the psychopath. Sex and death, embodied in a single mad mind."

"But your technique..."

"...will either liberate her or kill her. In either case, she will be better off than how she is now."

The doctor's assistant pushed a trolley from the side of the stage; a glittering array of blades covered the top and the doctor lifted several in turn, examining the edge or testing the jagged teeth against his thumb. He finally selected a small saw, placed it against the restrained woman's forehead and in a dozen quick strokes began his gruesome surgery.

The top of the woman's head fell to the stage floor, the sharp snap of bone against wood sounding like the crack of a rifle. Max jerked back in his seat, for a brief instant back in the trenches of northern France seeing Corporal Gerry McDonald collapsing in his arms, his face shattered by a sniper's bullet. Jacqui put her hand on his leg and gently squeezed it to bring him back to the here and now. He glanced at her gratefully; she knew what he was going through.

He was no stranger to violence, to the worst urges to which men and woman were prone, and now, more than four years away from the war, he had found a way to deal with it by bringing the culprits to justice. Surely this, which he knew was mere trickery, shouldn't bring back the memories he had, at first, tried to forget. He had moved beyond forgetting to understanding, largely due to Jacqui's help and the kindness of his friends.

Somehow what he was witnessing on stage was more real than real, it dug deeper into the sheer depravity of those who do terrible things while pretending their cause is just and good. Maybe that's why people flocked to this theatre; it gave them a chance to hate those who had led them into the bloodiest war in history without requiring them to do anything about it.

Then, the play was over, the mutilated corpse of the patient wheeled off-stage by the cackling doctor and his assistant, whose hunched body swayed sensuously as she pushed the gurney, her face mere inches from the gaping cavity where the woman's brain had been extracted. Sex and death in a single body.

In the brief intermission before the next performance, Max put his arm over Jacqui's shoulders and pulled her close.

"Sorry for putting you through this," he whispered.

"It's okay, Max." She tilted her head up and gently kissed him on the lips. "Do you want to leave?"

"Not yet."

When the curtain rose again, the scene had completely changed, the work of Carlos Herrera Max presumed. The walls were like that of a dungeon in a castle, large stone blocks with a single arched entrance. An emaciated corpse, little more than a skeleton draped in bits of flesh and tattered rags, was shackled to the back wall.

In the foreground, a woman, naked to the waist, was being held down by two men while a third danced around her body, his arms and legs making grotesque imitations of the graceful movements of ballet dancers. With a final pirouette, he pounced on the woman, pushing her legs apart. Though her body was obscured by the heavy coat he wore, it was clear from his motions and her cries and pleas that the was raping her. Max felt himself rise from his seat but Jacqui leaned into him.

"It's not real, Max, though what it depicts is all too real in this city of shadows."

Despite that, one couple seated in the row behind them suddenly leapt to their feet and bolted from the theatre.

The third play was even more grotesque than the first two. Set in what was clearly meant to be a ward in an asylum, patients acted out their mad fantasies as doctors watched on. Before the action had progressed very far, a sudden commotion from the seats of the orchestra section drew attention away from the stage.

A dozen men and women, who had been sitting in the middle of the first few rows had leapt to their feet and were yelling at the performers on the stage.

"Naturalism is a lie."

Some had also produced banners that echoed their taunts.

"The past is dead. The future in now."

Some members of the audience were heading for the exits. Others were pushing their way toward the protesters. Max spotted Tsara leaning against the wall farthest from the action. He was holding his ever-present sketchbook. He looked around the theatre until he spotted Max watching him. He made a small gesture with his head before returning his attention to the growing melee in the centre of the theatre.

"Thought is made in the mouth."

Some of those making their way into the turmoil had slogans of their own.

"Forget reality; only the surreal holds the truth."

One of the first group pushed one of the newcomers to the ground. "Dada is like your hopes: nothing."

On stage, the actors had formed a frozen tableau. Some had expressions of outrage on their faces while others were clearly amused.

"Perhaps we should get out of here before the swallows arrive and arrest us all," said Jacqui.

Max nodded. Jacqui was familiar with the indiscriminate approach of the police when rioters—no matter what their reasons—got out of control. He looked back to Tsara but the man had slipped away. He apparently had no need to see how this disturbance would be resolved.

Jacqui was already halfway down the stairs when Max's attention was drawn back to the stage by an angry bellow.

"Get out. Get the fuck out." It was Carlos Herera, standing on the edge of the stage. "Get out before I do something you'll regret."

Hererra jumped off the stage and began to move forward, the protestors stumbling over each other to get away. The Spaniard had a wooden club in one hand; in the other, the long thin blade of a stiletto gleamed in the lights from the stage.

MAX HAD BEEN TEMPTED to return and confront Herrera but he didn't want to abandon Jacqui to find her way home. Pigalle was not a safe neighbourhood for a woman alone, no matter how independent she was.

They slept late the next day, not rising until well past ten o'clock. The weather was cooler, aided by some light rain over night, but the day was still pleasant and sunny. By the time Max came out of the shower, Jacqui had gathered together a picnic basket, consisting of roast chicken, egg salad sandwiches, a hunk of hard yellow cheese and two bottles of chilled white wine.

"It's time I saw the park where this infamous murder took place. I've always wanted to see an artificial lake and an English garden."

The designer of Parc Montsouris, Jean-Charles Alphand had opted to recreate an English landscape garden, probably to show that what ever the English could do, the French could do better. It had changed considerably in the more than fifty years since it opened, with the addition of several works of art and other structures but the general plan of the park remained. Max thought it would be nice to explore the short trails and woods in the company of his lover, without, necessarily focussing on the grisly death that occurred there.

They had finished their lunch and were strolling around the perimeter of the lake—Jacqui insisted on seeing where the body had been found—and were about to head home when a familiar voice called out.

"Max! Jacqui! What a pleasant surprise." Ginger Buchan was approaching from the other direction, with a slightly older man who resembled Buchan closely enough to be his brother, which, in fact, he was.

"This is my brother, Sol. He's here with his wife and four children. Sol, this is my friend, Max Anderson and his, ah, wi... ah, friend, Jacqui Grandet."

Max shook the proffered hand. Jacqui smiled sweetly at Buchan's awkward introduction. "Pleased to meet you, Sol. Is that short for Solomon?"

"It is indeed, though I make no claim to wisdom. I leave that to my brother, the diplomat."

"What brings you to Parc Montsouris?" asked Max, always suspicious of chance encounters where Ginger Buchan was involved.

"My idea," said Sol. "After a week of art museums, monuments and cemeteries, I thought the children deserved a break, something more to their taste. Peter remembered you had told him about a puppet theatre here and that, plus some ice cream cones, have proved very popular. We were just heading back to collect them when he spotted you."

"Why don't you and Jacqui go ahead? I need to talk to Max for a moment."

Max watched Jacqui walk away on Sol's proffered arm and heard her laugh at some remark he had made to her. "What was it you wanted to talk to me about?"

"Just an interesting tidbit about your client and about the man whose murder she asked you to investigate."

"Go on."

"Helen Miller is a card-carrying member of the Socialist Party of America."

"I thought America didn't have socialists."

"They're like rats, they have no respect for borders. We try to keep them under wraps as much as possible, but you know, free country and all that. Their leader even ran for President in the last election, though his campaign was limited since he was in prison at the time. Didn't stop nearly a million people voting for him."

"All very interesting, or it would be if I was interested in politics. Helen Miller didn't bring up politics when she hired me. She just wanted to get justice for a friend."

"Then maybe this will interest you a bit more. Gladstone's original family name was Rubinovich. His grandfather was kicked out of Russia by the Tzar for sedition. Put those two facts together and they spell Bolshevik to me. Maybe you should take a little more interest in politics and find out the connection between Miller, Gladstone and the Reds."

Chapter 7 Monday May 7th 1923

Max woke with the dawn, his mind whirling with the experiences of the last twenty-four hours. He listened to Jacqui's gentle breathing for a few minutes but sleep did not return so he crept from their bed and dressed quietly in the small living room. He scribbled a note inviting her to join him for lunch at the Lux-Bar not far from their old apartment on Rue Lepic. Though they had been living in their new place for nearly four months, he still thought of Montmartre as his Paris home.

He wished Henri would return from his investigation in the north. Then, they would all gather at Le Coq Bleu where he could hash over the case with his most trusted friends. In the meantime, he would breakfast here on Rue Jacob and then walk from there to his office at Chez Jake. An hour on his feet would help burn off the excesses of the weekend and give him a chance to think through his next steps.

The bar was dark and quiet when Max arrived so he let himself in and gathered a few pieces of mail that had arrived with the early post. He made a cup of coffee in the kitchen before creeping up the stairs to his office, careful not to wake the denizens who were still sleeping off the Sunday night jam session that Smitty hosted while Jake was away. Jake rarely commented on Max's "other work," as he called it, but his observations were often sharp and to the point. Yet another absent friend whose advice he missed.

His mood brightened when he discovered that one of the letters was from Henri, who would return on the late train and would meet him at Le Coq Bleu for lunch the next day after the regular crowd departed. "I am sure," he finished, "to have this matter resolved by then."

The other correspondence consisted a request for help in a divorce case, which Max crumpled up and threw in the trash and several bills that needed paying within fifteen days. He set those aside for Jake's return which was scheduled for the end of the week. He took out his notebook and made a list of those he had to see, or, in some cases, find in the next few days.

At the top of his list was Yelena Semenova, Gladstone's reputed love interest. Although police "wisdom" claimed that poison was a woman's preferred method of murder, in Max's experience, women were not averse to using more violent means. Given the manner of his death, might not a lover be able to approach him from behind and deliver the fatal blow? Would she then be able to move the body into the lake? Max had his doubts but with only the vaguest description of Semenova, he would have to meet her to be sure.

Monday was typically a dark day for theatres but members of the cast and crew might still be found at The Grand Guignol, rehearsing or otherwise preparing for the week's performances. If he was lucky, he would find both Yelena and her so-called boyfriend at the same time.

Yelena was key to moving the case forward. If she knew anything about Gladstone's background, it might either confirm or discount Buchan's speculations. The man tended to see Bolshevik's hiding around every corner but he had proven right often enough that it was worth following up. If Gladstone was involved somehow with the Reds, Max could consult with some of the contacts he had made in the Russian quarter during a previous case. Chatting with Joseph Asper and Colonel Dominic Ledux might prove useful. He paused and stared at his growing list. It was a long shot, but he added the name of Jacopo Giamatti's eastern European friend, Madame Mira Novak.

Helen Miller had a few questions to answer as well, though as his client, he would have to find a delicate way of asking them. He would also still like to speak to Delacroix to get his insights into the tumultuous arts scene and what, if anything, Gladstone might have done to earn some enemies there. Of, course, he also needed to track down the young writer who apparently carried a grudge against the dead man.

That certainly left him with plenty to do for the rest of the week but he still had to make progress on the other three cases he had, perhaps foolishly, taken on. Henri might have solution to one, though he wouldn't know until he talked to him. Roget should report back on his task soon and he would need to check with Alain on anything more he had discovered with respect to the potential industrial spy. Hugo and Gaston should have finished their assignments over the weekend, which would hopefully shed light on the whereabouts of Cleroux's missing heiress.

He hesitated for a moment before adding Gertrude Stein to the list. It seemed unlikely but he had learned over the years that the most vital clues often came from the most unlikely sources.

BOTH SEMENOVA AND HERERRA were at the theatre when Max arrived, caught in a vigorous conversation, though Herrara was doing most of the yelling, in a mixture of Spanish and heavily accented French that Max couldn't decipher. Other members of the troupe stood around the stage and watched with bemused expressions. The discussion ended when the young woman slapped Hererra's face and stomped off across the stage. Hererra started to follow but Max intercepted him.

"Let me speak to her. I'll put in a good word for you. Stay here. I want to talk to you as well."

Hererra looked unhappy but he nodded his compliance and Max followed the woman into the backstage area. He expected to find her crying but, as usual when it came to women, he was wrong. She was with another woman, laughing at something she had said. As Max approached, the other woman nodded in his direction, said something too low for him to hear, and walked quickly out of the area.

Yelena turned to face him. She was, as Hererra had said, quite beautiful, and when she stepped toward him, he could see the athletic grace one might expect from a dancer.

"Yelena Semenova?"

"You are this detective that Carlos told me about? What do you want from me?" Her voice was pitched low, with only the hint of a Russian accent.

"You were a friend of Walter Gladstone?"

"Poor Walter, yes, a friend, I suppose, but not close, no matter what Carlos thinks. He has cast himself in the role of the jealous boyfriend, wrongly accused of a rival's murder. It would be a tragedy if it were not a farce."

"I was told that Walter was courting you."

"Yes, yes, some might think that. But it was as much of an illusion as what occurs on this stage. Walter and Carlos—and countless others—imagine they are in love with me. Worse they imagine I love them back."

"I thought Carlos was your fiancé."

Yelena held her left hand up and turned it back and forth as if trying to catch something in the light.

"Do you see a ring here? It is the fad now, you know, to give a ring when you propose marriage."

"Then Carlos has asked you for your hand in marriage?"

"In his mind, I am sure he has, but, in reality, he has not. Nor has he contacted my parents in Moscow for their permission, not that they would care." She looked away but not before Max saw the glint of a tear. "We are estranged."

"So, Carlos had no reason to be jealous?"

She turned back sharply, her eyes flashing. "When do men need a reason? Do not mistake me. I like Carlos well enough. He has his charms but he does not own me. I have no interest in being owned by a man."

"Did Walter have his charms, too?"

Yelena smiled wistfully, showing off the dimples that Carlos loved so much. She gestured to a pair of chairs and Max followed her lead. Once they were settled, she leaned forward and spoke in a low voice, as if she didn't want to be overheard.

"Walter was funny and he had money he was willing to spend on trinkets and treats. I don't think he was courting me, no matter what others think. We never talked of love, rather we spoke of being strangers in a strange land, both of us, living in Paris, speaking in French, but neither of us really from here. Do you know what I mean?"

Max nodded. He had come to Paris after the war because he couldn't bear the thought of returning to Canada and his family. For years, he had spoken nothing but French and had immersed himself in the culture of the city. It was the best place he had ever imagined, yet, sometimes, he thought he would never really be part of the city, like Yelena had said, a stranger in a strange land.

"Of course, Walter was obsessed with writing his novel. He had great ambition that way though whether he had talent, I couldn't say. I proposed he write a script for the theatre here, something I could take the lead in. He laughed and said that was a good idea, but I don't know that he did anything about it."

"Some of his fellow writers said he was putting something together." Max gave himself a mental kick. He had found the playscript in Gladstone's flat but hadn't read it. He wondered if it might contain a clue. Didn't writers sometimes include real people in their work, as a tribute or an insult. "That was it then. You would have coffee or a meal and talk about the theatre and being foreigners in your shared second tongue. It must have been difficult to—"

"No. That was the best thing about Walter. He spoke Russian. Better than French, I think. It was nice to talk to someone other than my cousin in my native tongue."

"There are plenty of Russians in Paris..."

"Tsarists!" She practically spat the word. "And those who spy on them."

"You don't support the White Russian cause?"

"Why should I? They are only in it for themselves. They yearn for the old Russia where they could have servants to serve them caviar and tea while serfs toiled in their fields. That Russia is gone, never to return. I don't support them. I don't even care about them."

"You prefer the Soviet regime."

"I'm Russian. I accept what is and get on with my life. Tsar or Commissaire, it is all the same to me. I want my freedom, a concept most Russians have a hard time grasping."

"But Walter grasped it?"

"Yes, I think he did. He wanted to be free, too. Free of his family and their history, free of America, free to be who he really was."

"And who was he?"

"A friend, not a lover. Not really anything but a man wrapped up in his own passion. Which, I assure you, was not for me." Her eyes misted again. "I will miss him."

Max resisted reaching out to comfort her. She clearly would take it the wrong way, as another man intruding on her freedom. He had learned something about Gladstone here though he wasn't entirely sure what it was. He wondered if he was one of those men who only liked women as friends, whose own deeper affections ran in a deeper direction. There had been no hint of it but, even in Paris, many choose to keep that part of them secret. He knew they had good reason; some would view it as a reason for murder.

"One last question before I go," he said. "You weren't seen around the city for a week after Gladstone was killed. Where were you?"

"Even actresses need a holiday. I took advantage of the warm weather and went to La Rochelle with a friend. Not someone who knew Walter in case you were wondering."

Perhaps but someone worth looking into if other leads didn't develop. He would be speaking to Semenova again.

AS IT TURNED OUT, MADAME Novak was no longer at the address that the Prefecture had for her and the concierge thought that she might have left Paris altogether. If he wanted to track her down, he would probably have to locate Giamatti. He likely had better sources of information but added his name to his list of potential contacts in case it came to that. He had only slightly better luck with some of his other contacts in the Russian community. Irina Pavlovna agreed to see him but not until the following Monday when she returned from Berlin. Baron Denidov simply didn't respond to his request for a meeting. Max knew he could probably find him in one of the gambling clubs in the Russian quarter but he doubted it was worth the effort; Pavlovna was the more connected source.

Colonel Ledux agreed to see him at four for cognac and cigarettes. That left Joseph Asper, whom he would try to track down at the Sorbonne after lunch. Helen Miller would have to wait until the morning and he made arrangements to see her at a café near where she was staying in the 7th arrondissement for a mid-morning coffee.

Jacqui was waiting for him at the Lux Bar, sitting at a table under the green awning to take advantage of the still pleasant weather. They had been regulars there when they lived just down the street and Daniel, the chef, was Josette's uncle and had helped her set up the food service at Le Coq Bleu. He was standing by the table chatting to Jacqui when Max arrived ten minutes past the hour. He greeted Max warmly with a bise on each cheek and promised to make them something special to celebrate their return to the neighbourhood.

While waiting for the food to arrive, Max told Jacqui of his encounter with Yelena Sokolov and her declaration of independence from any man.

"Maybe she's an anarchist. There are a lot of them in Russia you know. Bakunin and Kropotkin were both important to the establishment of anarchist thinking. The latter was imprisoned in Lyon for several years but still managed to produce significant books that are required reading for anyone interested in the cause. I can loan you my copy of *Words of a Rebel* if you like."

Jacqui and Henri had taken it upon themselves to further his education in French culture and politics. She recommended political tracts, often very obscure ones, while Henri was always producing a "classic" novel for his bookshelf. Max would dutifully read each one, usually in bed at night when he was having difficulty falling asleep. The books were more effective and healthier than a glass of brandy.

Chef Daniel delivered the food himself, a warm spring salad of arugula, baby spinach, sauteed mushrooms, toped with goat cheese and sandwiches of rillettes of rabbit on thick sourdough bread. A bottle of chilled Alsace Riesling was served with the meal, which Max thought was a perfect match but Jacqui found a little sweet. Still, she drank one glass "to be sociable," but refused a second. After lunch, both took the Metro to the other side of the Seine. She got off at Saint-Germaine-de-Prés to return home while he continued on to Cluny La Sorbonne.

Joseph Asper was half way through a lecture to about thirty students on the history of Croatia. Max took a seat at the back of the hall until he finished and even took note of several points of interest in the talk. It had been nearly a decade since he had sat in a university lecture hall and he felt a wave of nostalgia to be in the halls of academe again.

Asper finished the talk and handed out a reading list to those who wanted more information. Max took one and carefully folded it and slipped it into his jacket pocket while Asper finished his conversation with two of the students.

"I never thought I'd say this but I love teaching," said Asper, as they made their way out of the hall to a nearby bistro. "The pay, however, is execrable so I'd be pleased to provide you with whatever useful information I can, as per our usual agreement."

Asper had been one of Max's first informants back when he was investigating the death of Havel Barzani four years before. The rates had increased from fifty francs to over a hundred but the deal was still the same. Max paid for each useful fact or lead, but he got to determine what constituted useful.

Asper ordered a large lager and a charcuterie board, which he invited Max to share. "Lecturing is hungry work as is, I'm sure, detecting."

Max had a small glass of beer and picked at the olives and cheese to, as Jacqui put it, be sociable. Max explained the two cases that seemed to have some connection to the Russian community, both Gladstone's murder, and, more uncertainly, the industrial espionage case. "What rumours are circulating among Pavlovna and her friends?"

"I'm not as well connected there as I used to be but I still go to the Petrograd at least once a week; they have the best veal Orloff in the city."

The pay might be execrable at the Sorbonne but it was apparently good enough for the best meal in the house. Max could remember when Asper could barely scrape together enough money for a shared room in a bad neighbourhood. He didn't begrudge him his prosperity now.

"Pavlovna and Davidovitch are still plotting the overthrow of the new Soviet government in Moscow despite the final annihilation of the White army last October. However, they aren't the only ones in conflict with the new regime, or rather, I should say, within the new regime. The undisputed leader, Vladimir Lenin, has been ailing since he was shot in the assassination attempt of 1918 and, rumour has it, he suffered a collapse in March. He is still a force to be reckoned with but already the vultures are circling his body in case he doesn't make a recovery.

"Stalin seems to have the inside track for succeeding as leader of the party and, so, the country, but I wouldn't rule out the commander of the Red Army, Lev Davidovitch Bronstein, better known as Leon Trotsky. He proved a very able tactician during the various military conflicts and, was for a time, considered the heir apparent. Take nothing for granted behind the closed doors of the Kremlin."

"How does that relate to Paris and the cases I mentioned?"

"Sorry, I'm still in lecture mode. Trotsky is a proponent of international revolution whereas Stalin wants to consolidate power within the Soviet Union. There is a rumour that Trotsky will take a swing through western Europe, including Paris, this spring to drum up support for his leadership, among the members of the third International and to test the waters for a communist uprising in Germany in the wake of the occupation of the Ruhr.

"Meanwhile, Stalin is pushing for the rapid industrialization of Russia, putting a final nail in the coffin of serfdom while preparing for the inevitability of further conflict with Europe. They're starting at a very low bar so industrial theft is almost certainly one of their strategies to move forward quickly. If your engineer is working for the Soviets or, even aiming to sell to the highest bidder, it might explain his visit to the Petrograd restaurant."

"I thought it was a hangout for the White Russians."

"It is. What better place for Soviet agents to congregate than where the objects of their interest have drunken dinner parties? Information flows freer than vodka at the Petrograd."

"That makes sense. As we used to say back home: if you want to hunt ducks, you should go where the ducks are,"

Asper laughed. "I'll have to remember that."

"Have you heard of a woman called Yelena Semenova?"

"No, who is she?"

Max explained her role at the theatre and her relationship to Gladstone.

"A lot of young Russians, especially cultural workers, opposed the nobility, many of whom viewed artists as decadent and dangerous. They tended to gravitate towards the anarchist forces in Russia, as Jacqui so cleverly suggested, who supported the Bolshevik revolution initially but soon discovered they were largely unwelcome in their ranks. With the crackdown that occurred in 1918, many went under cover or fled the country. I can ask around about her if you like. I know some people who might be able to find out more."

Asper had told him little of value though it did open a couple of lines of inquiry. Besides, he had enjoyed seeing his old friend relishing his new found career as an academic, so he paid for his lunch and handed three hundred francs to Asper, with a promise that they would talk again soon.

COLONEL LEDUX WAS WAITING in his study when Max arrived. As usual, he was impeccably dressed and seated in his favorite chair, a cigarette in one hand and a full ashtray on the table beside the chair. The air was slightly blue with smoke but the valet who ushered him into the room opened a window near where Max was sitting. At a nod from Ledux, he poured them each a generous serving of the Armagnac the colonel favoured.

Max breathed in the fumes, appreciating the aroma, a pleasant change from the stale smoke of Ledux's cigarettes. He took a small sip, allowing the liquor to linger across his tongue before swallowing.

"What did you want to see me about, Max?"

It was almost as much of a ritual as the cigarettes and drink. He had given a general outline of his inquiries on the telephone but Ledux always claimed he got more from face-to-face meetings than from disembodied voices. Although the colonel had been blind since the war, he had told Max that his doctors could find no physical cause. "Perhaps," he had speculated, "I can actually see but my brain refuses to accept it. Instead, it translates my vision into other senses. In any case, I do perceive more when the person I am talking with is actually in the room."

Nothing about the human psyche surprised Max any more. The war had opened his eyes to the immense range of human behavior for good or evil. More often than not it was the state of mind that determined the path men and women took rather than sickness or health or any external factor. Nothing he had witnessed in the four years as a private detective had altered that conclusion.

Max outlined the two cases as he had done with Asper. Given the circles that he knew Ledux still maintained, though he seldom left the confines of his own house, he mentioned the missing English woman as well. He might well have heard something of her movements.

"Asper was correct in part. Trotsky was due to go to Germany, Switzerland and Paris in April but Lenin's sudden illness, which is far more serious than the Kremlin is letting on, forced the cancellation of those plans. Nonetheless, Soviet agents, some working for Stalin and others supporting Trotsky, linger in the city. I can almost smell the stench of cabbage and cheap vodka in the streets."

Ledux butted out the cigarette he was holding and reached for another, lighting it and letting out a long stream of smoke before continuing.

"I don't know this Gladstone but it is not an uncommon name for Russian Jews to adopt in trying to make a new start in England or America. You might want to dig deeper into the young man's origins. Of course, knowing that will not tell you which side his family was on in the complex political machinations of the new regime. Trotsky was born into a wealthy Jewish family but now declares he is an atheist. Others were, to a limited extent, supporters of the old system, or were active in Menshevik circles."

"They seem to be a very political people." French Jews were also very active in politics, mostly on the left. Meanwhile, the right saw every event that displeased them as part of a Jewish conspiracy. It often left him feeling bewildered.

"Every oppressed people—the Jews, the negro in America, the Irish—inevitably turn to politics. It offers the best hope for survival, though it has meagre results. But the Jews are no different from the rest of society, some good, some bad, the rest simply wishing to live in peace."

"That is a very... liberal view of humanity." Ledux had always struck him as conservative, not extremely so like Bucard or members of the Action Française but certainly a supporter of Poincaré and other leaders of the Bloc National.

"I have had plenty of time to contemplate the events of my life. When I was young and still active in the Great Game, it was easy to see things as black or white. It was easy to believe that I, as a Frenchmen and a European, had a duty to civilize the world. The Great War shattered the very idea of civilization, it mixed black and white and turned it all into shades of grey. Why should I consider my country, my continent, more or less 'civilized' than any other?"

Max leaned back in his chair and took another sip of the excellent Armagnac. Other men might have settled into despair losing their vision both literally but also figuratively. Ledux was no longer young, in his sixties at the very least, yet he was still willing to change his views without abandoning his values. He maintained his circle of contacts, listening as much as talking and he had a servant whose sole duty was to peruse the dozen or so daily papers and select articles to read to the colonel. His interests were broad and he had told Max that he spent most mornings "reading" or dealing with his extensive correspondence.

Ledux waved his glass in Max's direction. While he was refreshing their drinks, Ledux continued.

"Trotsky is a force to be reckoned with, a brilliant writer and speaker and a master of five or six languages. A story is told from his brief incarceration in Canada, in somewhere called Nova Scotia, while trying to return to Russia from New York after the Tsar was overthrown."

It was the first that Max had heard of it but he supposed that someone transiting the Atlantic might have been detained in Halifax. "Go on."

"He would gather what papers he could—almost entirely in English—and would read them to the German soldiers, translating as he went. If true, it was a remarkable feat. They also say he began to organize the enlisted men against their own officers. I suspect that's why they quickly sent him on his way."

"You think Trotsky will succeed Lenin if he does not recover his illness."

"Not in the least. Stalin is a thug and willfully ignorant but he is crafty and utterly ruthless. Through a combination of charm, bullying, favoritism and deceit, he has built a vast network of allies. He will easily outmaneuver Trotsky and eliminate him and anyone else who stands in his way. Stalin has, of course, produced his own manifesto, because that is what Marxists do, and you can take some clues from that which might shed light on your industrial espionage case.

"Stalin is determined to transform Russia from a feudal and agricultural society to an industrial one so that the dictatorship of the proletariat can be properly established. To do that in a decade will cause great upheaval and require him to acquire modern technology. The Soviets are both bankrupt and pariahs in the West, so, perforce, he must steal it. They have been recruiting heavily in the universities and technical schools, either to entice graduates to move to Russia or to become moles within national industries and governments. I am sure the engineer who was seen in the Petrograd will be one of those.

"I'm afraid young English ladies, even those from the aristocracy, are no longer within my purview but I have friends who might advise and I will ask them and get back to you in a day or two."

Chapter 8 Tuesday, May 8th, 1923

The unseasonable warmth continued and Max enjoyed the ten-minute walk from his apartment to the Bistro de Paris on Rue de Lille. The sun sparkled off the waters of the Seine and he took a few minutes to enjoy the pleasure of an early Spring before entering the café to meet Helen Miller.

Miller was seated by a lace-curtained window fidgeting in the bentwood chair. She smiled as Max approached and took the seat opposite. She already had a café au lait in front of her and he ordered the same along with a plate of pastries, his breakfast having consisted of a hard-boiled egg and a withered apple.

He quickly brought her up to date on his findings so far, limited though they were. "I'm waiting for Alec Minter to get back from Berlin. He and Carlos Hererra seem the most likely suspects in Gladstone's murder. I understand Minter tried to get fresh with you—"

"Fresh is the nicest way to put it!"

"—and Gladstone came to your rescue."

"Walter was a gentleman. Alec Minter is not."

"Was that when you and Gladstone began hanging around together?"

"We had already known each other a bit but I guess that was the beginning of our friendship."

"Gladstone was seeing another girl at the time." Max consulted his notebook. "Clarice Michaels."

Miller blushed and glanced away. "Walter had a weakness for a certain type of girl. Clarice was, how should I put it, a bit too fond of the men."

"One of them described her as wild."

"I suppose that Russian actress he started chasing was the same type."

Max wondered about that. He had the impression that Yelena Sokolov enjoyed the attention and especially the gifts but managed to keep both Hererra and Gladstone at arm's length while still letting them think she was interested in them.

"You wouldn't know where Miss Michaels lives?"

"No, though I understand you can find her most evenings in one of the bars in the Latin quarter. After her break with Walter, which was quite public and very nasty, she drifted from beau to beau. I can't imagine it makes her happy."

Max liked living on Rue Jacob but didn't care much for the constant sense of desperate celebration that permeated so many of the clubs in the area. His work often took him there and, since he would have to do the rounds if he were to track down Pierre Delacroix. He might as well add Clarice Michaels to the list.

"You spent a lot of time with Gladstone, didn't you?"

"I suppose. Walter had his writing to occupy his mornings, of course, and he would go out three of four times a week with Clarice or, later, that Yelena, but we dined at least once a week and had lunch about twice as often. He was always finding out-of-the-way museums or art galleries for us to go to."

"Did he share your socialist views?"

Miller gasped a little, raising her right hand to her mouth.

"How did you know about that?"

"It's my job to find out things, though I generally prefer my clients to be honest with me in the first place. You could have mentioned both Minter and Michaels to me when we first met. If I'm to find out why Gladstone was murdered and by whom, I need to know everything you can tell me about him. Was he a socialist or was he even farther to the left?"

"Walter had little interest in politics, or, at least he never expressed much to me. He knew I was a socialist and suffragette but didn't seem to care much one way or the other. He did tell me he had voted for the Democratic party but only because his father was such a staunch Republican. He seemed to find that ironic 'given our family history.' He never did say what that history was."

"His father's father, whose last name was Rubinovich, was expelled from Russia for sedition. I've heard suspicions that Gladstone might have been a Bolshevik."

Miller laughed. "I doubt if Walter would know what a Bolshevik was if he found one hiding under his bed. Honestly, all Walter cared about was his writing, the theatre and Yelena Semenova. He was utterly agnostic about everything else."

HENRI WAS AT HIS USUAL spot at the zinc bar in Le Coq Bleu when Max arrived shortly after one. He had a half-empty glass of red wine in his hand and another glass and the bottle in front of the neighbouring stool. His face was tanned and his eyes, twinkling; the trip north had obviously done him some good. He broke into a broad grin as Max took his seat. A moment later, Josette delivered a plate of sandwiches to the bar.

After making their selections—a roast beef on white for Henri and a ham and gruyere on rye for Max—and enjoying the first few bites in companiable silence, Henry began his report.

"Saint-Denis-le-Thiboult is a pretty little town and the people are the salt of the earth. I enjoyed the country air and the simple but hearty food but I would never want to live there. And neither did René Voisin."

"I thought no one in the village had a clue as to what happened to him."

"Villagers come in three types," said Henri. "Those who know, those who know but won't say, and those who don't know but make things up to cover their ignorance. The trick is to listen to the first, pry open the second and ignore the third. It took a few days but the real story emerged."

Henri never let the chance for a homily go by but he seldom made a mistake about people either. Max grinned and took another bite of his sandwich, washing it down with a healthy gulp of red wine.

"The blank look and staring into space his parents reported wasn't despair, it was heart break. Voisin's girl from before the war had returned to the village for a visit. He thought they could pick up where they left off but she rebuffed him and boarded the next train for Paris. A few days later, he got on another train in pursuit."

"Then he's somewhere in Paris."

"For sure. The woman's name is Marie-Claire Lavigne and she shares a flat with two other women, one from Saint-Denis-le-Thiboult and the other born in Paris, on Rue Poirier in the 12th. It's a rough part of town but the women all seem respectable. They work in shops in the area and the accommodation is cheap. I'll drop by there this afternoon. I'm pretty sure I'll find Voisin lurking on the street or in one of the local cafés. I'll gently remind him of his duty to let his parents know where he is. I'm sure he'll be embarrassed by the worry he has caused them. Love is a terrible affliction, is it not?"

Max had occasionally found it so though he was more than happy now.

"Excellent work, Henri. I knew this was the case for you."

Henri smiled. "I'm only getting warmed up. I can hardly wait for my next assignment."

"Careful, Max, you'll swell his big head," said Yesim, selecting one of the remaining sandwiches. "Before you know it, he'll be running your whole business."

Max hadn't really thought of it as a business but he supposed it was. He already had one full-time employee in Alain and he routinely hired other agents to carry out specific assignments. He had a dedicated office at Chez Jake with its own phone, used primarily for his detective work. What with salaries and expenses, paid informants and the like, not to mention the increasing correspondence success was bringing, he was spending more and more time doing his books and handling the administrative tasks of running the operation.

"That might not be a bad idea," he said. Both Henri and Yesim looked at him quizzically. "Not to run the whole business, no, but to manage my office. Henri already does the books for the catering business he and Josette run for you, Yesim, and he is a whiz at keeping track at details. He could run the office, make sure everyone reports on time and that correspondence is dealt with."

"I don't think I'd like spending my entire life behind a desk."

Max considered that. It would be waste of Henri's people skills if he was hidden away up a Chez Jake. Besides, the business had grown but hardly required a full-time office manager. "I don't blame you. What I'm describing takes me ten or fifteen hours a week, so I expect you could handle it in three mornings a week. That would leave you time to do some field assignments for me and still oversee Josette's work." Josette hardly needed oversight but she was fond of

Henri and wouldn't resent the helping hand. "You could even take the occasional shift at the train station if you like."

"I'll be seventy-three in July. I think two jobs will suffice, as long as you're paying a living wage."

"I'll do my best." Max smiled at Yesim who was looking a little crestfallen. "Don't worry, Yesim, you're a key part of the team, too. I don't know if I could have solved any of my cases if I didn't have the two of you to bounce ideas off."

Max outlined his progress so far on the Gladstone murder, the industrial espionage, and the missing Lady Wentworth. "The first two may be connected in some way I still don't understand and I'm waiting to hear back from Gaston and Hugo on the last one. They should report later today, either here or at my office at Chez Jake."

"You've talked to one of your main suspects, the Spaniard, but what about the other one?" asked Yesim.

"He is expected to return from Berlin this week, though the exact day is unknown. He has a room on Saint-Sulpice and he may be in contact with—" Max checked his notebook, "—Neil Herod. He's looking after Minter's cat so is the most likely person Minter will contact when he returns. Barring that, he might drop into a new bookstore called Shakespeare and Company on Rue de Odeon. The proprietor, Sylvia Beach, is friendly to ex-patriate writers."

"Do you want me to go and see if he's around?" asked Henri in heavily accented but understandable English. "As you see, when teaching you French, I pick up some English, too."

Yesim was staring at Henri as if he had grown a second head.

"What?" said Henri, reverting to French. "When you stop learning you may as well retire to bed and die."

Henri would clearly rather be out on the street talking to people than sitting behind a desk, but the more Max thought about it, the more he realized he really did need an office manager. "That would be helpful. Maybe you can meet me at Chez Jake tomorrow morning and report on those inquiries and how you made out with Voisin. I'll show you the books and the filing system."

Henri nodded his agreement.

"What do you want me to do?" asked Yesim. "I can't go galivanting around like Henri but I'd still like to help."

"If Alain, Hugo or Gaston drop by here looking for me, tell them to come to Chez Jake tomorrow morning. I've got quite a few errands to run myself and probably won't make it back here today."

That seemed to satisfy Yesim, who drifted away to greet several regulars who had come in for a post-lunch drink.

ROGET'S FLAT WAS ONLY a few steps away and Max decided to trudge up the four flights on the off chance that the agent would be there.

Roget looked readier for the day than the last time Max had seen him, clean shaven and dressed in a three-piece suit and spats, a rarity for a man who preferred more casual clothes and military style boots.

"I was just on my way out but I've got ten minutes. My report won't take long."

Max took a seat in the only chair while Roget sat on the edge of the neatly made bed. The small flat looked considerably different than the last time Max had visited, neat and tidy with everything in its place. There were even new curtains on the small window.

Roget noticed Max taking in the changes and blushed. "I met a girl. A nice girl for a change. She hasn't been here but if she does drop by... First impressions, you know."

Max smiled. Love affects us all, he thought, sometimes for ill but mostly for good. Roget had had a lot of hardness in his life. Perhaps, now he might find a little joy.

"Not much to report. It's a small sample but on Friday, Saturday and Monday, Pierre Caron worked late and went home alone. As you know, he lives not far from his place of work, a small cottage on Rue Ferdinand Roussel, and can walk there in five or six minutes. On Sunday, he went to early mass, returned home, where he stayed except for meals. He eats his breakfast and supper at one of three small restaurants nearby and presumably eats lunch at the factory. He lives alone. I wondered how he could afford an entire cottage as a recent graduate but it is listed as belonging to M. Caron, so I expect he is getting a family discount on the rent.

"Nothing special about the restaurants but on the three occasions I observed him he was eating alone, simple fare with a single glass of wine. On Sunday, he had a more elaborate meal and a demi-liter. I made discrete inquiries with the busboys at two of the restaurants and they have never seen him with a dinner companion though they all said he was pleasant enough and often chatted with the waiters when business was slow."

"Any idea about topics?"

"The only thing of interest about the man, so I was saving it for last. Caron is a supporter of the PCF and often spoke in support of Georges Marrane, who came close to winning the mayoralty in the last election. It appears our engineer is a Bolshevik, though as far as I can tell he doesn't attend meetings or pass out pamphlets. Nor does he entertain visitors of any sort, red or otherwise."

Yet another link between his two main cases and the Communists. The PCF were part of the Third International and were known to have ties to Moscow, though they always claimed to operate on the principle of France and its workers first.

"Good work, Roget. I'd like you to keep an eye on Caron, especially on the weekends to see if he breaks that pattern. I'm especially interested in the link to the PCF. Let me know if he does attend any meetings or has a visitor from the party. In the meantime, if you're still free, could you switch your attention to another person connected to the factory where Caron works." He handed Roget the photograph of Leo Duvalier, the youngest of the three brothers, who seemed the most likely candidate for being subverted by his family's rivals. "Report to me at Chez Jake next Monday morning on both of them."

"I'm a bit occupied today," replied Roget, gesturing at his suit as if that explained why. "But I can start first thing in the morning."

Max paid him for his report and gave him an advance to cover expenses for the following week. If he had a hot date, he might need a little extra cash. He got Roget to sign a receipt for both; if he was to have a business manager, he better start operating like a business.

MAX HEADED OVER TO Montparnasse, detouring on the way to Les Halles markets to pick up staples to replenish the pantry in the apartment on rue Jacob, including a brace of trout he would prepare for their dinner tonight. He and Jacqui shared the cooking on those days they didn't go out to eat. With both of them working, dinners out were an enjoyable and affordable luxury. It also meant they could afford a woman to come in three times a week to keep the place clean. The rest of the chores they split evenly between themselves, although Max was sure that she still did more than him but Jacqui seemed satisfied with the arrangement so he wasn't about to rock the boat.

Once he had dropped off the food, he headed for Le Dôme to see if he could track down Clarice Michaels among the crowd of Americans and Brits who began to gather there at about four in the afternoon. He had no luck and was about to head across the street to La Rotonde when he spotted the elusive Pierre Delacroix, accompanied, as he often was, by several handsome young men. Although he had celebrated his fiftieth birthday the year before, Delacroix was still handsome, with even features, large dark eyes, and a thin mustache over a strong mouth. His hair was dark with a mere hint of silver at the temples and his clothing was stylish and had been carefully tailored.

Max intercepted him on his way to a large table near the bar. "Can I have a few words, Pierre?"

"It would be my pleasure, Max. Shall we take that booth over there; it's a little more private." He gestured to the young men to be seated and waved over a hovering waiter. "First round of drinks is on me, Enrico."

One of the young men, a blond whom Max had seen in Delacroix's company before, glared at Max and then pointedly turned away. Max suppressed a smile at the obvious jealous pique. Over the years, Max's attitude toward men who loved other men had shifted, from disapproval to tolerance to simple acceptance. Love came in many forms, he had concluded, and as long as it was open and genuine, who had the right to complain about it?

"Are you working on another case?" Delacroix asked after Enrico delivered his usual tipple, a coupe of champagne. Max ordered a small beer; he still wanted to track down Michaeal and preferred to be sober if he did.

"I'm looking into the murder of a young American writer, Walter Gladstone."

"Never heard of him. Why do you think I can help?"

"He was interested in theatre, notably Le Grand Guignol. He was rumoured to be writing a play for them. He was also interested in a young Russian actress, Yelena Semenova, a regular at both the theatre on cite Chaptal and the tamer puppet show in Parc Montsouris. His body was discovered in the lake there."

"Ah, yes, Montsouris. It has recently been the scene of some Dadaist demonstrations, criticizing the art work that has recently been installed there. They consider it a paean to the past and an affront to the future—or something like that. It's a spent movement, don't you know, despite what Tsara says. The surrealists, who are all the present rage, show up whenever they hear about it and taunt the poor fellows. It has even been known to come to blows."

"I witnessed that, both in the park and at the theatre. Are they seriously violent or is it all a show?"

"Something more serious." Delacroix finished his drink and waved over the waiter. "Surprise me with something new. Max will have another beer.

"Depends on whom you mean. Certainly not Breton and Ernst or Deschamps and, for that matter, Tsara, though he sometimes egged them on. Still, violence seemed to accompany them and was often a feature of the early cabarets, held in the middle of 1916. Violence was often a theme though seldom a manifestation, despite them calling it a 'war on the war.'"

The French approached most things in life seriously though they seldom allowed themselves to take it too seriously. Food, drink, love, politics, and especially art, it was all part of Parisian life. Still, it was not uncommon for innovative artistic events to erupt in violence that spilled out of the gallery or theatre and on to the street. People still talked about the riot that followed the premiere of The Rites of Spring in 1913. Max had gone to a remount of the show in 1920 and while the strange music and dancing kept him awake, it didn't provoke riotous feelings.

The waiter returned with Max's unordered beer and a tall tumbler of clear sparkling liquid.

Delacroix laughed. "Aren't you clever? The champagne was already open so you added some gin and a bit of lemon juice."

"And simple syrup to balance the flavor. The bartender says it is called a French 75—one of the Americans showed it to him."

"When people can't legally drink at home, it must spark their imagination. Send a round of these to my table and tell them I'll be joining them soon."

It was clear that Max's time with Delacroix was limited. He could not compete with the young men in Delacroix's circle for long.

"As I said, I've seen a few of these fights but no weapons were being wielded, at least not by the artists. It was all pushing and shoving and the occasional punch thrown. Does it ever get more violent than that?"

Delacroix paused for a few minutes and took a long sip of his drink before shaking his head.

"It's possible though I can't think of an example. Why use a knife when a cutting remark will do? Why bludgeon someone's head when it is their ideas you wish to crush. They attack each other's art not the actual artist. More often than not, the focus of their rage is those most impervious to their outbursts: the rich and powerful, the church, state or industry.

"I suppose some actual violence is done but only on the fringes, among the hangers on or those whose minds and souls are too weak to grasp the central message of the avant-garde: Change in any direction, by any means, is essential because the status quo will kill us. Fights among themselves over method or interpretation are futile. The weak cannot afford to fight among themselves. And yet they do.

"As for me, I'm perfectly happy to stand on the fringes and cheer or boo and make money from magazines for doing so. Now, if you'll excuse me, I must do as I always do, eat, drink, be merry and hope for enlightenment. Tomorrow."

Max remained in Le Dôme for a few minutes, finishing his beer and watching young men and women come and go but none of them were Clarice Michaels. She wasn't at La Rotonde or any of the other half-dozen clubs that had sprung up in the neighbourhood in the last year. At eleven, he gave up and returned home to find Jacqui already asleep in bed. He crawled in beside her, feeling too edgy to sleep. He listened to her breathing until it turned into the wind, blowing distorted birds across a crimson sky.

Chapter 9 Wednesday, May 9th, 1923

Despite the late night, Max was awake before seven and by the time Jacqui was washed and dressed, he had breakfast on the table, in the form of a truffle omelet served with fresh berries and half a baguette of bread that he had cut into rounds and toasted in their small oven.

"It's not my birthday, is it? Or some arcane Canadian holiday?"

"It is. It's national 'tell your lover you love them day', celebrated every May 9th in every province except Quebec."

"I thought Canadians didn't believe in lovers."

"We believe in them but only a lucky few of us have them. And only I have you, which makes me the luckiest Canadian of them all."

"You clearly should spend more time hanging around writers and artists. It's good for your imagination."

It was true. Although he was getting nowhere with his investigations, the complexity, variety and the strangeness of them had stimulated something in him. He had not only woken early; he had woken with a mind full of possibilities. It was as if he had crossed a threshold from his old life to a new one. Everything now was in front of him and he could hardly wait to plunge into this brave new world.

Jacqui was finishing her second cup of coffee when Max sprang to his feet, kissed her lightly on the forehead and hurried out the door, with an over the shoulder promise to meet her in the

Luxembourg gardens for an afternoon walk. The heat had broken in a sudden downpour in the early hours but it promised to be a fine spring day and the gardens would be bursting with blossoms. "We can have a late lunch at Aux Charpentiers near the Saint-Sulpice church."

Henri was sitting on a bench across from Chez Jake when Max arrived shortly before nine.

"Smitty would have let you in if you had rung the bell."

"I'm sure they need their sleep—I know the hours they keep. Besides it was nice to sit here in the cool morning air after sweltering all weekend. Spring shouldn't be so hot; it leaves nothing for summer to do."

Someone was stirring in the kitchen so he asked them to put together a tray of pastries and cheese and an urn of coffee. The long walk had revived his appetite and he was sure Henri, who lived alone, had not yet had breakfast. In any case, coffee was always welcome at any time of day.

Henri had been in Max's small upstairs office many times, but today it was as if he were looking at it with fresh eyes. He opened each of the drawers of the wooden file cabinet and took the chair behind the desk as if getting comfortable with the idea of it being his workplace. *Well, I did ask him to manage my office. I guess I'll need to find another place to sit.*

"What do you want to do first, teach me the ropes or hear the results of yesterday's inquiries?"

The food arrived and Max poured them both a coffee. "Why don't you tell me what happened while we eat? We can do the boring stuff after."

"Suits me." Henri selected an apple tartlet and swallowed a large gulp of coffee. "It was as I anticipated. Voisin was sitting in a café across from the young woman's apartment with a love-sick expression. He jumped up when I called him by name. I'm not sure who he thought I was, the girl's grandfather or a police agent but I could see him eyeing the exit so I put my hand on his shoulder and told him to sit down and listen."

"Did he?"

"Yes, though reluctantly. I told him that Marie-Claire had made her decision and that all his mooning was going to do was make her afraid of him. He was shocked by that. I suppose he thought he was a character in a romantic book, somehow believing he could make her love him if he only persisted. I then told him he had someone who loved him, who worried about him, and to whom he owed a duty. 'Who?' he asked me, as if it were a mystery. He glanced around the café and out onto the street, as if this person would suddenly appear. When I told him that his parents were worried he had done himself harm, that they were frantic over his sudden disappearance and subsequent silence, he looked stunned.

"Go home, I told him. If Marie-Claire changes her mind, she will return to Saint-Denis-le-Thiboult and find you. If she doesn't, well, you are still young and unblemished by the war. There is a surfeit of young women who would be happy of your attentions. Open your eyes and you will find love. It was as if I had thrown water in the face of a sleeping man. He grasped my hand and thanked me, promising to take the next train home. He was genuinely sorry at the hurt he had caused his parents, even though I think it will still take him a while to get over Marie-Claire."

"You handled it better than I ever could. You have a way with people."

"I've had forty more years than you to learn—mostly from my mistakes. I always hoped I would become a wise old man, rather than a foolish one. Though I wish I could have done it without the stiffness in my joints."

Max smiled at his old friend, the first person he had met when he got off the train in November 1918. He had always thought of him as somehow ageless, and until a year or two ago he still worked full-time at the Gare de Nord, hauling heavy trunks and dishing out good advice to innocents abroad. He had slowed in recent years, taking fewer shifts, though he always said he would take more if they offered them, but Max had never heard him complain. Henri might prefer to be out and about, but perhaps this job as office manager would do them both good. Pushing paper across a desk had to be physically easier than pushing a luggage cart and figuring out Max's files could be just the challenge Henri would enjoy.

"Did you have any luck with Alec Minter?"

"Some. He has returned from Berlin according to his friend, Mr. Herod, who has been relieved of his pet care responsibilities. However, he wasn't in his room when I visited. I went to the bookstore with the funny name. They knew Mr. Minter but hadn't seen him in a few weeks. Apparently, they lend books as well as sell them. For a small subscription fee, you can borrow one or two books at a time. Mr. Minter has two books overdue." Henri smiled. "I subscribed myself for twelve francs and borrowed two books, recommended to me to help improve my English, one by Charles Lamb and another by Madame Christie. I must return them within the month or I will be as scandalous as Mr. Minter."

Max had spent months under Henri's careful tutelage to master the finer points of the French language. He had the basics when he came to Paris just after the armistice was signed but only enough to order food, ask for and understand directions and engage in the simplest conversation. Henri had been a good teacher and, now five years later, he was fluent, though no one would confuse him for a native speaker. Henri, of course, had known a few phrases in English, Spanish, Italian, even German, enough for him to do his job as a porter but no more. While his English was still not as good as Max's French, he had essentially taught himself a second language at the age of 70. Max doubted he would have been able to achieve such a thing.

As Henri finished speaking, Smitty appeared at the office door to announce the arrival of two young men to see Max. A few minutes later, Hugo and Gaston could be heard clomping up the stairs.

Hugo arrived with a big smile on his face though Gaston still looked nervous.

"I take it you had some success with your assignment, Hugo."

"Not me, Max, Gaston. I'm pretty sure he visited four places for every three I made it to and emerged with twice as much information."

Max looked at Gaston expectantly. The young man, glanced at the floor, at Hugo, at the filing cabinets, anyplace but at Max. "Well, um, I..."

"I think he's afraid of you," said Hugo.

"Me? Why would he be afraid of me?"

"My fault, I guess. I told him you had a gun—"

"Two," added Henri, causing Gaston's head to jerk up.

"When I told him you carried it with you and had actually shot somebody with it, well—"

"Three, I think." Henri was grinning now. "Or was it four? And he only killed one of them."

Gaston went pale and collapsed to the floor.

"Give him some brandy, Henri." Henri had been in the office often enough to know where Max kept his liquor. He fetched the bottle and two glasses from the desk drawer.

"Nobody should drink alone, even medicinally." He poured two healthy portions, took a sip of one and placed the glass on the desk before kneeling beside Gaston and lifting the brandy to his lips. He took a sip, almost automatically, coughed at the harshness in his throat and then, at Henri's urging, took another more careful one.

Max knelt beside Gaston and put his hand on the man's shoulder to reassure him. He was glad Gaston didn't flinch away.

"You weren't in the war, were you, Gaston?"

"No, I was too young. My two brothers were. They didn't come home. Both shot dead in 1916. I know that is part of what happens in war, but somehow... I grew up in a small village. Most men there were hunters before the war but few carry it on now. Some were wounded; others did the wounding. I have never held a gun, let alone fired it. I'm sorry but I guess I'm not fit to work for you, not brave enough to shoot other people."

Max sighed. It had taken him years to overcome his feelings about the war and his part in it. He had taken lives in battle, though he seldom saw the men he killed. He carried a gun because others did. Some men did not miss the war. Some men—and a few women, too—did not flinch at taking another's life. Max hoped he never became one of those.

"Most days, my two revolvers are locked away in my safe. On some days, when I know my life or the lives of innocents might be at risk, I go armed. On four occasions since the war, I have shot another human being. Once was an accident, the other three a necessity.

"Most of the work we do is not dangerous and, in any case, I would never put you knowingly at risk or ask you to carry a weapon if you didn't want. For now, why don't you report on what you found out about Lady Wentworth? Then we can discuss your future employment."

Max helped Gaston to his feet and saw him settled in the extra chair. Hugo stood behind him and rested his hand on his shoulder. The young man looked up at Hugo with a grateful smile. Their shared assignment had created a bond between them.

"I did as you asked, visited all the shops and galleries on the north side of a river where a young lady might find something of interest. I started with the large department stores like La Bonne Marche, Aux Galleries LaFayette, La Printemps and so on. I spent half a day questioning sales staff and floor managers but without much luck. Then I thought, this woman we are looking for, she is an aristocrat, an art lover, maybe someone with specialized and expensive tastes. I switched my attention to the small exclusive dress shops, millineries and perfumeries, to book stores, to galleries and any place really that might catch the eye of a young woman. I have an aunt who lives part of the year in Paris and I tried to remember the things she used to talk to my mother about.

"In any case, I soon struck it lucky. Lady Wentworth had purchased a number of dresses and several hats in three shops, all within the last few days, all near the Tuileries. On Monday, she visited a luggage shop and purchased a small trunk and a suitcase. I asked around some of the hotels in the area and she was staying, under the name Caroline Akerman, in a small hotel on Rue de la Sourdiere. She checked out Monday morning and left no forwarding address.

"She also dined at several cafes in the area, generally alone though on Monday, she had a companion, a swarthy gentleman, whom the maitre d' thought was perhaps Spanish or Italian. He was well dressed and did most of the talking. So that proves she is still in Paris or was as late as early Monday afternoon."

"Did she leave the restaurant with her lunch companion?"

"I wondered about that so I returned to the café and asked everyone who worked there if they could provide additional details. He left first. He was seen checking his watch several time and left in somewhat of a hurry, as if he had another appointment. He apparently left her to pick up the bill, so perhaps gentleman was the wrong term to describe him. The waiter who had served them had just come on shift and was able to tell me a little more. He was a big man, though more broad than tall. He had unusually large hands and a ready smile, enhanced by a gold tooth or two on the right-hand side of his mouth. Dark curly hair, going a little grey. His French was good but the waiter was sure he was Italian because he mentioned Rome and Venice."

The description could be any number of men but it could also be one man in particular. Jacapo Giamatti, who might or might not be Cosa Nostra but was definitely well connected in the Italian government, now that Mussolini was in control. If it was Giamatti, what was his interest in Lady Wentworth? More important, what was her interest in him? There was only one way to find out: ask him.

"That was solid work, Gaston. You certainly earned your pay. I'd be happy to have you work for me as the need arises. In the meantime, Jake is always looking for staff, if working in a restaurant interests. The pay is not much better that working on the docks but you get some free meals and you can rent a room out back cheaper than what you're paying in the 11th."

"Thanks. I'll think about it." For the first time since entering the office, Gaston relaxed and even gave Max a small smile.

Hugo reported that Lady Wentworth had been seen at a couple of cafés on rue de Varenne the previous week though not since Friday. Other than that, she hadn't been anywhere south of the river as far as he could find out.

"The Italian embassy is on rue de Varenne," said Henri. "I'd be happy to pay it a visit if you like."

"Thanks, but I'll handle that visit myself."

After the others had left, with a wallet full of francs and a promise to check in later in the week to see if he had further work for them, Max spent an hour showing Henri the filing system and his rudimentary set of books, a pair of journals showing in-goes and out-goes, a chequebook and a manila envelope stuffed full of receipts. Henri shook his head at the mess but swore he would whip it into shape in a week or two.

Max sensed that his comfortable office had now become Henri's comfortable office so he headed down to the kitchen to ask Smitty if there was another place he could use for interviews. The big man showed Max a room on the second floor, a few doors down from where Henri was ensconced, that had been used for storage before the last expansion of the premises. There were still a few boxes and a sagging set of shelves.

"It's a little dusty but we can get it cleaned up in a day or two. You'll need to get some furniture and another telephone line but I think it will serve the purpose."

The room was larger than his old office but it had no window and only a single electrical outlet. As part owner of Chez Jake, taking over a little more space was within his rights but he would send a telegram to Jake's hotel in London so there would be no surprises on his return.

He returned to the office to ask Henri to make the arrangements to furnish the office. Henri was just hanging up the phone as he entered.

"That was Alain. He said he had a report to make on Dupont but promised Josette he would have lunch with her at the Lux and wondered if you could meet him there at 2 this afternoon. Also, I went through the stack of correspondence: a couple of overdue bills, a thank you from a previous client who mentions he has recommended you to a neighbour with a similar problem, a request from said neighbour plus another request involving a missing soldier, this one from a village on the west coast. There were four divorce cases as well which I reluctantly placed in the trash can."

"You're a fast learner, Henri. I'll take the two requests with me and look them over while I have lunch at Le Coq Bleu; Yesim may need some back-up with Josette away. I'll meet with Alain, drop by the Italian Embassy and then return to the bar where I will buy my new office manager a celebratory drink."

JOSETTE HAD STAYED long enough to handle the lunch rush at Le Coq Bleu. Max arrived just in time to say good-bye as she rushed out to meet her cousin at the Lux a few blocks away. Yesim waved away an offer to help with the remaining few tables.

"Besides, you have company." Yesim gestured to a heavily bearded man seated at Max's usual table beneath the neon parrot. "I don't like the looks of him." Yesim laid his length of iron pipe on the bar in case looks weren't deceiving.

The man stood as Max approached and stuck out his hand in greeting. "Ivan Rubenstein. You are Max Anderson." His voice was low, his accent not quite recognizable.

Max took the hand and was surprised to find Rubenstein's grip was gentle but firm, the hand quite soft. Someone who works with his head rather than his hands, thought Max.

"How can I help you?"

"You are investigating the death of Walter Gladstone, are you not?" The investigation was hardly secret but Max was surprised that a complete stranger could know about it.

"I am. Unless you are friend of my client or a police officer, I'm not at liberty to discuss it."

"But I am Walter's cousin."

"From Chicago?"

"Well, perhaps more distant cousins." Rubenstein grinned showing a mouthful of large crooked teeth. "And family is family. I must insist you tell me what you know."

"Do you have any proof of your relationship to Mr. Gladstone?"

"You doubt my word?" He made an effort to look hurt though Max thought it looked more like gas.

"Cynicism is an unfortunate side effect of being a detective. Now, if you'll excuse me, lunch is waiting for me at the bar."

Rubinstein laid a hand on Max's arm to restrain him. Max's glare shifted from the hand to the bigger man's face and back to the hand until he let him go.

"I'm sorry. But I and the family are distraught. This client of yours, a woman, yes? Helene Muller?"

Close but no cigar, an expression Max heard all too often when Jacqui dragged him to a summer carnival. Rubenstein knew something about Gladstone's murder, though what it was or whether it was valuable was yet to be seen.

"What else have heard about it?" Max said without correcting Rubenstein on Miller's actual name.

"Not much. He was found in a lake, in a park somewhere. The police declare it was an accident and the case is closed. That's all they would tell me at the Prefecture, though one Sargeant directed me to you if I had any doubts. The police are right, aren't they? Nothing but an accident."

Max would have to remember to thank LePêcheur for sending him a possible lead. Or curse him if was a waste of time.

"Do you know why Gladstone was in Paris? What he might have been doing in that park?"

Rubenstein looked evasive, as if he were trying to find something to say that would garner him more information than he gave. "I think his family in Chicago sent him here. For what purpose I do not know. Now, please tell me what you have discovered that would cause you to continue investigating something the police in their wisdom deem an accident."

It was almost as if Rubenstein wanted the death to be accidental. But why would a so-called cousin want that, unless he was somehow involved? Max purposefully looked around the bar at the remaining diners. He leaned into Rubenstein and spoke in a low voice.

"Listen, I get that, as a cousin, you would be concerned but I can't talk here. Too many interested ears." Max's efforts to appear clandestine had the desired effect; most of the patrons had ceased their own conversations and were staring at the two men at the end of the room. "Perhaps, if you left me word of where to reach you?"

Rubenstein nodded and whispered back. "I don't have a calling card but I'll leave a note at the Petrograd—do you know the restaurant?"

"I'm sure I can find it." He shook Rubenstein's hand and watched him leave the bar. He couldn't have looked more furtive if he tried.

"What was that about?" asked Yesim, as he placed a large sandwich and a glass of beer on the zinc bar.

"I haven't a clue but I intend to find out."

MAX HAD FINISHED THE last swallow of beer and was about to rendezvous with Alain at the Lux when Henri came through the door, his face flushed and his breath short.

"Thirsty, already?" asked Yesim, reaching for a bottle of pastis.

"Always, but that can wait. Max, I tried to call but the operator said the line was disconnected." Henri glared at Yesim whose face darkened.

"You know I only have that thing so I can call out." Nonetheless, he put the receiver back on its hook.

"What was so urgent you had to run all the way here?" Max wasn't sure if *he* could run all the way from Chez Jake to Le Coq Bleu even though it was downhill most of the way.

"Mr. Herod called. He sounded frantic so it took a few tries to understand what he was on about. Mr. Minter has returned to his apartment. Mr. Herod says he is acting strangely and that he might be dying."

Max leapt to his feet.

"Yesim, see if you can get an ambulance to Minter's place on Rue Jacob. Henri will give you the address. Henri, go to the Lux and tell Alain I will see him later today or, perhaps, tomorrow."

He hurried into the street. As luck would have it a motor taxi was letting off a passenger a few doors down. Max leapt into the back and gave the driver the address. "Get me there in under twenty minutes and I'll double the fare."

The driver took every short cut he knew, taking him through streets and alleys Max had seldom seen in his five years in the city. He screeched to a halt in front of Minter's apartment building eighteen minutes later and grinned as Max, still recovering from the ride, pressed a wad of francs into his hand. Neil Herod was pacing outside the front door, while the concierge gazed worriedly at a second-floor window. There was no sign of an ambulance.

"Thank God you're here, Mr. Anderson. He's quiet now but he was standing at that window a few minutes ago, screaming incomprehensibly and threatening, in his more lucid moments, to kill them if they came for him. I have no idea who they are and I'm not sure he does either."

"When did this start?"

"I'm not sure. I heard at Le Dôme that he was back in his rooms and so I thought I'd bring Queen Sheba back to him." He nodded at a small enclosed basket where a cat could be heard howling angrily. "He was like it when I arrived. He had driven poor Madame Debané into the street and was racing back and forth upstairs. I could hear him running into things and crockery breaking."

"Perhaps you should take Madame into that café a few doors down, away from all this noise. I'll look in on Mr. Minter."

"What about Queen Sheba?" Herod looked like he might collapse if not taken in hand.

"Perhaps you could continue caring for her. I'm sure she needs comforting."

Herod nodded and seemed a little stronger now that he had a duty to perform. He took the cat carrier in one hand and the concierge's arm in the other and made his way toward the indicated café. Max took the steps two at a time and pulled up in front of Minter's closed apartment door.

Faint moaning came from within and, when Max tried the handle, the door swung open. Minter was collapsed in an overstuffed chair, vomit spilled down his front and his eyes wide and staring. His breath came in quick hard gasps and his hands and feet were spasmodically twitching.

"Mr. Minter?"

Minter's head jerked around at the sound of his voice. He mumbled something Max couldn't make out and waved one hand toward a jug of water on a small table by the window. Max poured a glass and helped him drink it. Minter slumped back with his eyes closed as if the effort of swallowing had exhausted him.

The apartment was small and had likely been carved out of a larger space by a landlord eager to cash in on the flood of foreign tourists. The living area consisted of a small sitting room with a couple of chairs with side tables. The one next to where Minter was sitting had been knocked over and a broken vase had scattered bits of crockery and dead flowers across the floor.

The kitchen barely deserved the title. A sink for washing the few dishes that could be held in a small cabinet above it and a single alcohol-fired burner for warming soup or making coffee were apparently sufficient for a single man and his cat. A free-standing pantry held a few cans of food and tins for dry goods and a tray for cutlery.

Two doors, both open led to a small bedroom and a miniscule bathroom with toilet, sink and shower. Max didn't bother to explore either as his attention had been drawn back to the dining table that had held the jug of water. Beside it were three small vials, two empty and one still filled with a white powder. Max picked up a few grains from the tabletop with a moistened finger. The taste was bitter and numbed the tip of his tongue. He quickly rinsed his mouth with water and spat it into the sink.

Cocaine or something similar. Although the drug had fallen out of popularity since the end of the war and its sale and distribution was now a criminal offence, cocaine was still found in certain clubs and, according to rumours he had heard, was common in night clubs in Berlin. Minter had recently returned from Germany and might have picked it up there, but if the empty vials were any indication, was unfamiliar with its use and overuse. Max swept the detritus off the table and dumped it in a kitchen drawer.

Max looked out the window but there was still no sign of the ambulance. He returned to Minter's side. The man was calmer now, though his skin was flushed and his breathing was still ragged. His eyes were open but unfocused. Max lifted his head to give him a few more sips of water. Minter's face was hot to the touch so Max wetted his handkerchief and lay it across his brow to cool his fever.

"Who are you?" These were the first intelligible words Minter had uttered and Max hesitated while he considered how best to answer. He didn't want to further agitate his troubled mind.

"Did they send you? Did they?" Minter pushed weakly against Max's hand resting on his chest.

"No. I'm a friend of... Neil Herod."

"He has my cat."

"Yes." The faint cry of a siren reached him through the open window. "Help is on the way."

"Is it the police? I can't be—"

"It's an ambulance. You've been sick."

Minter giggled and waved his hand weakly toward the table. "Sick is a good word for it."

Feet were pounding up the stairs. Minter jerked and tried to stand but then collapsed back again. The flush had faded and his skin was pale and clammy. Two uniformed men burst through the door carrying a stretcher.

"Cocaine overdose, I think," said Max, standing to let the men work.

"Did he lose consciousness?"

"No, not while I was here or according to witnesses on the scene when I arrived. Extreme agitation, expressions of fear, vomiting as you can see. His breathing was rapid but it's calmer now. I gave him some water and tried to cool his fever."

"Who is he? And who are you?" The larger of the two men was clearly in charge.

"His name is Alec Minter. He's American. Speaks some French I think but not well. I'll cover his expenses for now. I'm a friend of a friend. Mr. Herod is in a nearby café and can verify my identity." Max produced his identity card, which he had recently renewed to reflect his new address. "Can I ride with you?"

"Sure, since you're paying the fare. It will be crowded but we're taking him to Salpêtrière in the 13th, so the drive will only be twenty minutes or less."

Max helped them load Minter onto the stretcher and down the stairs to the black and white ambulance. It was cramped in the back of the vehicle with Minter and one of the attendants but he was determined that now he had found one of his primary suspects, he wasn't going to let him go.

THE DUTY NURSE WAS less sanguine about allowing Max to accompany Minter into the wards but a quick word—and transfer of cash—with the administrator gained him permission to stay at least until visiting hours, normally restricted to actual family members, ended at eighteen hundred. The nurse administered a mild sedative to calm Minter's racing pulse and reduce his fever. The young man fell into a light doze despite Max's attempts to question him.

Two hours later and Minter was still drifting in out of consciousness and visiting hours were almost over. Max was about to see if he could get an extension, when Minter sat up in bed.

"Where am I?" His voice was raspy but his words clear.

"At the Salpêtrière hospital."

"Are you a doctor. You don't look like one."

"No. My name is Max Anderson. I'm a private detective investigating the death of Walter Gladstone."

"I heard he was dead. Drowned or something, right before I went to Berlin."

"Did you also hear that a number of people suggested you had the most reason to see him dead." Minter looked confused. "To kill him."

Minter's already pale skin blanched further and he fell back onto his pillow. Max thought for a moment he might lose consciousness but his eyes were wide and his lips twitched as if he couldn't make them form words. Was he about to confess?

"I didn't kill him."

Max sighed. It was never that easy.

"You accused him of thwarting your career and later of stealing your girl. There was an altercation and you threatened him."

"I never did!" Minter's voice raised to a screech drawing an admonishing glare form the ward nurse. "He attacked me."

"After you laid your unwanted hands on Helen Miller."

"Who says they were unwanted?"

"She did."

"Well, she would say that but—"

"Listen! I don't care about your romantic delusions or, for that matter, your foolish adventures with dangerous drugs. A man was murdered, his body dumped in a lake, and I intend to find out who did it." Max didn't like threatening people but sometimes, when you knew someone was a louse and a coward, it was the easiest way. "And if I have to slap you around a little to get you to give me straight answers, well..."

"Can't you see I'm sick, I..." Minter's eyes began to well. Max poured him a glass of water from the pitcher on the table. Minter sat up again and took several sips. "Alright, ask your beastly questions."

"You confronted Gladstone several times, often in the presence of other writers, Neil Herod and Ernest Hemingway, for example—"

"Hemingway remembered me?"

Max remembered the cruel nickname the other writer had applied to Minter. "Yeah." Minter looked pathetically grateful and Max began to have his doubts that this was the man he was looking for.

"Were you trying to boost yourself up by putting Gladstone down?"

"I can see it would look like that but you didn't know Gladstone. He was a real charmer when he wanted to be—the woman liked him and the men admired him, even when they resented him. But he could be a right bastard, too. When I first met him, he seemed a good sort and I gave him a couple of my short pieces to read. He gave them back with the words 'Utter shit!' scrawled across them and went around telling *our* friends what a talentless lug I was. Turns out, they were all his friends.

"I admit I hated him but I was a conchie during the war—yes, I know, 'a coward,' I've heard it all. I spent my war working on a military farm. I wouldn't trade my values for a rotten beggar like Gladstone. He struck me; I never struck him back."

Max had known some conscientious objectors both before and even during the war. Some had served their country by working in the ambulance corps, going into no man's land to rescue the wounded and recover the dying. None of them were cowards as far as he could see, just men of principle who stood their ground no matter the abuse they took from their own countrymen. Whatever flaws this man might have, and Max was sure he had plenty, he was no murderer.

"Why did you leave Paris?"

"Word got around about my views on the war. Most people didn't seem to mind now that it's all over but those who did, well, they managed to make life unpleasant. I thought I'd go to Berlin to see the face of the 'enemy.'"

"Did you?"

"No, the language was different but the faces were just the same."

Chapter 10 Thursday, May 10th, 1923

Max had walked home from the hospital. The steady drizzle and dropping temperatures fitted his mood. Jacqui's usual inquisitiveness was supressed by his apparent unhappiness and she didn't try to quiz him on the case or lighten his mood by talking about her day. Instead, she made him a light supper of potato soup and ham sandwiches and sat with him in silence until he finally said. "Tomorrow is another day; it can't be worse than this one."

He slept fitfully but he slept, not rising until well after 9. Jacqui left him a note saying she had to go to a pre-production meeting but would meet him at a café she had discovered not far from the Opera at 1 that afternoon. "Drop a note at the box office if you can't make it."

There was a basket of fresh pastries on the table and the makings of coffee on the sideboard. Max savoured a raspberry tart and reviewed his notes while waiting for the coffee to perk. The loss of Alec Minter as a primary suspect was depressing. He supposed the man might be lying but his story was easy enough to check. He would question Herod again and some of the others as well though he suspected it was a waste of time.

If Minter was uninvolved, who did that leave as suspects? Hererra was now number one on the list but Max was doubtful. Gladstone had been flirting with Yelena for some weeks. Why would the stage manager choose one particular day to wreak his jealous revenge. If something had changed, no one had mentioned it but he would now focus his attention more carefully on the actual day the crime took place.

He bit into his third pastry and refilled his cup. He would have to think about a return to Kid O'Brien's gym if he kept this up. Maybe he could entice Hemingway into the ring to see if the man was as good with his fists as he was with his mouth.

The way Gladstone had been killed troubled him. Stabbed from behind and then dumped in an out-of-the-way lake did not fit with an act of passion. Herrera was a big man and physically confident in his strength. He would have confronted Gladstone directly and, if it came to knives, the assault would have come from the front. This was more like an assassination.

What about the man who had approached him the day before? Ivan Rubenstein claimed to be Gladstone's cousin but he only had his word for it. He would arrange a meeting in the next few days, after he had a chance to check out his background with Ledux or some of the Russians, since it seemed likely their connection, if there was one, came from Russia and not America. He had no reason to think the man had committed murder but somebody had and he had few other avenues of inquiry.

What about Tsara and the other artists who liked to fight in parks and theatre houses? Tsara was not a big man; he might resort to a stab in the back but what was his motive? A disagreement over art and its purposes seemed like thin soup but murders had been committed for lesser things if the argument intersected with opportunity. The man had not struck him as someone whose passions ever left the sphere of the intellect but like the so-called cousin, the conflict between the dadaists and the surrealists was another line of inquiry, no matter how lightly drawn that line might be.

Next to murder, the industrial sabotage which was undoubtedly being carried out by Dupont for persons or persons unknown seemed trivial. However, he was being paid quite handsomely to put an end to it and he would meet with Alain this morning, if at all possible, to see if he had further leads. He should see if Roget had anything to say about the younger brother as well.

At least, the missing Ladyship seemed to be on the verge of being solved. She was either planning a trip to Italy or had already left. A quick inquiry at the Italian embassy, quite possibly to his old "friend," Giamatti, might wrap up that case. He hoped the two other cases he had decided to take on would resolve as easily.

MINTER'S BEHAVIOUR still bothered him. If the man was so eager to kill himself—as his flirtation with drugs suggested—he should have simply joined the army. He could have avoided killing anyone himself. The Bosch would not have been so delicate. Perhaps, he was missing something. None of the artists he had met in the last few weeks seemed completely sane. Was there something in the artistic temperament that might drive a person to murder? Jacqui had certainly told him some odd stories from her time working at the Opera and the behavior of the artists in the park and the performers at the theatre bordered on the bizarre.

Perhaps he should take Miss Stein up on her offer. She might be able to enlighten him on the inner workings of the artistic mind. He retrieved her card from his wallet: Salons held every Saturday beginning at 1600 and ending when the last person left. He would drop by sometime on Saturday and see if he could get a few minutes alone with her, before her guests arrived.

In the meantime, he would drop by the Italian Embassy on Varenne to see if he could discover the whereabouts of Lady Wentworth.

Max gave his card to the uniformed aide-de-camp manning the front desk. He picked up a phone and spoke rapidly in Italian, paused, spoke some more, then nodded and hung up the receiver.

"Follow me, the assistant to the Ambassador will see you," he said in excellent French, leading Max up a broad stairway and down a hall to a spacious office.

"We meet again, Mr. Anderson." Jacapo Giamatti was leaning against an ornately carved desk, smoking a large cigar. He was wearing a similar uniform as the man at the desk, though with more decorations on the breast and sleeves. He gestured to a pair of wing-back chairs facing each other over a low table. "Come in, have a seat. Do you want anything? Cigar? Pastis?"

"Perhaps a coffee?" Drinking in the morning seemed like a dangerous way to start the day.

Giamatti pressed a button on his desk and, moments later, a young woman, also in uniform, appeared at the door. "Due caffè e qualche pasticcino."

"Are you in the army now, Jacapo?"

"Naw, el Duce likes us to look like a martial people. You should see the get-up the ambassador has to wear. Sit! Sit!"

Giamatti had the good grace to stub out his cigar before taking the chair opposite Max. He leaned back with his fingers steepled over his expansive girth and gazed at Max speculatively.

"It looks like the diplomatic life has been good for you."

"Too many state dinners. My brother says I should start an exercise program, starting with pushing away from the table." Giamatti laughed at his own joke. His formerly solitary gold tooth now had a couple of neighbours. "But you didn't come to discuss my eating habits. Is there a murder you want to accuse me of."

"No, I save those kinds of accusations for Andre Bucard."

"How is my old friend, Andre?"

"Retired and living on an estate south of the city. He has decided to leave the spotlight to his nephew."

"Good decision. Marcel will go far. Now, I have another meeting in 15 minutes. Perhaps we should get down to business."

"I'm trying to locate Lady Evelyn Wentworth."

"Never heard of her."

"You were seen having lunch with her last week."

Giamatti laughed. "If I had your network, I could ferret out every secret in Paris. Okay, sure, I guess I can help you. She didn't exactly ask me to keep our business secret."

"What kind of business?"

"Exactly what it looks like. Consular business. She wanted help arranging a visit to Italy."

"She has a British passport. Surely getting a visa wouldn't require much help."

"Easy. Even you could get one, Max. She wanted me to arrange a meeting with Benito."

"Mussolini?"

Giamatti laughed again. "Got it in one. We had a long chat about the party and our philosophy. She seemed fascinated. We have a lot of admirers among the British aristocracy, according to her. I'm sure we'll have one more once she meets El Duce."

Max tried not so show his disgust. He found the French far right ugly and dangerous; the Italian version was likely to be just as bad. Or worse. He'd have to mention Wentworth's trip to Buchan. He was sure to have some use for the information.

"I expect her back late next week. But there was something else. Have you heard about the guy who stole the Mona Lisa? Became a national hero when it was found out. Of course, the previous government didn't have the courage to keep it in Italy where it belonged."

"And?"

"Lady Wentworth had become infatuated with a young Italian artist—if you can call his ugly daubs art—who will be traveling with her to Rome."

"What's the connection?"

A soft knock at the door was followed by the entrance of the young woman, carrying a tray, which she placed carefully on the table in front of them. Giamatti made a great show of choosing one of the pastries until she had exited the room and closed the door behind her. Max took a sip of his coffee, much better than what he had made for himself.

"Well—and you didn't hear this from me—Enrico Carletti has even bigger plans. To, as he calls it, repatriate all the great Italian masters for museums in Italy. Me, I think it's asking for trouble. It will all come back to us eventually, you wait and see. Now, excuse me, I have to review some files for my next meeting. Take a couple of these things with you. Otherwise, I'll eat them all myself."

THE WALK FROM THE EMBASSY was a long one and Max was pleased the heat spell had ended. By the time he reached the café where he was to meet Jacqui, he was slightly winded and even more determined to return to his exercise regime. He arrived just in time to meet her coming the other way and they entered the café together. It was a place Jacqui had visited a number of times with her workmates but it was Max's first time there. He paused a minute at the door to admire the clean lines of the art deco décor, all metal and glass and colorful geometrical panels.

The maître d' greeted Jacqui warmly and led them to a table near the back, well away from the kitchen and the prying eyes of other customers. The chairs were at an angle so their legs almost touched and they could lean into each other if they wanted. He placed two menus on the table with a flourish and gave a small bow before leaving them to consider their lunch options.

"I'm sorry, Max, but I don't seem to have much appetite today. I'll have the soup—the menu board said it's a creamy mushroom—and some bread. And no wine. Sparkling water, I think. Don't stint yourself because of me."

He had noticed that her eating habits had changed recently. Sometimes she ate heartily and others merely picked at her food. He might have suspected she was unwell but her color was good and he had seldom seen her skin so radiant. Perhaps, it was the irregularity of their schedule or the stress of preparing for the upcoming premiere.

He looked up from the menu to find her smiling at him, her eyes glistening as if on the verge of tears. The waiter was standing a discrete distance away, waiting for their decision.

"Try something different, something you've never had before. I always love to watch you explore something new."

Max nodded and glanced back at the menu, though he had already decided to do exactly as Jacqui had suggested. Not for the first time he wondered if she could read his mind. He waited until Jacqui had placed her order before announcing his choice.

"I'll have the Hare á la Royale. I think a demi-liter of Burgandy would go well with that, don't you?"

"The gentleman has a discerning palate. It is what I would have chosen myself." Max glanced at the older man and, though Paris waiters were notorious for their ironic rudeness, he could see that the man was sincere. It made him feel oddly like he had only now come into his adulthood.

Max described the meeting with Minter, with its shocking conclusion and the man's confession of pacifism.

"It is so dramatic, Max. Surely, he would not confess to such a thing—to a decorated soldier no less—if it were not true."

"I doubt he would have known about my few decorations..."

"Still, he must have guessed as much, given your age and carriage and those very attractive scars you carry on your face like a badge of honour."

Max felt his face grow hot, and hotter still when she up and caressed the aforementioned three pale lines that ran from his temple to the middle of his cheek. He clasped her hand and pressed his lips into the palm.

The waiter cleared his throat as he delivered their meals. He poured Max's wine with a flourish and smiled at them both.

"Don't worry," he said, looking at Jacqui. "Your appetite will return soon."

Max thought it was an odd comment but Jacqui nodded and smiled back.

"What happened this morning?"

He quickly summarized what he had learned from Giamatti about Lady Wentworth.

"Aristocrats!" She practically spat the word. "The gentry long for a return to the old days when the working classes knew their place and were seemingly satisfied to stay in it. I'm sure they are blithely unaware of what is said about them beneath stairs."

Max knew better than to argue politics with Jacqui. Despite her best efforts to instruct him, he knew he could never match her knowledge or passion on the subject.

"What are your next steps?"

"I'll see if I can reach Roget today and then go to Miss Stein's to get some further insights on the world of artists. Is it all talk or do they really intend to tear every thing down and start the world anew? Would they resort to violence to do it?"

"In the heat of the moment, anything is possible. There were many who follow the Black Flag, even those who first called for the end of the propaganda of the deed, who when things grew urgent, would still raise their fists, only to look embarrassed a few minutes later. I learned a lot about what was going on in those moments."

Max looked at her thoughtfully. He had always been told that people would tell him things they would not tell anyone else. "You have an easy face to talk to," was how Henri put it. Maybe it was the same with Jacqui. He had never felt so...comfortable with anyone. *She and I are a perfect match.*

"I was thinking. I need someone on the inside, in fact, I need two people, one to get to know these artists, to see if any of them knew Gladstone as his friends imply, to see if any of them might, either in the heat of the moment or in a more calculating way, have struck the fatal blow. You were leaving as Tsara approached me at the Murphy's and he might not make the connection. Would you—?"

"I thought you'd never ask! Of course I want to help you, be part of everything you are and do. How do I begin?"

Max laughed. "We could start by finishing lunch. I've got an address where Tsara works. You could visit him there and, maybe, tell him you want some advice on artists to patronize or whatever seems right at the time. I trust you will think of something cleverer that I could."

"I doubt that but I'll do my best. You said you need two people?"

"I would like to get an insider at Le Grand Guignol. We were seen there together or I'd ask you to take that on, given your experience at the Opera but—"

"What about Hugo? You said he did a good job searching for the English woman. I'm sure he can use the work. As could Gaston, I'm sure, but Hugo is, well, more presentable. He could work front of house as well as backstage and they would be more likely to take him on. He would be expected to volunteer at first, of course, but since you would be paying him, that would be fine."

"Is that common? Asking people to work for free?"

"Too common, I'm afraid, though less so since the war. After a couple of weeks, to see if they fit, volunteers soon move into paying slots."

France had lost so many men during the war, more than six million killed or wounded, some so severely they still were unable to take jobs. Buchan had told him that in America, all the women who had taken factory jobs had been sent home when the troops returned. In France, many women continued to work, as he had seen in the car factory. He suspected that some employers were glad of that; the women did just as good a job but at three quarters of the wages.

"Hugo it is, then. I'm sure I'll find Gaston something to do before long, so he doesn't have to take any more work on the river." If this keeps up, soon I'll be employing half the city to watch the other half.

MAX RETURNED TO HIS new office at Chez Jake to find it furnished with a solid desk and chair, a file cabinet and two beige arm chairs on either side of a small table. Alain Laurent was sitting in one of them, consulting a notebook, and sipping a cup of black coffee. The coffee was kept warm by a small candle under the carafe and Max poured himself a cup of the steaming liquid, savoring the aroma and bitter taste.

"Have you had lunch?"

Alain nodded absently, still reading his notes. He flipped a final page before closing the book and looking up. "I ate at Le Coq Bleu with Gaston. He's back working on the docks but the shifts are irregular. I think they do it to prevent the men from joining the union."

If so, there will be trouble soon. The unions were strong in France and didn't much care for the tricks employers used to limit their membership. He couldn't blame them; there was plenty of money to be made in Paris and working men and women seldom got their fair share. Still, Gaston deserved better than that. He would remind him of the offer to come to work here or find him some additional detective work to do, even if he had to accept a divorce case or two.

"What have you found out about Dupont and the others?"

"Not as much as I'd like. I tried to find Roget to see if he had any news of the younger brother, but he hasn't been in his room for a couple of days and there is no sign of him in the bars he is known to frequent. So, Leo Duvalier remains a viable, though unlikely suspect.

"Andre, however, seems in the clear. Not surprising, of course. Why would he risk the family enterprise by stealing his own inventions? Still, I checked up on him. He lives a quiet life with his wife and two children in the 14th arrondissement. His neighbours say he is friendly but often distracted. His close friends all seem to belong to a bicycle club. He arrives by bicycle—odd, perhaps, for a man who builds automobiles—each day, including Saturday, at seven in the morning, give or take a few minutes, according to the woman at the front desk. He departs at eighteen hundred hours, noon on Saturdays, by the same conveyance. His evenings are invariably spent at home and his weekends participating in bicycle rallies or watching races at a local velodrome. I showed his photograph to the bookies around the track but none of them knew him. He served in the army for two years before being released to do 'war work.' Clean as a whistle as far as I can see.

"Jordain Lefebre, the foreman, has been with the company since it's founding, and is described by the other employees as 'firm but fair' and 'impeccable' when it comes to protecting the company's interests. Like the oldest brother, he was too old to fight, but in addition to his work at the factory—they made ambulances during the war—he served in the home guard. He and his wife and their four children live in a small village south of the city, close enough that he can drive to work everyday. Again, good reports from his neighbours and the local constable told me he had never been close to breaking the law. He's either innocent or a very good actor."

"That leaves Jean Dupont and, as you say, Leo Duvalier, as possible suspects in the thefts. Anything more on Dupont?"

"Not a lot. He went out of town last weekend but didn't go far. He took a train to the coast after work on Friday and returned Sunday night. I suppose he was taking advantage of the nice weather to go to the beach. I called hotels in his final destination and he stayed in one of the better establishments for the two nights. They couldn't, or wouldn't, tell me anything more over the phone. Do you want me to head down there and see if I can find out anything more?"

"No. I think the answer to this lies in Paris. Anything else?"

"Last night, I followed Dupont to a restaurant in the 7th. I watched from across the street but I had a clear view as he and his companions were sitting in the window seat. He had supper with a man and a woman, perhaps the same ones he met in the Petrograd. The woman was fairly tall and attractive for someone her age—about fifty, maybe—and the man was big, over six feet, with a heavy beard. Part way through supper he and Dupont started yelling and Dupont leaped up and stormed out. The man rose to follow him but the woman restrained him. They resumed their meal, their heads tilted together in close conversation. I followed Dupont but, after roaming around a bit to let off steam, he went home."

A large man with a heavy beard. It could be Rubenstein but what would Gladstone's cousin have to do with Jean Dupont? It was Max's turn to scribble in his notebook. It was a connection worth exploring. "It's a long shot but go back to the factory with the photo of Gladstone to see if anyone ever saw him around." Alain looked puzzled but said he would do it before they closed for the evening.

Before heading home, he asked Henri to look into the theft of goods from a local warehouse. It involved, among other things, missing cases of cognac; a subject Henri could throw himself into with relish. It was almost certainly an inside job as there had been no evidence of a break-in. He sent a note to Hugo to ask If he would take on the job of infiltrating Le Grand Guignol. He would investigate the missing soldier himself. He often found comfort in those kinds of cases. Maybe it would relieve his growing sense of frustration over the Gladstone murder.

Chapter 11 Friday, May 11th 1923

Max was enjoying a quiet breakfast with Jacqui, who was telling of her first meeting with Tsara, when the telephone buzzed for his attention.

"Hold that thought," he said, as he crossed the living room to answer it. It was Helen Miller.

"I need to see you. Can you come to my apartment at 10 this morning?" Max agreed, took the address and returned to the table.

"Sometimes, I think Henri is right, that thing is more trouble than it's worth."

"Don't be silly, Max. It's a useful tool but like any tool you have to know when to use it and when to put it down."

He supposed she was right but ever since he had had one installed in their old apartment on Rue Lepic, he could never resist answering it no matter what time of day or night it buzzed. Perhaps there was a way he could have someone else answer his calls and pass on the messages. He would ask Henri to look into it.

"What was your impression of Tsara?"

"A strange little man, though no stranger than a lot of other anarchists I've met."

"He's an anarchist?"

"He doesn't call himself that but if you look at the core of his ideas—opposition to bourgeois capitalism, the embrace of independent thinking, rejection of conformity, continual clashes with those who strayed from the purity of the cause—what else could you call him but an anarchist? One of his mentors, Hugo Ball, is well known in German anarchist circles.

"In any case, I found him strangely compelling. He certainly believes in his beliefs, while at the same time criticizing the idea of belief. He said to me that to understand dada truly is to reject the very idea of dada."

"That doesn't make sense."

"I think that is the point. The effort to make sense of the world through reason and logic and the worship of efficiency over all is what led us into war, what will continue to led us into violence. Anarchists embrace much the same ideas, at least those who have rejected the propaganda of the deed."

"So, you don't think Tsara or his followers are capable of violence. They certainly seemed to want to start a fight at the theatre the other night."

"But they didn't, did they? A lot of yelling and insults but no punches were thrown, at least not by Tsara and his friends. I only spoke to him briefly during one of their manifestations but I did read the tract he gave me and arrange to see him again at his studio. I can probably tell you more after that."

Max wasn't sure he liked the idea of Jacqui going alone to an artist's studio. Henri had regaled him with wild stories of the goings on at Le Lapin Agile, a bar and artist hang-out near Chez Jake. He remembered the acquisitive way Picasso had looked at Jacqui at the Murphy's party; he had been a denizen of that bar before he moved to nicer digs in Montparnasse. But he had learned long ago that Jacqui was more than capable of sensing and avoiding danger or dealing with it if it came to that. Perhaps, Alain had another cousin, one Jacqui didn't know, to keep an eye on her while she kept an eye on the artists. Though if she found out...

THE CONCIERGE AT HELEN Miller's upscale apartment on boulevard Raspail greeted him as he approached the entrance and led him up the stairs to the flat on the third floor. The door was ajar and the woman knocked lightly before ushering him in, closing the door behind her as she left.

The apartment was sparsely furnished with a mix of traditional and more modern pieces. Miller was reclining in a chaise lounge, gazing out the window onto the street below. She had a flute in one hand; an open bottle of champagne was on the floor beside her. Three suitcases, packed and bound in leather straps, along with a set of golf clubs, were against one wall, a travelling cloak draped across them.

"I don't normally drink in the morning but today is a special day. I'm leaving Paris and I'm not coming back. There's another glass on the table if you care to join me."

"Thanks, but no. Drinking in the morning doesn't agree with me."

"You clearly haven't embraced the ex-patriate lifestyle." Miller smiled sadly and finished her glass.

"Did you ask me here to say good-bye?"

"Yes. No. I don't know. I… I think you should stop looking into Walter's death. The police are probably right. Death by misadventure. That would make a good novel title, don't you think?"

"I wouldn't know. But I do know that Walter Gladstone was murdered, no matter what the police say. And you know it, too."

"What does it matter? France is full of dead young men. What difference does one more make?" Miller poured another glass of champagne, spilling half of it on the floor. "Christ, what a waste."

Max took the glass from her hand and moved it and the bottle to the side table. The young woman fell back onto the chaise, her hand across her eyes. He stayed by the table, uncertain. His client, or was she his ex-client, now, was clearly distressed. She had been drinking for awhile; the champagne bottle was less than half full.

"Perhaps, we should go to a café. Have you had breakfast yet?"

Miller laughed. "I wondered if you were? A gentleman, I mean. Half the men I know would, you know, take advantage of this situation."

"I'm happy to be in the other half." Miller was crying now and Max crossed back to her to offer his handkerchief. "Why are you leaving?" If he knew that he would probably know why she wanted him to stop investigating Gladstone's death.

"There's nothing left for me here. I'd hoped Paris would help me forget Henry—my fiancé—but everything reminds me of him. Even the things he would have hated remind me of him. I thought Walter—it doesn't matter. Walter wasn't interested in me, didn't care about the things that mattered to me. It was just fun to him. Maybe, if we'd had a little more time. Don't you see, everything is ruined and I'm afraid..." She put a hand to her mouth as if to stop further words from emerging.

"Afraid of what?" Fear would explain why she was leaving, why she was upset enough to drink in the morning, why everything felt ruined and hopeless. He knew what fear looked like; he had seen it often enough in the mirror.

"Nothing. Nothing that matters. You should go. I did what I could to get you to stop. It's all on you now." She thrust his handkerchief back at him, her face blotchy but composed.

"Did someone ask you to stop me? Did Gladstone's cousin, Rubenstein, speak to you? Did he threaten you?"

Her composure shattered at the mention of the name, her eyes flicking from side to side as if it would evoke the man himself.

"You... you've met him then?" She shuddered and seemed to fall in on herself. Max slid in beside her and put his arm across her shoulders.

"Did he come here?"

He barely heard her whispered yes.

"Then you can't stay here. And you shouldn't go where he might follow, away from anyone you know, anyone who could protect you. I can find you a place that is safe, away from the heart of the city but close enough I can keep in touch. I'm getting closer to the truth everyday." Max wasn't sure of that but he knew she needed to hear it. "I don't know why Gladstone's cousin—"

"He's not his cousin. He's something else."

"Yes. Will you stay, until this all gets resolved?"

"I'll be safe?"

"Safe as houses."

Safe as one house in particular, at least. Henri had a small rowhouse on the far north edge of Montmartre. Max had been there only once, while recovering from a bout of the Spanish flu in 1919, and there was little now to connect him to it. Though Henri maintained the place as a memorial to his dead wife and daughter, he seldom stayed there anymore, preferring to sleep in a small room Yesim had prepared for him above Le Coq Bleu. Helen Miller would be perfectly safe there.

MAX CALLED HENRI FROM a post office on rue Montparnasse and arranged for him to come for Miller in a cab. "Make sure you're not followed to your house. We need to keep her safe and secret."

Stopping for a bite to eat at Le Select, he was surprised to see a familiar face. Erich Harvey had put on a few pounds and his color was healthier than when he left Paris, but Max would have recognized his long equine face and hunched posture anywhere. He was at a small table in the corner, his notebooks sprawled across the surface leaving hardly any room for the large glass of beer and small plate of sandwiches that comprised his lunch.

"Erich. You've come home."

"Hah!" Harvey barked a laugh and pointed to the seat opposite. "You're looking well, Max. Married, I mean, handfasted life clearly agrees with you."

"I thought you were happily settled back in Chicago with your brother."

"Families. You can't choose them the way you can your friends. Robert got religion and kept trying to drag me to church. And, you can't get a drink in Chicago without associating with gangsters and their purchased politicians. Given my previous brushes with the law and disdain for the governing class, I found it disconcerting. But it was good in one way, it broke the habit of drinking in the morning."

"What will you do back in Paris?" Max knew Harvey had found it difficult to eke out a living as a journalist, especially after the influx of young Americans who all thought they could write. Most had allowances from home and could afford to take a pittance for their efforts.

"The same as every other ex-pat in this benighted city, I'll write the great American novel.

"But..."

"My brother's new found faith had a silver lining. Literally. My parents had left a modest inheritance for me, held in trust by Robert. He had neglected to inform me but now feels duty bound to come clean. It's not a lot but should see me through to my decrepitude."

Max laughed. He had missed Harvey though it took meeting him again for him to realize it. "You could always supplement your income. Even with a year's absence, your contact list must still be substantial."

"You only like me for what I know." Harvey smiled as if such a motive was enough.

"No doubt. Though it isn't your only redeeming feature."

Harvey's smile broadened. "Well, I've only been back in town a few days but I'd be happy to help."

Max quickly outlined the two main cases he had been working on. Harvey nodded sympathetically at Max's frustration at his lack of progress, especially regards the murder of Walter Gladstone.

"I know a family of that name in Chicago, not well but I met them at a few charitable events my brother organized. A couple of about my age or a little older and their married daughter. Someone asked about their son but only got a cold stare in response."

"Any idea what the father did?"

"A businessman, a fairly successful one, making furniture, household goods and, this may be relevant, parts for automobiles."

"He manufactured automobiles?"

"No, he built the seats and some of the other accessories—an extension of his furniture business, I suppose. There were over two dozen factories making trucks and automobiles in Chicago before the war though most of them have failed or been bought out by the big companies out of Detroit. Still, from what I heard, the elder Gladstone, his brother and their father before them had made a good part of their fortune investing in those early factories and continue to prosper from their sale of parts to their rival metropolis."

"Then Walter Gladstone's money, he apparently was well-heeled for an artist, came from the automobile business." That was an interesting twist. Although the young man had apparently been estranged from his father, he might still have an interest in the business, perhaps with hopes to inherit some day. He would have to see if Alain's queries turned up anything but, if Gladstone was involved with Dupont, he had another witness, or possibly suspect, to add to his growing list.

WHEN HE STOPPED AT Chez Jake to see if Henri had any further information on the missing soldier, Alain was waiting for him, beaming from ear to ear.

"Gladstone visited the factory several times in the weeks before his death. He even took a tour of the factory floor, conducted by none other than Jean Dupont. According to the very informative young woman at the front desk, the pair had lunch together on at least two occasions."

Max felt a small frisson of satisfaction. It was time he talked to Jean Dupont.

Chapter 12 Saturday, May 12th to Sunday, May 13th, 1923

Dupont was not at the factory when Max arrived. The informative young woman thought he might be home sick—he had been sneezing frequently the day before. Duvalier came down the stairs before Max could make his exit.

"Mr. Dupont said he might need to take the day off. He didn't mention sickness but rather a family matter that would take him out of town. Mlle. Janvier is a very capable young woman but she is not a nurse. Should I be concerned about Dupont's absence?"

If Dupont was responsible for the thefts, his absence did nothing except assure there would be nothing taken this weekend. If he wasn't, and the younger Duvalier might still be a possibility, Max didn't want to make a false accusation.

"No."

"Have you made no progress on this matter?" Duvalier's face had grown red.

"Considerable progress. Have you implemented the security measures I suggested?"

Duvalier nodded. "There have been no further missing prototypes or plans."

"Good. I expect to finish my inquiries in a few days. If all goes well, I should be able to deliver the culprit and return the stolen plans in a few days." And if it doesn't, he doubted he would get another job of this magnitude for the foreseeable future. Gaston might not be the only one trailing wayward spouses for a living. Duvalier seemed mollified, at least temporarily.

The concierge at Dupont's apartment building had seen him leaving the evening before with a small valise in hand, confirming Duvalier's report of a weekend excursion. She turned up her nose at a hundred-franc bribe to gain access to his rooms, either out of principle or because it wasn't enough.

To make matters worse, the turn in the weather had delivered a chill rain that soon soaked through Max's light jacket.

Although the hour for Miss Stein's regular salon was still some way off, he decided to drop by her lodgings at 27 rue de Fleurus. She had warned him that she did not appreciate impromptu visitors interrupting her work but he thought her expressed interest in detectives might cause her to make an exception for him. The door was answered by the diminutive woman with dark hooded eyes he had seen at the Murphy's lunch party. Alice something.

"I'm sorry, we were about to sit down for lunch. Miss Stein does not accept uninvited guests for lunch."

"Who is it, birdie?" Stein's voice was distant but distinct.

"That detective you told me about, lovie. The Canadian." Alice spoke loudly over his shoulder. Max's assessment of Alice shifted from servant to something much more intimate.

"Bring him in."

Alice sighed audibly but did as she was requested. His first impression of their quarters was that of a comfortably furnished art gallery. Paintings of all sorts hung from the walls, some of which looked similar to a few he had seen during the visit to the Louvre he had made with Jacqui. He remembered Asper telling him that Stein was an avid collector of art and, according to one of the young

American writers, of artists as well. He wondered if she was adding detectives to the list.

Stein was still sitting at the small kitchen table but it appeared that lunch was over. An empty soup bowl and a plate containing a few bites of a beef and tomato sandwich had been pushed to one side. She put down her coffee cup and gestured for Max to follow her down the hall to a large studio space where art covered nearly all the available space. Alice joined them a few minutes later, bringing more coffee before taking a seat against one wall, almost seeming to disappear into it.

"I had been expecting you, though perhaps not until the start of this evening's gathering. I do not like unexpected visitors as it interferes with my writing but, this once, I will make an exception. I have, as I promised, made some inquiries."

"I'd be happy to hear whatever insights you can give me. About American writers, the expatriate community or about the avant-garde artists who you obviously know so well." Max gestured at the paintings on the wall. His eyes were drawn to one in particular, a dark portrait that he immediately recognized as that of Stein, which held pride of place above the heavy chesterfield where Stein was sitting.

"Picasso painted that," she said, "when we first became friends, nearly twenty years ago now. He might be here tonight. One never knows what Saturday will bring.

"I expect Hemingway might also drop by, he's a regular when he is not galivanting around for the newspaper he works for in Toronto."

Max smiled at the Canadian connection, although he himself had never been farther west than Montreal. "He seems to be well-liked and respected by his fellow writers."

"Liked by some, I suppose, respected by most, if only grudgingly. He is only now coming into his own. McAlmon is bringing out his first book next month but more will follow soon. He is a cut above the others who spend their days scribbling in cafes and their nights drinking or worse in the bars and clubs of Montparnasse."

"Was Walter Gladstone one of those?"

"In part. He certainly spent some of his days scribbling and had several poems and a very short prose piece published in small but respectable magazines. However, he seemed to have other interests as well. He was an habitue of Le Grand Guignol—"

"He was interested in one of the actresses."

"Perhaps. But according to McAlmon, he approached him about publishing a novel based, in part, on the conceit that the horror depicted on the stage there was actually an imitation of actual crimes. Robert quite rightly refused to have anything to do with the venture, refusing even to look at the manuscript."

"How did Gladstone react?" If Gladstone had made threats, it might have led to his own death.

"He laughed. 'Your loss!' Whether he had another publisher lined up or planned to have it printed at his own expense, we'll never know for sure."

"There was no sign of a long manuscript in his effects. Only a few notebooks, with some poems and a few pages of a play as well as notebooks with brief sketches of things he had seen in Paris."

"Perhaps one of his rivals stole it. There are those so desperate to appear in print that would steal the work of others."

Max made a note to follow up with the group of writers he had met at the Murphy's party. When he looked up Stein was looking at him with a curious half-smile.

"Have *you* ever considered writing a book? Your life seems perfectly suited to turning into fiction."

"Is that what writers do? Turn their lives into fiction?"

"The first thing beginning writers are told is to write what you know. If it were literally true, literature would be nothing but a dull recital of uneventful lives. Given the paucity of middle-class existence, we would be lucky to have any books at all. Rather, the adage should be: write what you can learn, discover, observe, imagine. Isn't that how you solve the crimes life presents to you? You surely don't have to be a criminal to think like one."

"I hadn't thought of it that way. By the same token, I suppose you could be a detective, turning the tools of the writer into that of a sleuth."

Stein laughed. "I think I shall make an exception for you, Mr. Anderson. You may admit him anytime he comes by, Alice."

"I hope he won't be stopping by after midnight or before breakfast." Max was suddenly taken by the deep richness of the voice and the way the inflections contained both humour and admonishment. There was more to Mme Toklas than met the eye.

"I promise not to abuse the privilege."

"Now I have some correspondence to attend to and we must prepare for this evening's salon. If there is nothing else..."

"One more question—if you can?" Stein nodded. "I have twice seen groups of artists almost come to blows over... well, honestly I don't know what they were fighting about."

Stein paused for a long moment, her gaze flicking from one painting to another along her studio wall.

"The war caused a great turmoil in the lives and thoughts of men and women. France today is not the France I came to in 1903. Then, the Belle Epoch was coming to its close but what was to replace it had not yet fully formed. Impressionism which marked the end of that era's rejection of the traditional had run its course but what was to follow had not yet been fully formed or understood. The war forced the new age to be born, fully formed but unprepared for the world. It was a dramatic break from the past but one that still yearns for a reformed future.

"Vision tumbles upon vision, new forms emerge before the previous one has finished its work. Ten years ago, Dadaism had not appeared and now it is dying of old age and, like all old men, it clings desperately to life by rejecting the emergence of its children. The emotional conflicts are real but the physical ones are staged, all for show. As you said yourself, they *almost* come to blows.

"Of course, I am only telling you what I've observed, what I've learned from talking to the practitioners, from collecting their art around me to make it part of my story. Picasso, who I know better than any of the rest, might be better placed to answer your question."

"Is he a violent man?"

"Pablo? All his fury and force are poured into his work and all his passion is poured into his mistresses. I doubt he even knows how to make a fist."

Max doubted that. He was a man after all and had almost certainly been taught by other men to form a fist.

"Perhaps, I will try to come back tonight or if not, then next Saturday. You've given me a lot to think about, and a lot to do. I'll leave you both to your work and I'll get on with mine. Thank you for your hospitality and your help."

Stein nodded and Alice stood, leading him back to the entrance, unbolting the door to let him out.

"The collection is valuable," she said. "It drove a wedge between Gertrude and her brother and has, sometimes, sent artists into paroxysms of jealousy when she declines to include their work on her walls. I have a less sanguine view of the passivity of artists. But, from what you've said, there is nothing to explain why an artist might have decided to kill this writer. Other than proximity, what is the connection?"

Indeed, thought Max, what was the connection?

NEIL HEROD WAS STILL taking care of Minter's cat. The latter had not returned to his flat though Herod didn't know if he was still in the hospital or had been sent to another facility—one that dealt specifically with drug addicts. He seemed vaguely uneasy at Max's continued interest in him and his friends but eventually suggested that he might try to find Archie Roberts, the young man who had shared a berth and, later, apartment with Walter Gladstone.

"He can usually be found around Le Dôme or one of the other bars in the area. He's taken up with Clarice Michaels and, from what I'm told, has been spreading nasty rumours about Walter. Speaking ill of the dead is hardly a gentleman's occupation."

"What has he been saying?"

"I didn't hear him myself. I don't hang with that crowd anymore. I really want to be a success, you know? I try to find quiet places where I can read and think and try to write. I got an acceptance of two poems yesterday, so I think it's working."

Max wished him well and headed for Le Dôme in search of Roberts. Before he got there, he spotted the young man in a sidewalk café, bundled up against the chill and the threat of showers. He had a notebook open in front of him but all of his attention was focused on an attractive redhead who was leaning across the table, talking while gesturing emphatically with her hands. He recognized her from the Murphy's party. She had been the red head at the bar. Clarice Michaels had been within his grasp all along.

"Mr. Roberts, may I have a few words. If you don't mind, Miss Michaels?" As he had with Stein, he spoke in English, his own language still feeling odd in his mouth.

"Have we met?" she flashed him a bright smile before furrowing her brows.

"Almost. We spoke once at La Rotonde and—"

"You were at that party, the Murphy's, wasn't it?"

"Yes, you were talking to the bartender. I noticed you but didn't make the connection. I'm afraid I was focused on Madame Stein."

Michaels spat a nasty phrase. Roberts looked startled.

"Please, Clarice. We'll never get invited nice places if that gets around. Just because she gave you the brush—"

She held up her hand, then blushed, pulling her jacket closer and crossing her arms.

"You may as well sit down," said Roberts. "The return of winter has driven away the usual clientele. A waiter will arrive before you're settled in your seat."

Robert's prediction proved accurate. Max had not eaten since breakfast and ordered a bowl of onion soup and some bread, along with a small beer to wash it down. Roberts and Michaels accepted his offer of lunch and each opted for a Croque Monsieur and a glass of red.

"I understand you've got additional information about Walter Gladstone."

"Who told you that?" Michaels answered before the young writer could respond.

"Paris is a big city but the Americans in it are a small town. Word gets around. About a lot of things."

Michaels looked like she might have more to say but Roberts leaned across the table to pat her shoulder. "It's alright, Clarice. I don't mind talking to Max. I can call you Max, can't I?"

"It's my name. What have you got to talk about?" He took out his notebook and opened it to a fresh page, writing the initials of the two witnesses at the top.

"Do you remember I told you that Gladstone was incredibly lucky at cards?"

Max didn't though he had probably made a note about it. He jotted it down again. "So?"

"So... I ran into a couple of fellows we played with aboard ship. Like you say it's a small town. A few days after Gladstone asked me to leave his apartment, they caught him cheating. They challenged him on it and it would have come to blows but a couple of the waiters at the club where they were playing intervened and threw the accusers out. Gladstone was allowed to stay. Maybe the club was in on it or maybe he was paying the waiters for protection.

"It's not like Gladstone even needed the money. He always seemed to have lots of it. Now I wonder where he got it."

"I thought he had an allowance from his family. Some even said he had been paid to leave Chicago by his father."

"I thought that, too. But I asked around and he seemed to have some pretty shady friends. Foreigners by the sound of it. Maybe cheating at cards was only the tip of the iceberg. Maybe he was going to write about crime because he was writing what he knew."

The food arrived and Max paused to sample it. The rain had held off but clouds were threatening in the west. The soup was dark and rich with a slight caramel flavour. The bread was a little sparse but the layer of melted gruyere was thick and flavoured with red wine. It was almost hot enough to burn his mouth but was cooling quickly. Roberts ate half of his sandwich before even looking up but Clarice Michaels only picked at hers.

"Paris is full of foreigners." Max picked up the conversation where they had left off. "Including us."

"Americans are never foreigners," said Michaels. "It's everyone else." Her voice was slightly slurred and Max guessed that the glass of red wine, which she had almost finished, was not her first of the day.

"Any idea who these 'foreigners' were?"

"Haven't a clue. I never met them. Someone said they didn't sound remotely French."

"Do you remember who?"

"No. It was a party. You only remember half of what you hear and never who it was that said it."

Not the most reliable of witnesses. Still, if these friends of Gladstone didn't sound *remotely* French, they probably weren't Italian or Spanish, either. Russian was the obvious choice; Yelena had mentioned that Walter spoke Russian and his so-called cousin could have been Russian as well.

Max finished his soup, hoping Roberts would have something further to add during the ensuing silence but the man seemed to have run dry. Max gestured for the waiter who arrived promptly with the bill. Max closed his notebook and made to rise but Michaels put her hand on his arm.

"Archie isn't the only one who hears things." Her voice was pitched low as if she were afraid of being overheard. "Walter Gladstone was a Red!"

"A communist?" exclaimed Roberts in a shocked voice. It was apparently news to him.

"That's why he was kicked out of Chicago by his family. Alex Minter told me."

"You've seen Minter lately." Asked Max.

"I ran into him at the bar at the Ritz. He was by himself and looked pretty peaked so I took pity on him."

"I thought he was someone young women had to be wary of. Gladstone knocked him down for making unwanted advances on Helen Miller. Did he ever try that on you?"

"Sure, his face should have had 'slap me' written on the cheek." Michaels shrugged. "Things like that happen. It doesn't mean you should give a guy the cold shoulder when he's looking ill."

"Why was Minter at the bar?"

It was one of the nicer places in town and the drinks weren't cheap.

He said he was waiting for friends but nobody showed up while I was there. We had a bit of a chat and I asked him what he knew about Walter's death, you know, because they had that bit of history. I wondered if he had, you know, gotten his revenge. He was pretty embarrassed getting knocked down like that. He said and I quote 'that Red got what he deserved. I only wish I'd had a hand in it.' I was a bit taken aback."

"I thought Minter was a pacificist."

"Yeah, he tells that story but only because it's easier than admitting his father bought him a deferment. He might not want to fight men but I know a few girls he slapped around. He knew better than to try that on me."

"Did he say who he was waiting for?"

"No. But the longer I sat there the more nervous he got, like it was someone he didn't want me to see. But the way he was acting, I figured it was someone I knew. One of the other girls I guess."

Someone she might recognize. Max wondered who it was.

THE RAIN HAD FINALLY arrived in the form of a light drizzle. At least the day was warmer than the previous two and, with his coat wrapped around him and his fedora keeping the worst of it off his neck, Max was happy enough to walk along the Seine, watching those whose work required them to be out in all kinds of weather, cargo handlers, fishermen, and, of course, police officers in their long black cloaks that gave them the nickname of swallows. Several of them greeted him by name and he was surprised that he could return the favour. It reminded him that he should check in with LePêcheur and see if he had any further tidbits that might help him with his cases.

The walk, which he had hoped would help clarify his thoughts, stretched into the late afternoon. When he reached the Eiffel Tower with no revelations, he decided he might as well head to the Russian quarter on the off-chance that that Pavlovna had returned to the city ahead of schedule and would be willing to see him. He slipped into the Metro at Quai de Grenelle, changing at Etoile to arrive at Corcelles a few minutes later. The rain had stopped and the sun was struggling to peer through the clouds as he walked the short distance to Irina Pavlovna's luxurious flat on rue Daru in the 17th arrondissement.

He had maintained a cordial but uneasy relationship with the Russian aristocrat and her cadre of counter-revolutionaries since their involvement in the murder of a former American diplomat a couple of years before. Russia and its discontents had preoccupied them (as well as his friend, current diplomat Ginger Buchan) since before the end of the Great War and, if a Soviet agent was involved in the murder of Walter Gladstone, they were bound to know something about it.

Pavlovna was indeed home and willing to speak to him. A dour looking butler took his coat and offered him a pair of slippers to replace his wet shoes and ushered him into the parlour where she was holding court with a number of her friends and supporters. Baron Denidov and General Chersky he had met before but the other three, two men and a woman, he did not know.

"This is my cousin, Adrianna Semenova, and her friend, Vladimir Alexei Andropov," said Pavlovna, indicating the youngest of the men. "And this is Captain Dominik Fyodor Novikov, General Chersky's adjutant. Max Anderson, a Canadian private detective of my acquaintance."

"You know the most interesting people, Irina," said Andropov.

"It pays to maintain a wide circle when living in a foreign city."

"Are you related to the actress, Yelena Semenova," Max asked the young woman.

She made a sour expression. "Is that what she claims to be now? A distant cousin. We do not travel in the same circles."

"I suppose not." Max took a seat near the fire place and accepted the offer of a small vodka. After the obligatory toast to Mother Russia, he briefly described the two cases, leaving out details he felt were either still confidential or not pertinent to his inquiries. When he described Walter's putative cousin, Ivan Rubenstein, Denidov's face flushed.

"Is that bastard still in Paris? I thought we had sent him packing."

"Ivany spoke to him but Volodin is a slippery character. He may have left only to return."

Ivany Fedorov had apparently done the same thing, leaving town to escape police questioning in the St. John case before returning to resume his post as, well, whatever, Pavlovna wanted it to be.

"I take it Volodin is Rubenstein's real name."

"Yes, Peotr Nikita Volodin is a Cheka agent who made a hobby of threatening those of us with little power to resist him. His threats became a nuisance to me and so we, politely, asked him to return to Moscow. He apparently declined or came back with a new mission in hand. Certainly, none of us have seen hm."

"Any idea what that mission was?"

"To me, one Bolshevik is much like another but I understand, like the pack of dogs they are, they fight among themselves to see who shall be the leader. Volodin is loyal to Stalin. If he is back in Paris, it has to do with the struggles back in Moscow."

"Trotsky?"

"You see, my friends," said Pavlovna, smiling broadly. "Max always knows more than he lets on. I can assure you, the reputed visit of Lev Davidovitch Bronstein, known as Leon Trotsky, is what has brought this snake back to Paris."

THE RAIN HAD RETURNED by morning and Max lingered in bed until he heard Jacqui starting to prepare breakfast in their small kitchen. Sunday breakfast had become a tradition for them over the last year with each alternating as chef from week to week. He stumbled to the bathroom to relief himself and run brushes over his teeth and through his hair. Dressed only in his robe and slippers, he took his seat at the table as Jacqui served up.

The main course were poached eggs served with a puree of mushroom and truffle and a side of toasted brioche. A platter of fresh fruit, small pastries and a few select cheeses plus a large urn of hot coffee rounded out the meal. They both agreed not to talk about work during the hour or so they spent enjoying their late breakfast and Max had taken to preparing conversational tidbits to prevent him from breaking the rule.

This morning, the conversation drifted from possible trips they might take in the summer when Paris grew too hot to bear to the latest dance craze as reported in the more frivolous of Paris newspapers. When they had poured the last of the coffee, Jacqui signalled the end of the morning's respite by asking how the case was going.

"Cases," he reminded her. "I think I've gotten to the bottom of the industrial espionage case. At least, I'm pretty sure who is doing it and for whom. Getting the evidence for an actual conviction might be hard but I think I can gather enough for the company owners to deal with the problem. Another few days should do the trick.

"The murder case is more complicated. Every time I think I've eliminated a suspect, new information turns up to put them right back in the picture. Even what I know about the victim keeps changing, which of course, creates new motives."

He reported on the three separate conversations he had had the day before. Jacqui was particularly taken with his description of his visit to Gertrude Stein and her comments on the competitive side of art.

"Maybe we can visit her salon one day," she said.

"She gave me an open invitation. I'm sure she'd be as happy to meet an anarchist as a detective."

"I'm sure I wouldn't be her first. I, for one, would like to meet this Alice Toklas. The way you describe them they sound like an old married couple."

He supposed she was right. He wondered what they would sound like after twenty years together. A warm glow suffused his chest as he thought of that far off future.

AFTER BREAKFAST, JACQUI, dressed in raingear and carrying a large umbrella went off for a long-scheduled stroll through the Luxembourg gardens with old friends from Marseilles. Promising to be back after lunch, she left him to go over the file on the missing soldier he had agreed to try to find.

Corporal Jacques Gibot had never returned to his parents' home in St. Rogatien, a village near La Rochelle in the department of Poitou-Charentes. They had received a letter from him in early 1919, stating he had been discharged in Paris and would be home in a month or two "once I have seen enough of the city lights." They had heard nothing further from him directly and only a few rumours since from a few of his comrades who had eventually drifted back to village life. He had escaped form the war unscathed and had seemed determined to return home and work in his father's boulangerie. "It was all he talked about."

Four years later, they had given up hope when a young man, only recently released from a Paris hospital for the severely wounded, had wandered into their shop looking for Gibot. The lad, Albert Braque, was missing one leg and the left side of his face was covered in a metal mask. "He visited me often in the hospital. He gave me the courage to get well again. When last I saw him, six months ago, he insisted I come see him when I was strong enough." His disappointment in his friend's absence was washed away by the joy his parents showed at the news.

The matter was perplexing. Gibot had no apparent reason for staying away from his home. Indeed, by all reports he was eager to return. According to Braque, he was alive and well when he had last seen him at the invalid hospital in the 5th arrondissement. That was where he would begin his search on Monday.

Satisfied he had made progress on the case, Max decided to reward himself by going to Kid O'Brien's gymnasium for a long-promised workout. The late morning crowd was thin and none of his usual sparring partners were in attendance. He had been working on the heavy bag for about ten minutes, when he spotted a familiar face. Hemingway was without his usual entourage as he filled the door to the gym, pausing to take in the array of equipment, from punching bags to a rack of free weights, that surrounded the two boxing rings. When he spotted Max, he sauntered over with a broad smile splitting his handsome face.

"You've worked up a fine lather," he said by way of hello. Hemingway was dressed in casual slacks, an open-neck white shirt and a brown corduroy sports jacket.

"Here for a workout?" Max glanced significantly at the ring not currently in use.

"I'd be happy to meet you in the squared circle one of these days." Hemingway mimed a quick combination. "I heard this was one of the better places to practice the gentleman's sport and wanted to look it over. Any good?"

"Kid O'Brien is a good teacher but he's no gentleman." Max laughed, remembering the times he had been sucker punched by O'Brien, until he had turned the man's dirty tricks back on him.

"I'll keep that in mind. Stein told me last night you'd dropped in for a chat. About the young American writer who was dumped in the lake."

"Yeah. She was... helpful."

"Any progress?"

Max shrugged. He still wasn't sure he liked Hemingway but Stein thought he was smart and he had served in the war—earlier than most of his American comrades. "Every time I think I'm on track, some new complications pop up."

"Life seems complicated, yet it's not really. If you can hone in on the telling detail, the key moment, the truth of everything emerges. That's what I try to do when I'm writing; push all the little details beneath the surface so the truth emerges on top."

"Like an iceberg."

"That's a good way of putting it. Simplify everything, Max, and it will all become clear.

Easier said than done but good advice nonetheless.

Chapter 13 Monday, May 14th, 1923

The visit to the Val-de-Grace hospital provided few clues as to the whereabouts of former-Corporal Gibot. One of the attendants did remember Braque. He had been written off as unlikely to improve until a series of visits by a young man seemed to bring him back from the edge. Those had stopped a few months before his discharge but he had continued to rally on his own and often spoke of his "guardian angel." As to who the visitor was and where he had gone, no one could offer an idea.

"I've seen it before, of course," said the attendant. "Patients often improve when family or friends visit on a regular basis but this young man was a stranger according to Braque. Maybe he really was an angel."

Max had his doubts about divine intervention but had himself experienced the power of connection to heal the damaged spirit of several injured soldiers. Gibot had somehow chosen to visit Braque and then moved on. But where had he moved on to?

Max was still considering his next step when he arrived at his office to find Hugo waiting for him as if called there by Max's thoughts. He had met Hugo Pomeroy at The Invalides hospital during a search for another missing and badly wounded soldier. His visit—and the connection he was able to make to the man's past—had sent the man back to the arms of his parents. Perhaps Hugo's appearance was an omen of future success in Gibot's case.

"That happened several times in the years after the war," said Hugo. "An unexpected visit from an old friend or a comrade from the trenches seemed to hasten their recovery. Once, a person dropped by to see a friend only to find he had been discharged. Rather than waste the visit. he made the rounds of the ward like a visiting doctor or priest. He soon had us all laughing and I'm sure several of the men found comfort and healing in the hour or two he was with us."

Max made a note to check with the half dozen hospitals and care homes in the city that still held the most severely wounded from the war. Perhaps Gibot's visit to Braque had been repeated elsewhere.

"What have you learned as a volunteer at the theatre?"

Hugo smiled broadly. "More than a volunteer now. They've offered me a part-time job, helping here and there as needed. One day, I'm hauling the curtain up and down, the next I'm showing people to their seats. The pay is meagre but it all helps these days. Between that and the hospital and what work you have for me; I feel I can start planning for my future."

Hugo's smile and optimism was contagious and Max felt his own lips quirking up. "And what future do you have planned?"

"Well, there's this girl..." Hugo's face had flushed. "But I don't want to say more before things are more certain."

Max recalled Hugo's reaction the last time he had been in Le Coq Bleu. Could Josette be the girl in question? Life was full of mysteries to solve, but those of the heart were the most difficult.

"In any case," Hugo went on. "I like working there, now I've gotten used to the kind of things they do on stage. It's all fake, of course, and most of the writers and actors take their work seriously without being too serious about it. Lots of laughs, lots of big ideas, you know. They seem to feel they are doing the city a service, relieving the terror most people still have of the war."

Max supposed it was possible that they felt that way but he had seen few former soldiers in the audience on the night he was there. Those who had truly experienced the horror of the trenches might not see it as a service.

"You've made friends?"

"Started to, though it is hard to say. People you work with sometimes seem like friends until you get another job."

"True enough. I had several close friends in the army but haven't exchanged more than a postcard with any of them since the war ended."

"The only person I haven't warmed to at all is the one you sent me to watch. Carlos Herrerra is a trouble maker. He teases people to the point of brutality and always eggs on any little dispute that comes up in the course of a day. Theatre is a driving ambition for most of them, so there is always a little tension over this and that. Herrerra seizes on every opportunity to make it worse."

"Why would he do that?"

"I don't know. I thought some people were just mean that way but one of the actors, Arno DeClercq, said he thinks Carlos is frustrated. He feels his talents are wasted on helping design sets and manage the shows. He has ambitions to be an artist, has even been taught by Picasso, who comes from the same town in Spain. I did notice, after that, he does tend to go after people who dismiss his efforts as secondary to the real work of the theatre."

Would those people have included Walter Gladstone, who, in his competition for the attention of Yelena Semenova, might well have found it useful to denigrate his rival? Perhaps, he had been too soon to dismiss the Spaniard as a suspect.

After Hugo left for a shift at the Invalides, Max wandered down the hall to talk to Henri and review the morning's mail. He found him poring over the account books and muttering to himself.

"You look troubled. Is there a problem with the books?"

"Other than you don't seem to know the difference between a debit and credit and your handwriting is nearly illegible to boot. What does this say?" He pointed to a scribble beside an entry for 200 francs.

"I'm not sure. But see it has a minus sign beside it so it was a payment of some sort." He squinted at the note and then nodded. "That's a C and there's a J. So, it was a cheque to cover some expense at the club."

Henri threw up his hands in frustration. "That's what I thought! You jumble them all together, Chez Jake, Le Coq Bleu, the detective agency and even personal expenses. I think it's why you are paying too much tax."

"I don't mind paying taxes." Max knew enough to know he should keep better records but had thought of all his income and expenses as "personal." It all came from the same back account.

"Very admirable. Everyone should pay their share. But if you want to make charitable contributions, there are better places to give your money than the government. Don't worry, I'll sort it all out. Fortunately—" Henri paused to glance meaningfully at two large boxes stuffed with paper. "—you seem to have kept every receipt and cancelled check since the end of the war."

"I think Yesim and Jake keep proper records for the business..."

"Yesim is meticulous that way. He knows the history of every franc. I once caught him cursing over his accounts because they were out by nine sou. I suggested he look for a transposition error, you know, writing 43 when it should be 34. You would think I had found a pot of gold under the bar. I will ask him about your contributions and I will ask Jake as well when he returns."

"No need to wait. Smitty does the books." Max had only discovered that recently when Jake announced he was making a trip to London and would likely be away for more than a month.

"Smitty? The giant who guards the door and deals with troublesome clients?"

"And manages the cellar. He has a beautiful singing voice, too."

"Ha! I should know not to be fooled by appearances. The clothes do not make the man."

Henri closed the account book and set it to one side. He handed Max a small stack of letters and two sealed envelopes, both marked "personal." One was a letter from René Voison, thanking him for returning him to the arms of his family. "I have discovered that misplaced love can leave you blind to other possibilities." Max handed the note to Henri.

"It is always the way. One lost and ten found."

The other letter was from Jake. He was having a wonderful time in London but would return within a week or ten days. He had a great idea for expanding the bar's business and would tell him all about it when he returned. Max smiled at that; while Jake's ideas usually panned out, they always required a significant upfront expense.

"The others are the usual. A couple of possible cases—I disposed of the three divorce ones as instructed—plus some bills, which I have set aside to pay when due. Also, Cleroux called about the missing aristocrat. I told him you had solved the case and would drop by first thing tomorrow."

Max made a note of the appointment in his notebook and handed the two case requests back to Henri.

"These look interesting enough but my mind is too full to consider it. Why don't you see if it is something fairly straight forward Gaston could take on. Otherwise, respectfully decline."

Henri gave him a broad smile. "It would be my pleasure."

MAX NEEDED SPACE TO think on his own so he returned to the apartment on rue Jacob with the intention of making himself a sandwich. He could go over his notes in the comfort of his favorite chair with a demi-liter of white wine by his side. He was surprised to find Jacqui there, ensconced in the selfsame chair with a book on her lap.

"Not working today?" Jacqui had been gone before he got up, not unusual as the days grew longer. She liked to walk the length of the Tuileries Gardens on her way to the Opera House, stopping at one of the little cafés on Rue de la Paix for a pastry and coffee before her day began.

"I walked all the way there only to find that the master costumer is away for a few days. We weren't all needed to complete the work he left for us. Giselle, the assistant to M. Turgot, said I should go home and take it easy."

Jacqui had returned from her walk the day before well after lunch, tired and out of sorts. She took a long nap before rallying long enough to go out for a light supper but had gone straight to bed as soon as they were home. He had been worried she might be coming down with something but she had assured him she was fine. Now, she had been sent home from work "to take it easy."

"Are you alright?"

"Yes, but... there is something I need to tell you, but I'm not sure how you'll take it."

Max had an ominous feeling. He loved Jacqui and knew she loved him but he always feared he would not be enough for her. "Go on."

"Two things really." She hesitated and glanced away.

Max pulled a second chair close so he could sit opposite her.

"I was telling one of the girls at the Opera about the murder case. They all think what you do is so exciting."

Max's tension released. He didn't like Jacqui gossiping about his work but if that was all it was...

"She knew this Yelena Semenova. They had needed to fill out the chorus at one of the shows last year and Yelena got the part. They got quite friendly and, well, to put it simply, Yelena didn't care for either Gladstone or Herrera, they were merely amusements to her."

"She had another boyfriend?"

"Not at all. She doesn't have boyfriends. She has girlfriends, including my friend at the Opera."

Max was surprised but mostly at himself for not realizing it. Despite his years in Paris, where values were far more liberal that those he had grown up with, he was still sometimes oblivious to the different way people lived and loved.

"That certainly puts a different spin on things." It did, though Max was not quite sure how.

"You said there were two things."

"As I was finishing my walk in the Luxembourg Gardens, I ran into Pablo, M. Picasso. He invited me to come and see his new studio. It wasn't far and on the way back here, so I didn't see the harm in it."

"You were alone with him?" He had heard rumours about Picasso and his way with women.

"Not at all. Several other artists were there as well as a couple of women who were modeling for them. I was introduced quickly but can't remember all their names, Irene was one of the women and one of the painters was named Braque. I remember him because he was visiting from Normandy and he and Picasso acted like old friends at a reunion. They were both quite excited about another painter named Enrico Carlotti. Picasso, Braque and the two others got quite heated about his proposal for repatriation. I couldn't follow the whole argument but it was clear Braque was opposed and one of the others in favour."

"I've heard of Carlotti—he's Italian."

"Yes. Anyway, after a bit it all calmed down. Picasso said 'we came here to paint, not fight and we have such lovely models to inspire us.' They set up their easels and Irene and the other woman shed their clothes and, well, it seemed so comfortable, I did, too."

"You what? You took your clothing off in front of a bunch of men."

"A bunch of painters, Max. Once they had brushes in their hands, we might have been bowls of fruit. 'Move here, turn there, now be still'. After a while, I got cold, so I put my clothes back on and came home.

"I was a bit embarrassed though when Picasso ran after me and pressed thirty francs in my hand to pay for my time. Oh, Max if you could see the look on your face."

Max opened his mouth to speak but he couldn't think of what to say. He stared at Jacqui, seeing her for an instant how others might see her, so delicate and fresh except for the steel in her eyes. He opened his mouth again as he saw how his silence was hurting her and wondered what he could say to show he didn't care, that he loved her and trusted her.

"Thirty francs, eh? Maybe I should take up this modelling business."

They were both still laughing as they tumbled into bed.

IT WAS LATE AFTERNOON by the time they roused themselves, too late for lunch, too early for supper. Max's notes were calling to him but he felt a more urgent summons. He pulled Jacqui on top of him. She had gained a little weight in the last few months and he enjoyed stroking the enhanced curves of her body. He wondered if this is what lovers did as they aged; each changing and the other finding new delights in the changes.

After, he decided that he had needed this more than he needed to sort out the accumulating information into some coherent pattern. Maybe he needed to follow Hemingway's advice and allow the details to sink below the surface of his conscious mind until the truth emerged. In any case, the day was almost over and their bodies craved sustenance.

"Josette always prepares a hearty stew on Monday afternoons," Jacqui reminded him. Stews could be stretched if custom was busy and reused the next day if it was slow "Let's go to Le Coq Bleu for a drink and an early supper."

The rains had paused for the day and the late afternoon air was fresh and clean. The walk to the little bar would take an hour, uphill most of the way, so they decided to use Jacqui's modelling fee for a taxi.

They were greeted by the aroma of bay leaf and thyme and beef broth. Only one table was occupied. A trio of men in rough clothes leaned over their plates, scooping spoonfuls of dark stew into their mouths, punctuating their food with hearty gulps of brown ale. Yesim was at the bar, talking to Josette in low tones. He placed his hand over hers and she did not pull away. Rather she smiled at him, and he, in a rare show of delight, smiled back. It seemed that Yesim's reluctance to have a woman working in the restaurant had been transformed over time into a much different feeling. Max hoped that it wasn't Josette that Hugo had set his heart on. He exchanged a glance with Jacqui; her eyes were gleaming and her lips lifted in a smile.

"Do you have anymore of that stew? It smells glorious," said Jacqui, as if they hadn't witnessed the moment of intimacy. Yesim jerked his hand back and cleared his throat, a faint flush rising on his cheeks, as if he were a school boy and not a man of fifty.

"Plenty, plenty!" he exclaimed. "So good to see you, Jacqui. Married life, or whatever you call it, suits you."

"Married is fine for me," she said, looking up at Max and squeezing his hand. "And happily, so happily."

It was Max's turn to blush. Then he laughed. Who was the school boy now?

Chapter 14 Tuesday, May 15th, 1923

B laise Cleroux was already in his office when Max arrived. His assistant promised coffee would be ready in a few moments as she waved Max through. The lawyer was in his usual place behind the paper strewn desk, making notes in a thick file perched precariously on a stack of ill-assorted books. Max shifted another stack of books off a chair and took a seat near a small open patch of the desktop in hopes it would soon be occupied by a steaming mug of coffee.

"I thought I might have to wait to see you," he said, when Cleroux finally looked up. "I didn't take you for an early riser."

Cleroux held up his hand until the assistant brought the carafe to the sideboard and poured them each a mugful mixed with warmed milk. Cleroux didn't speak until he had drained half the steaming liquid. He belched and declared: "No wonder they call you a detective. Unfortunately, the judge I have to appear before this morning *is* an early riser. Needs must, as they say. Now, what did you want to see me about?"

"You called me about Lady Wentworth. I have a report."

"Good, Lord Robert is coming to Paris this weekend and I'd like to deliver her to him."

"It may work out then. She's currently in Rome but is expected to return by Friday. I expect she will return to the Meurice. She has nothing if not expensive tastes."

"Why all the secrecy? I'm sure her travelling companions would have enjoyed a week in sunny Italy."

"She is travelling with a young man, an Italian artist named Carlotti, a bit of a dubious character by all accounts. I doubt if her chaperone would have approved."

"No, I suppose not. Anything else I should know."

"She went to Rome to meet with Benito Mussolini, the new Prime Minister. She is apparently a great admirer of his thinking."

Cleroux's face darkened. While Max had never been entirely sure of the man's politics, he knew he had little sympathy for Les Camelots de Roi and other actors on the far right. Too many of his clients had suffered beatings at their hands for him to approve.

"Will her father be upset?"

"I no longer know him well enough to judge. As a student, he spoke like a radical but, now that he has settled into his peerage, he has become more conservative, though we seldom let our correspondence extend beyond family matters and the latest football scores. Nonetheless, I will dutifully report your findings."

Cleroux took out his cheque book and wrote a scrip for half the promised amount. "Half now, the rest when the Lady is back in the arms of her family. I'll mail the remainder next week if that is agreeable."

Max would have been happy to settle for half—the work had not been onerous—but it would set a bad example if other jobs came up. He finished his coffee, shook Cleroux's hand and grabbed the Metro up to Montmartre.

ALTHOUGH THERE WERE performances scheduled for the evening at Le Grand Guignol, the resident stage manager was nowhere to be found. He had finished clearing up after the Saturday night shows but no one had seen him since.

"It's not uncommon for him to miss the Sunday rehearsals but he should be here now," His assistant looked nervous at the thought of having to run the stage that night. "Maybe the director knows where he is."

Camille Choisy, despite the name, was a man of medium height with a pencil mustache and piercing blue eyes. Max found him inspecting an arcane device that looked like a cross between a guillotine and a catapult. Max wondered if it was used to launch severed heads into a terrified audience.

"Hererra?" He said, barely looking up from his work. "He asked for a week off during the intermission on Saturday. Said he had family business back in Spain. More likely he wanted to get away from Yelena. She's slated to perform every night this week. Never get involved with actresses."

"Is she here today?"

"I haven't seen her but she is likely around somewhere. Try the actors' lounge.: He gestured vaguely to his left and Max headed that way until he came to a door, labelled: "silence, les génies se préparent à l'éclat." Despite the warning about geniuses working, Max rapped softly on the door. A quiet voice bid him enter. Yelena Semenova was seated at a dressing table, peering at herself in the mirror. An actor, middle aged and paunchy was reclining on a couch, sipping coffee and chatting to another actress, the one he had seen with Semenova the last time he spoke to her.

"Can we speak in private Mme Semenova?"

"Anything you want to say to me can be said in front of my friends. We have no secrets."

"This is delicate..."

"No matter. You want to know about my relationship to Gladstone and Herrerra. The truth is, they were mere conveniences. Places exist where a young woman cannot go by herself. It is useful to have someone's arm to lean on. It was also useful to have one to play off against the other. I cared for neither of them."

"I understand you don't care for men at all." Max felt his face grow hot.

"Nonsense. Jerzy there is one of my closest friends. But I wouldn't want him in my bed."

"I am deeply hurt, my darling." Jerzy placed the back of his hand on his brow. "Well, fortunately, Rosa is always willing to oblige." Rosa gave him a playful slap on the top of his head.

"You see, no secrets and no judgement. Paris was always a city of love; the war has only made it more so."

"And was that how Herrerra felt?"

Yelena made a spitting noise. "He was a Spaniard. He could not believe he couldn't make me love him. I didn't disabuse him. Perhaps if I had, he might not have killed Walter in a fit of violent rage."

"You have proof of that?"

"No, nothing concrete, but a woman learns to read a man's looks, his moods. He must have killed Walter. It's only natural."

Max didn't think there was anything natural about killing another human. Men did it, some eagerly but most regretfully and spent the rest of their lives trying not to think about. It was why so many soldiers wouldn't talk about the war; others could talk of nothing else.

"Did you ever see them argue? Did you see them fight?"

"I saw them snarl at each other once or twice. I saw them bump against each other at parties, like animals trying to impress their mate. I was not impressed and it never went too far. People were watching, but alone, in a park..."

"Did you see them the night Gladstone died? Did you see them in Parc Montsouris?"

"No." Yelena hesitated, her brow furrowed in worry. "I did see Walter there. I was meeting with the puppeteers to discuss an idea

I had for a show. I saw Walter walking along the path by the lake. I followed him. I was going to finally tell him we were unsuited for each other. But he was distracted, worried, I think. He behaved like I wasn't even there. I asked him what was troubling him.

"Then he laughed and said he was meeting someone. It surprised me, made me feel strangely jealous. It must have shown on my face because he assured me it was 'nothing like that.' He had some business to settle."

"Did he say whom he was meeting?"

"No, I assumed it was Carlos but when I said that he laughed again and said he would 'settle with Herrerra later,' but I am sure he was meeting Carlos but didn't want me to see it."

Max was far from sure that Gladstone had gone to meet Herrerra in the park. Why would he risk an encounter with someone who clearly was better in a fight than he was and who had sworn on several occasions to kill him over Yelena Semenova? No. he was literally meeting some one to settle some business. A deal perhaps or the end of a partnership gone sour? He would check with Herrerra if he ever came back to Paris but, now, he had a stronger suspect in Gladstone's death.

Jean Dupont.

ROGET WAS WAITING FOR him when he returned to his office, sitting in the spare chair with his feet on the desk, cleaning his nails with the blade of a pocketknife. Max cleared his throat and Roget leaped to his feet; the knife now clutched in one hand.

"You shouldn't sneak up on a man when he has a knife in his hand."

"I'll remember that." Max picked up the phone and buzzed the kitchen. "Double that order, if you please." To Roget: "I'm having a sandwich and a beer. I assume you would take a little lunch while giving your report."

"I learned in the army never to turn down the opportunity for a free lunch."

Max thought of telling Roget it would come out of his wages just to see the expression on his face.

"What have you learned about Leo Duvalier?"

"Little enough for what you're paying me. I was initially suspicious because he was flashing around a lot of money, enjoying a bit of the high life. I have an old friend who works in a bank and he knew someone who knew someone so I was able to find out that young Duvalier's regular wages were decent but insufficient to manage his life style."

Max was impressed. Apparently, his chequered career had provided Roget with a broad range of useful acquaintances. He wondered whether there was a business case for taking the man on full-time.

"It turns out he has a knack for picking winners at the track, where I followed him on several occasions. I talked to a couple of bookies—he apparently spreads his bets around—who say he must have a system but, sadly, they couldn't tell me what it was, only that, nine days out of ten he goes home with more money than he came with.

He spends the money, as young men do, on wine, women and song but he doesn't have a regular bar or a regular girl as far as I could tell from observing and chatting with the staff. In the week I've been following him, he's gone out five nights. The other two nights, Wednesday and Sunday, he had dinner at his brother's house. The middle one, Andre, though on Sunday there was an older man in attendance. Strong family resemblance."

"Probably the eldest, Charles."

"Leo brought flowers for his brother's wife both nights and was greeted at the door by two young children. Judging by their enthusiasm, I think he had treats hidden in his pockets. In my opinion, Leo is very close to his brothers, not the type to steal their livelihood or his future."

"Very good work. I think you're right." Max doled out the agreed payment, again getting a receipt for his expenses. "I may have more work for you soon. I'll add 500 as a retainer against future assignments. Check in once a week."

Roget pocketed the money and rose to leave. At the door, he turned back, his face wearing a puzzled expression. "I told you I've met a girl. She asked me to meet her parents. No one ever asked that before. What does it mean?"

Max laughed. "It means you may soon need a bigger apartment."

Roget looked even more puzzled. Then he smiled and headed for the stairs, whistling a tune as he went.

Chapter 15 Wednesday, May 16th 1923

Finding Dupont was now at the top of his list but it was easier said than done. According to Alain, he hadn't returned to either his apartment or his job at the factory. Duvalier would want more than Max's opinion on the man's guilt; he would, at the very least, want to prosecute the man and, if possible, recover any of the drawings and models still in his possession. Without informing the police, which his client explicitly told him not to do, he couldn't legally enter the man's residence. Although housebreaking wasn't out of the question, he would rather lay his hands on Dupont himself. If he was responsible for Gladstone's death, there was more to this matter than some stolen automobile parts.

If Gladstone had some business relationship with Dupont, one that had gone seriously astray, then maybe some of his friends and acquaintances could shed light on it. Le Dôme was a favorite hangout for most of them and if that didn't work out there were a dozen other bars and bistros the new American crowd frequented. He might also run into Erich Harvey; he had thought of a few more questions for the old journalist.

He saw no one familiar at Le Dôme but at the nearby La Rotonde, a substantial pre-lunch crowd had gathered, with the largest group at a table with Pablo Picasso at its head. He briefly thought of confronting the man about his use of Jacqui as a model but then thought better of it. Perhaps he was becoming more

Parisian than the Parisians, for he felt no twinge of jealousy at the idea of his wife—and he always thought of Jacqui that way, though he never said it in her presence—posing naked in front of a group of men. Why not, anyway? She was a beautiful, vibrant woman who made her own choices. And she had chosen him.

He couldn't help smiling as he drifted further into the bar. Hemingway was there, too, with his wife and the tall man, called Ez, who had been with him in the gym the first time they met. Ez was doing all the talking while Heminway nodded seriously. The conversation was too intent to interrupt and, besides, Hemingway was not on his list of either suspects or useful informants.

Erich Harvey was sitting by himself in a booth at the very back of the restaurant, near the door to the kitchen. Max headed in that direction only to pause when he heard the familiar high laughter of Pierre Delacroix. "Mr. Minter," he said in English, "you say the most amusing things."

"I do my best, Pierre."

Max spotted the pair at a table a dozen feet away. He stopped behind Minter's chair. Delacroix raised his eyes and opened his mouth to speak to him but Max shook his head and Delacroix coughed and covered his mouth.

"You haven't caught a spring cold, have you?"

"Allergies. There must be something close by that set them off." Delacroix smiled at his little joke. "Now, what were you saying about getting your book published?"

"It's almost done. A mystery set in Paris in the style of Edgar Allen Poe. Do you know his work?"

Walter Gladstone was a big fan of Poe, Max recalled.

"I've heard the name but..." he paused, glanced at Max who nodded at him, hoping he would keep the conversation going. "...why don't you tell me about *your* book?"

Minter spoke in fits and starts, sounding, to Max's ear, less like an author than someone who had read someone else's work and was trying to describe it. Had Minter stolen Gladstone's manuscript and, if so, had he done so before or after the man's murder? Keep it simple had been Hemingway's advice. It had seemed like good advice but that was before Minter had put himself back in the frame. Minter or Dupont—it had to be one of the two but which one?

"And you have a publisher for this novel?"

"No, that's why I invited you to lunch. And I meant it too when I said you can order anything on the menu. Eat, drink, it's all on me. I'm hoping you can help me find a publisher. Everyone says you know every one who's anybody in the arts in Paris, both French and English."

"Why stop there? I make sure I do the rounds of the national flags. Picasso over there, from Spain, Dalgliev from Russia and even some writers and painters from Germany. There is nothing I won't stick my... nose in. I'm sure we can find someone, provided the manuscript is worth publishing."

"Yes, well, it's pretty good, I think. The thing is, I've got the money to print it myself but I wanted someone else to take it on, someone who can spruce it up a bit, you know and give it credibility."

Delacroix laid a finger across his nose and winked. "Oh, I see. I think I can find someone like that."

"Wasn't Poe one of Walter Gladstone's inspirations?" asked Max. Minter twisted so sharply in his seat that he almost fell out of it.

"Oh, Mr. Anderson, have you been standing there long?"

"Long enough. I'm glad to see you looking so well. And so prosperous. Some of the items on the menu are too expensive for my taste."

Minter glanced from Max to the smiling Delacroix who was obviously enjoying the younger man's discomfiture.

"Oh, don't worry about me, dear," he said. "I would never think of taking advantage of you. Not financially, at least."

Minter was turning red, whether at Delacroix's inuendo or the surprise of finding out Max had practically heard him confess to stealing another writer's work. Max didn't care why Minter was embarrassed. It was something he could use. He pulled out a chair and sat down.

"Mind if I join you? Don't worry, dear," he said, laughing. "I'll buy my own lunch."

On cue, a waiter arrived with the menu board.

True to his word, Delacroix ordered the daily soup and a Croque Monsieur. Minter satisfied himself with a bowl of the soup—a mussel soup made with shallots and saffron—and a small basket of bread. Max had only had coffee and a slice of day-old brioche for breakfast and ordered an entrecote with red wine sauce. It came with a side of seasonal vegetables and a slice of dark bread, more than enough to fuel him for the day. He ordered a glass of Bordeaux while the others had the house white.

"Did you acquire Gladstone's manuscript before or after you killed him?"

"After, no, wait, I didn't kill him. I was in Germany, remember?"

"Your friends all say you left Paris after the body was found."

"You should get better friends," said Delacroix. "It's what I do whenever one of my friends betrays me."

Minter looked like he wanted to bolt. Max put his hand on his shoulder. "You still have a debt to pay." Minter's eyes widened. "You promised Pierre lunch."

Minter slumped into his seat, a resigned look like that of an animal in the jaws of a predator. "Walter and I made up before he died. It was a stupid thing anyway, fighting over a girl neither of us really wanted."

"Which girl was that, Clarice or Helen?"

"Does it matter? Nothing came of it. Helen chose Walter for all the good it did her and Clarice did what she always does, move on to the next victim."

"Are you saying Walter gave you his manuscript?"

"Sort of. It was peace offering, I guess. One way that writers show their friendship is by letting people read their work. It's an act of faith, that they won't steal it or maybe that they will have a thought or two how to improve it. I took it with me to Berlin. I didn't know Walter had been killed until I got a telegram from Helen."

"Yet, Clarice claims you said, 'that lousy red got what he deserved, I wish I had a hand in it.'"

"That lying putain!"

"Well, at least that clears him of the deed," Delacroix smirked.

"Look," said Minter, his eyes flicking from side to side. "I said that, yes, I said it, but... it's complicated. Walter did give me the manuscript and I was supposed to give it back but after... I don't know. Maybe I thought I'd get it published, as a kind of tribute to the friendship that might have been."

Max wondered if all the young Americans he had met were liars. They certainly all had a different spin on things. Clarice and Minter especially seemed to be at odds with each other. Maybe somewhere in the middle the truth lay hidden, so covered in deceit that it barely knew its name. Keep it simple. Forget the manuscript, forget the jealousy, forget the apparent lies.

"Was Gladstone a Red?"

"Maybe. He told me his grandfather was kicked out of Russia by the Tzar. The Okhrana chased him all the way to New York."

"So that he changed his name and moved to Chicago."

"I guess. He must have been a red, right?"

"Or a Menshevik, or a prying journalist or a Jew," added Delacroix. "Or maybe all three. The Tzar exiled plenty of those before the 1905 revolution. Reformers, writers, Jews, homosexuals, they were all considered enemies of the state. But Paris welcomed them all."

"You never cease to surprise me, Pierre."

"I do my best."

"Archie Roberts said Gladstone cheated at cards. He hinted at something bigger. Can you shed light on that?"

"You're not the police. I don't have to—"

"Have you forgotten the ambulance ride?"

Minter's face flushed. "Oh, that was you."

Delacroix raised an inquisitive eyebrow but kept silent. Max was sure he'd be asked about it later but now was not the time. At that moment, the food arrived, forcing a brief break in the conversation, giving Max time to gather his thoughts and, he hoped, for Minter to consider his debts.

"I said it was complicated," Minter said, when half his soup was gone. "But really it was Walter who was complicated. He was like a chameleon, always changing who he was to suit the background. He may have come across as some sort of socialist but he always had lots of money in his pockets. He could be talkative one minute, close-mouthed the next, charming and boorish in the space of an hour. He hung with our crowd but he had other friends too, people you might not want to hang with.

"Solve the mystery of Walter and you'll solve the mystery of his death."

Most people were murdered by spouses or family or neighbours but Gladstone hadn't been killed by any of those. Gladstone had been playing some kind of game and the stakes had proven too high for him to survive. But what was the game and who had he been playing it with? Surely not the disgruntled card players he had cheated and even more surely not Alex Minter, who, whatever else he was, wasn't a killer. Not a nice man but not a killer. It didn't matter how Minter had suddenly come into more money than his small allowance from home could explain. He suspected none of the Americans he had met were involved in the death, except perhaps his client, who was playing her own game.

This went beyond writers fighting for attention like dogs fighting over scraps, beyond spurned affections and hurt feelings, beyond artists' manifestos and fake blood in the theatre. Something darker lurked below the surface of these events, darker than the waters of Parc Montsourris.

It all somehow came down to Dupont but whether he was the killer or merely the motive for killing, Max still didn't know. He had to talk to Dupont.

He paid his bill and left Minter and Delacroix to their conversation, the former still pursuing the possibility of publishing the stolen manuscript and the latter pursuing seduction in a desultory way. He suspected they would both wind up disappointed.

On his way out, Harvey spotted him and waved him over to his table. He was surprised to discover the old journalist with nothing in front of him but a large milky coffee. Harvey grimaced. "Still morning by my clock. Chicago was the cure I could never find in Paris."

Max was pleased Harvey had maintained his new habit of abstinence, even if it only lasted until noon. "Paris is a cure for a lot of things, but not self-indulgence."

"Still, I feel better for it. A beer at lunch and then nothing until supper. A kind of reward for working all day."

"You've been working?"

"Yes, I've surprised even myself with my dedication. Five hundred words a day, every day including the Sabbath. I don't know if they are good words yet but it feels good to set them down. But I didn't call you over to brag about my scribbles. I've been in touch with my brother and have news about your murder victim."

"Go on."

"I mentioned that Gladstone was estranged from his family."

"Yes, something about differing politics."

"In a way. My brother says Gladstone, senior, Erik as it happens, with a k rather than a ch, clams up as soon as his son's name is mentioned. The excuse is one is a Democrat and the other Republican, but no one seems to know which is which. Erik Gladstone seems to avoid politicians as assiduously as I do. However, his brother, Thomas, your Gladstone's uncle is more than happy to talk about his nephew. Apparently, Gladstone's interest in writing a novel was peripheral to his real ambitions. He was recruited out of Princeton, where he was studying law, to a position in the Harding administration. No one knows what it was, but it was what was behind his move to Paris."

Ginger Buchan had been recruited out of Princeton by then President Woodrow Wilson, who had been the university's president before entering politics. Buchan had claimed not to know anything about Gladstone. Lies seemed to cling to Walter Gladstone like cat hair on a dark suit. *I wonder if Ginger will continue to lie if I confront him directly.*

"That's very helpful, Erich." Max took out his billfold and dropped two hundred francs on the table.

"That's not really necessary, son." Harvey's hand twitched toward the money. "Friends help each other out."

"Yes, they do, but I know the cost of transatlantic cables. Take the money Erich. Think it as my contribution to the writing of the great American novel."

"Thank you, Max. I appreciate that."

WHEN BUCHAN'S ASSISTANT told Max that his boss was too busy to see him and he should make an appointment for the following week, Max said: "Tell him I know about Walter's job."

Five minutes later he was sitting again in one of the leather wingbacks, though this time the drinks were Armagnac. Buchan was flushed and didn't meet Max's eyes.

"What kind of job do you think Gladstone had?"

"I think you know better than I do. You were the one who recruited him out of your old alma mater."

Buchan carefully set down his snifter on the side table and opened and then closed his office door. "The walls have ears and the keyholes have eyes. You know how it is."

Max didn't but he nodded and waited to see what else his so-called friend would reveal.

"I'll deny I ever met you and make it stick if this comes out."

Max nodded again.

"I did recruit Gladstone. One of the professors at Princeton keeps an eye out for prospective candidates. Usually, they don't pan out but sometimes they are ideal. Gladstone was one of those. Smart, fluent in several languages, including Russian, and intensely loyal to democracy and freedom. He was politically obscure, able to play the role of conservative or socialist as the situation warranted. A chameleon."

That was the second time that day he had heard Gladstone described that way. He wondered if Minter was somehow connected to Buchan as well.

"What did you recruit him for?"

"If I knew, I might even tell you. Some people who operate for the government you won't find on any organizational chart or payroll account. Their assignments are deliberately vague so they can appear as almost anyone. Gladstone was sent to Paris because the President, for all his talk of isolation from the affairs of the world, knew the world had no intention of letting America alone. Gladstone had a general remit to identify Soviet activity and do what ever he could to thwart it."

"Even using violence?"

"I don't know and if I did, I wouldn't admit to it. Friendship only takes one so far. I told you where to look for Gladstone's killer, didn't I?"

"You sent me after Helen Miller to see if she and Gladstone were connected to the Reds."

"Two birds, one stone."

"Meaning she isn't exactly what she appears to be. Though on the other hand, I suppose she is. A dedicated American socialist who will do anything to advance the cause at home. Even commit crimes for cash.

"You think she had something to do with Gladstone's death?"

"Something. She probably, unwittingly, introduced him to his killer." Buchan paused to swirl the snifter under his nose before taking a healthy sip. *He's enjoying this.* "I assume you've met Alec Minter."

"I just had lunch with him."

"Slippery little bastard, isn't he?"

Max couldn't disagree. Everyone was playing an angle, presumably including Buchan. "Did he have something to do with Gladstone's murder?"

"Not even indirectly. By all accounts the man is a physical coward and sybarite. I've had him interviewed a few times, once before his trip to Berlin and once after they released him from hospital."

Buchan didn't know of Max's involvement in the latter incident and, as he had said, friendship only takes one so far.

"What's your interest?"

"He's a bad one, Max. I don't know exactly what he's up to but I'm sure it is something neither of us would approve of. I would take it as a personal favour if, in the course of your investigations, you could bring him down."

MAX SPENT THE WANING hours of the day visiting four of the hospitals on his list. At each of them he was told of cases of patients, who had been deemed irrecoverable but had rallied after a series of visits from a young man. None of them knew the connection between the man and those he visited but, in each case after a few, or as many as a dozen, visits, the patients would make some progress toward recovery and the visits would stop. Within weeks all of them had been sent back to their homes, most crippled or horribly scarred but with a newfound lust for life, whatever that life would bring them.

None of the attendants—and in all four hospices, there was only ever one who had met the stranger—knew the visitor's name or give much of a description. The only thing they truly remembered about him was his unblemished face and his brilliant smile.

Chapter 16 Thursday, May 17th, 1923

Early the next morning, Max was in his office, going through some of the correspondence Henri had sorted and left on his desk. He had even drafted a few replies for Max to sign, banging out the letters on a Contin typewriter he had recently purchased "to make the agency look more professional." Only a few mistakes made it into the final drafts which Henri promised would disappear once he had finished reading the "Learn to Type" manual that had come with the machine. Max had no doubt Henri's typing would improve at the same rate as his English, that is to say, quickly if unevenly.

The more complex inquiries he had left to Max and he was in the middle of drafting a reply to a private investigator in Cologne when Alain burst into his office. His lip was swollen and he had a scrape above his left eye but the smile on his face suggested the fight had been worth it. He dropped a bundle on Max's desk and dropped into the chair opposite with a satisfied sigh.

"The stolen plans," he said. "You better put them someplace safe. I expect Dupont is hot on my heels looking to recover them."

"How exactly did you get your hands on them?" Alain's breath was short and his forehead was sheened with sweat. Max poured him a large glass of water; Alain drank half of it in a single gulp.

"I broke into Dupont's apartment last night, late, a little after three-thirty in the morning. It was easy enough; I used a grappling hook to haul down the fire escape ladder and climbed up to Dupont's window, which I had noticed was open a few inches. There were no lights on so I assumed he was either still away or asleep, the former as it turned out."

Max leaned back in his chair and fixed what he hoped was a stern glare on his face. "Breaking and entering is a serious offence."

"Surely stealing from a thief would be a defence. And Dupont is unlikely to go to the police to complain about losing the stolen plans."

Max doubted the former and was uncertain about the latter. He nodded for Alain to continue.

"There was a heavy wooden desk with brass trimming along one wall. I tried the desk drawers but they were locked. It was pretty dark; the moon was almost new and the streetlamps only provided a glimmer of light. I was nervous about turning on the lights in case Dupont had someone watching the place in his absence. The battery was almost dead in my flashlight but it gave enough of a glow I could see a letter opener in cup full of pencils."

Alain's voice had taken on the character of a stage detective and Max fought to keep a smile off his face. The story so far hadn't explained the young man's bruises but Max decided to indulge him and let Alain tell the story his way.

"I reached for the opener but knocked over the cup spilling the contents across the almost empty desk top. Imagine my surprise when the light caught a brass key. A brass key for a brass trimmed desk. The desk was jammed with the sort of things you might expect in that of a young man living alone. A couple packs of cigarettes, a flask of cheap brandy, a few notebooks and pens, a dozen postcards of the type you can purchase in the clubs of Pigalle. But in the lowest drawer, I discovered this bundle of papers. You can see the Duvalier name at the bottom of each sheet along with the company emblem.

"With the plans in hand, I quickly searched the rest of the apartment for the missing models. The place was small and the furniture sparse but there was a heavy oak wardrobe in the tiny bedroom, so big it covered part of the small window. It was secured with two heavy padlocks. Further search of the desk revealed no additional keys. Dupont had either done a better job of hiding them or he had them on his person. I decided to return to my own flat for tools I could use to break into the wardrobe."

Alain paused to have another long draught of water. He had still not explained the marks on his face and Max suspected he was nervous about telling what came next.

"The plans were enough to prove Dupont was the thief, maybe not to the satisfaction of the Prefecture but to our client, which is all we need care about." Max refilled Alain's glass, and poured himself a small glass of pastis which he topped with a generous dollop of water. It was too early in the day for drinking but Alain's continued hesitation worried him.

"You are probably right and, as you've likely guessed, it was a mistake to return but I was worried that if Dupont discovered the plans were missing, he would dispose of the models, perhaps even hasten his planned sale to whoever he was hoping would buy them."

While Max was certain money was involved in the thefts, he wasn't convinced it was the only or primary motive.

"It took two hours to cross the city, gather my tools and return. It was nearly dawn when I next climbed through the window. Dupont must have returned in the interim and heard me climbing the fire ladder. Some instinct made me jerk to the side as soon as I was through the window or I might not be telling you this story at all.

"Dupont had a club of some sort in his hand but my sudden move caused him to strike only a glancing blow. The force of it threw him off balance and, thanks to the training you gave me at Kid O'Brien's, I was able to recover before he regained his equilibrium. Two quick body blows and a clean uppercut put him on his back. He was struggling to regain his feet. I could hear him yelling imprecations and threats as I took off down the street. I think his feelings were hurt more than anything else."

Max took a quick glance at the plans to make sure they were what Alain claimed before taking them to Henri's office and locking them in his safe. He put on his jacket against the morning chill and slipped his five shot Kolb in his pocket in case Dupont was armed.

"It's time I had an extensive chat with Mr. Dupont. There's more to this than simply industrial espionage. Come along Alain, you've started the ball rolling, you may as well see where it stops."

"Good. I'd like to recover my tools. I dropped them in the scuffle."

A chill ran down Max's spine. He flagged down a cab outside Chez Jake. The ball had taken a dangerous swerve. Dupont and the models might well be gone, in one way or another.

A BLACK MARIA WAS PULLED up in front of the building, two uniformed police officers lounging beside it. An ambulance was parked beside it but the attendants were standing nearby, smoking cigarettes and passing the time with a concierge lingering in a doorway across the street.

"It looks like Dupont called for help," said Alain. "All a show, I guess to cover his own guilt. He's probably telling them he had brought the plans home to—"

"Stay here, Alain, until I know what's happening." The constables in charge of the police wagon were lurking outside, some one must have ordered them to do so. Max climbed the stairs to the second floor, leaving Alain to wait nervously in the street.

One door was open, another swallow standing guard outside. The low mumble of voices drew him closer, then one rose above the others. Captain Marcel Fontaine's distinctive tones told him all he needed to know. He only investigated murders; hence, Jean Dupont was dead.

Another voice, that of a woman, rang out from the bottom of the stairs. "That's him! That's the man who was lurking about last night."

Max was caught between the two voices. He wanted to confirm that Dupont was indeed dead and, if so, what had caused his death. But he knew whom the woman had identified. The sound of a scuffle below made up his mind. He dashed down the stairs in time to see Alain being bustled into the back of the police wagon, protesting his treatment, still unaware perhaps that he wasn't being arrested for theft but for murder.

"A friend of yours." Fontaine's voice was now directly behind him.

"He works for me but, yes, Alain is a friend." He turned to find Fontaine standing on the step behind him, using the elevation to compensate for his small stature.

"Are you now in the assassination business, Max?" Fontaine's demeanour didn't quite match his words. A faint smile was visible below his mustache.

"Alain didn't kill Jean Dupont."

"Are you sure? We now have a witness who saw him in the area. And there is a bag of tools on the floor beside the victim, with a name tag sewn to the handle. A. Laurent. Is that Alain's last name?"

Max nodded.

"The man was stabbed to death, once in the chest and again in the back of the neck as he tried to get away. We haven't found the murder weapon but it could be a screw driver or even a small chisel. Perhaps taken from that bag."

Fontaine came the rest of the way down the stairs into the street. "Take him to the Prefecture. I'll want to question him myself, once I'm done here." He waved at the ambulance attendants, who hurriedly butted their cigarettes and crossed the street. "Take the body to the morgue for the coroner to look at. No-one will be able to say I was not thorough."

"Were you aware that M. Laurent was planning to break into this Dupont's apartment last night. More importantly, did you send him to do it?"

"No on both counts." He didn't bother to add that he had explicitly told Alain not to enter the place. "He reported to me this morning. He admitted fighting with Dupont, who had attacked him—"

"Because he had interrupted his attempt at theft."

"Yes. Alain knocked him down and escaped. Dupont was in his window, swearing and quite alive."

"As you were told. Hearsay is not admissible. No-one had reported hearing Dupont and, even if they did, it could have been his death cries."

Fontaine had become a better detective over the years but old habits die hard. Once he had a credible suspect, the case was closed and his mind with it. He would listen to contrary evidence but he would not go out of his way to find it.

"What was Laurent here to steal?"

Max had been asked not to go to the police but now the police had come to him. He had learned the hard way that lying to the police never turned out well for private detectives.

"He was here to recover some plans and prototype models Dupont had stolen from his employer."

"Did he succeed?"

"He recovered the plans. They were in the desk drawer; Alain found the key and took them. They are now in my office safe but—"

"They will soon be in a safe at the Prefecture. To be released after the trial. Don't worry, I don't think the magistrate will deliberate for long."

"Alain recovered the plans, but not the models," Max continued, determined that Fontaine should at least hear the whole story, even if he didn't believe it. "He suspected they were in a padlocked wardrobe. He returned home to get some tools and came back to try to open it. Dupont, who had been away for several days, apparently returned and attacked Alain. They fought, Alain dropped his bag and fled."

"The desk had been ransacked, papers scattered everywhere. The wardrobe you mentioned had been shifted but no serious effort to open it had been made."

"Doesn't that seem strange? The necessary tools were right there in the living room."

Fontaine gave an elaborate shrug, then paused to watch the two attendants wrestle a limp, blanket-shrouded form into the ambulance.

"People panic, especially when there is a body in a growing pool of blood in the next room. Your friend was confronted by Dupont, they fought, he stabbed his victim—twice—and then decided discretion was the better part of valour and fled the scene. The simplest story is usually the correct one."

Fontain had always bragged about being well-read. Max wondered if his reading included the few published stories of Ernest Hemingway.

"Deliver those plans to me by the end of the day or I'll arrest you as an accessory. And don't try to enter Dupont's apartment. I have two constables collecting evidence and I wouldn't want it to include evidence of you."

Fontaine raised a whistle to his lips and gave two quick blasts. A black police car pulled around the corner and Fontaine climbed in the back.

"Don't forget, Max." Fontaine gestured for the driver to proceed. Max stood in the street and watched until the car turned the corner and disappeared. He re-entered the building and stood at the foot of the stairs. He listened to the two swallows stomping around the apartment above before heading back to his office, his heart heavy at the thought of Alain in the police cells, ones he himself had too often occupied.

THOUGH RELUCTANT TO part with the hard-won stolen plans, Max did not relish the idea of spending more time in the Prefecture's cells. He returned immediately to his office to retrieve them and to ask Henri to get hold of Gaston and have him come to Chez Jake at his earliest convenience. He left a telephone message with Cleroux to engage him in Alain's defence.

When he arrived at the police headquarters on L'Ile de France, Fontaine had already returned to the crime scene. Sargeant Ferdinand LePêcheur was on duty and took the plans, signing the receipt Henri had prepared. Max watched as his friend placed the plans inside a large envelope, wrote "PROPERTY OF MAX ANDERSON" in block letters on it and stowed it in the safe in the evidence room. Satisfied that he would get the documents back, Max thanked LePêcheur and headed toward the home of Irina Pavlovna to ask further questions about the activities of Russian agents in city.

He was quickly ushered into her study. She was alone, sipping coffee on a chaise longue and gazing out her window onto the quiet street below. Pavlovna had recently risen; the remains of a small breakfast tray was perched on a nearby table. He was surprised to find her still in her dressing gown, her hair down and her face free of makeup. Exile and loss weighed heavily on her and, though she remained a striking woman, she appeared, for the first time since he had first met her, dispirited and exhausted.

"Is this a bad time?"

She gazed at him over the rim of her cup. "Are there any good times left?"

"I can come back—"

"No, please stay. I need..." She paused, as if not quite sure what she needed, though it seemed his presence would suffice. "There is coffee in the samovar and I can order some breakfast if you like."

Max declined breakfast but poured himself a cup of coffee. It was still hot and he added a small dollop of cream, making it sweet enough not to need sugar. He took a seat near her in an armless Louis Quatorze chair covered in pink brocade.

"My friend, Sergei, died last night," she said, still gazing out the window.

"Baron Denidov?"

She nodded. "It is growing very lonely in Paris but I have no where else to go. I'm told my ancestral home has been turned into a hostel for war veterans. I suppose it could be worse. The tales we hear out of Russia..." She turned to look at Max. Her eyes were misty but no tears fell.

"Was it..." Max wasn't sure what to ask. He had come here to ask about the possibility of Russian involvement in Gladstone's murder.

"Murder? They say it was something he ate but, then, poison is something, isn't it? I prefer to think he died of natural causes. Weak hearts—brave but weak—run in his family and he never did as his doctor told him. It doesn't matter. Dead is dead."

Max hoped she wouldn't ask him to look into it. He was struggling to get to the bottom of one murder and now had that of Dupont to worry about, too. He had to discover who killed the thief if Alain was to be exonerated. They sipped their cooling coffee in silence, save for the ticking of a large clock on the mantle.

"We will have a gathering here after the funeral on Sunday. You did not know him well but I think he would be happy to have you come."

Pavlovna was an important figure in the Russian community and a useful contact but, over the years, he had also come to respect her, even like her, so he agreed to be there with Jacqui at three.

"Now, what did you want to see me about?"

"Have you heard more about the activities of Peotr Nikita Volodin?"

Pavlovna straightened in her seat, the mist in her eyes replaced with a spark of anger. "I expected you would come to ask about him again so I had Fedorov make some inquiries. Volodin is keeping a low profile but he is still lurking in Paris. Word has it that he was sent to watch several followers of Trotsky here in the city, to report on them and, perhaps, threaten them into silence."

"Threaten them with violence?"

"More likely to threaten their families still back in Russia. The Cheka is utterly loyal to Stalin; their mere presence in the doorway is often all they need to get their way. Of course, Trotsky himself shows no fear. As much as I despise the man, he has earned my grudging respect. It was after he took command of the Red Army that our cause was finally lost."

That would explain why Trotsky still posed a threat to Stalin. The latter might control the secret police but Trotsky must still have admirers in the military. Max didn't know much, and understood less, about the labyrinthine politics of the Soviet Union, as Russia was now called, but he understood military loyalty.

"Would Volodin use violence if his threats failed to achieve his results?"

"Yes, of course, if he could escape unscathed. Things are changing rapidly now that the White Army has met its final defeat. Soviet efforts at world revolution are faltering and are likely to cease if the government in Moscow falls into disarray, and, especially, if Stalin becomes the supreme leader.

"Though France officially still refuses to recognize the new regime and the government disavows the visits of French communists to Moscow, talks are underway to restore relations, and, most importantly, international trade. Even communists can heed the siren call of capitalism. Volodin would not want to get in the way of that."

Max considered whether involvement in international espionage in the aid of the desired trading relationship would be within the man's purview. He had expressed interest in what progress Max was making in solving Gladstone's murder but had then dropped out of sight, though he had apparently made threats to his client, Helen Miller.

Someone resembling Volodin had been seen meeting with Dupont. Dupont reportedly lunched with Gladstone on several occasions. Had Dupont killed Gladstone only to be killed himself by the Russian agent, perhaps because he failed to hand over the plans? Or had Volodin killed both men, for reasons he was yet to discover?

Who else could it be? Minter? Herrera? One of the fractious members of the Paris arts community or another of the American writers? And what wasn't his client telling him? Was Miller involved in some convoluted way? None of that made much sense anymore. Hemingway had told him to keep it simple and the simple solution was Volodin had killed both of the men.

He shook his head. Nothing was ever simple, maybe in a story but never in real life. All he could do was uncover the facts until the important ones emerged.

GASTON WAS NERVOUSLY pacing the floor in Henri's office when Max arrived. Henri was talking on the telephone but hung up when he saw Max.

"That was Cleroux. He says Alain is fine and ridiculously positive about your ability to clear him. His words not mine. I have every faith in you."

Max could always count on Henri to support and correct him in equal measure.

"Gaston. I'm glad to see you. I hope I can count on you over the next few days."

"I don't know. You said there would be no violence but now my cousin has been arrested for murder."

"But he didn't do it. Alain is not a killer. You know that, don't you?"

Gaston looked uncertain but nodded his head. "What can I do to help?"

Max wasn't sure. With Hugo still on the lookout for Herrerra and his concern about Roget's heavy-handed ways, Gaston was his only hope. He was young and inexperienced but he had done a good job in the search for Lady Wentworth. What he had in mind was similar and should, he hoped, be relatively safe.

"I need you and Henri to go to Dupont's flat. Gain access if you can to see if there is anything the police have missed. If it is still under guard, don't force the issue. Canvass the street and ones on either side to see if anybody saw or heard anything, anything at all, no matter how trivial it seems, between 10pm and 6am last night. Report back as soon as you can."

Gaston wrung his cloth cap in his hand. "Shouldn't the detective from the Prefecture be doing that?"

"Indeed, he should," said Henri. "But we are talking about Captain Marcel Fontaine. Go on, I'll tell you all about him on the way."

Chapter 17 Friday May 18th to Sunday, May 20th, 2923

Max was awakened by the buzzing of the phone. Jacqui moaned, rolled away from the sound and pulled the pillow over her head. Max squinted at the clock on his bedside table. Barely six a.m., the sun wasn't even up yet. The phone buzzed again and he crawled from beneath the blankets, the morning air cool against his bare skin. He staggered into the living room, closing the bedroom door behind him. Jacqui had not slept well the last few nights and he saw no need to disturb her.

"Max Anderson."

"LePêcheur here. I hope I didn't wake you."

Max resisted making a smart remark. LePêcheur wouldn't call him so early if he didn't have a good reason. "It's fine."

"Captain Fontaine has ordered Alain Laurent to be moved to more permanent accommodation in the 16th arrondissement so he's serious about the conviction. He has secured the agreement of a magistrate to proceed with a trial. It will begin Monday. I thought you would want to know."

"Thank you, Ferdinand. I owe you a debt."

"Repay me by finding the actual murderer. Alain is too nice a boy to go to the guillotine."

Fontaine had made up his mind; Alain would suffice and the captain would look no further. He had until Monday to discover the truth.

After the call, Max did a quick wash and shave, pulled on his robe and started making coffee. He needed to think and this early in the day, that meant he needed coffee. Jacqui had bought croissants the day before and he put them in the oven to freshen them up while he set out pots of butter, jam and honey. By the time the coffee and pastries were ready, Jacqui had emerged from the bedroom, her hair tousled and sleep lines still pressed into her face.

She grunted at his morning greeting and wandered into the bathroom and emerged a few minutes later, her hair combed and her eyes awake if not lively. "I'll have my coffee with lots of milk. I need something to settle my stomach. And just a plain croissant will do."

Max had anticipated the request and had milk on the stove to heat. Jacqui had never truly been a morning person but lately she had struggled to face the day, sometimes skipping breakfast altogether.

"Who was on the telephone? I hope it was important."

Jacqui always wanted him to unplug the phone at night and he usually complied except when he was deeply immersed in a difficult case, when a call might mean the difference between solving it or not, or even between life and death.

"LePêcheur. The trial will begin on Monday." Max poured equal amounts of coffee and warm milk into a mug and put it in front of it. Jacqui sniffed, took a sip, then held it out for more milk.

"Poor Alain. It must be awful. I remember how cold and damp those cells can be."

Jacqui had spent a few days in the cell at the Prefecture two years before and even longer at the more comfortable women's prison in Saint Lazare.

"Maybe I should visit him."

"They've moved him to the prison past the Bois du Boulogne. I'm afraid they won't let you see him; only family, lawyers and, I hope, employers allowed. I'll tell him you were thinking of him."

"You'll see him today?"

"I'll go as soon as visiting hours begin. At ten, if memory serves."

Jacqui nibbled at her croissant. Max slathered his with strawberry jam and crammed a third of it in his mouth. Jacqui smiled and reached across the small table to stroke his hand. "We could go back to bed until then."

Max paused in mid-chew, surprised by the sudden turn in her mood.

"After you've regained your strength, of course." She stood, drawing him after her.

Some things, he thought, are more invigorating than coffee.

MAX SPENT MOST OF FRIDAY dealing with Alain's impending trial. After his brief visit to the prison, cut short by a surly guard, he went to Cleroux's office to arrange for Alain's defence. He told the lawyer about his own efforts at investigation and Cleroux made some additional suggestions: witnesses to attest to Laurent's character and situation, a letter from Max concerning the work Alain had done to capture criminals.

He returned to his office at the end of the day to see if Henri had returned with a report on their activities. Smitty told him that he had come by a couple of hours after noon and asked him to let Max know they were making progress but some of the neighbours are reluctant to speak to them. Dupont's apartment was still occupied by "a swallow so fat he looked like a pigeon."

Henri had also left him several cheques to sign and letters to approve but Max's head wasn't in it. They could wait until he had Alain back.

Jacqui was still at work when Max returned to the apartment on Rue Jacob. With the opening of the new show imminent, she had been working a lot of overtime and often returned home late, so exhausted she simply fell into bed. He walked down Jacob to one of the new bistros that had recently opened in the newly popular district. He ordered a salad comprised of lettuce, sliced tomato, chicken breast and ham with a glass of chilled Chablis to wash it down and went over his notes.

The arrest of Alain Laurant weighed heavily on his mind but he used his worry productively. Alain's arrest was directly connected to Dupont's murder which, in turn, was linked to his investigation of Walter Gladstone's death. Both, it seemed, were connected to the theft of plans and prototypes from the Duvalier car factory. Circling this central problem were the suspicious activities of Alec Minter as well as the questionable motives, perhaps mixed, of his client, Helen Miller. What was her actual relationship to Gladstone and did it relate to his mandate to watch for Bolshevik agents? What threats had Volodin made to her to drive her into hiding in the small extra bedroom in Henri Compte's house?

He had ruled out Herrerra as a suspect in Gladstone's murder and his absence from Paris during the murder of Dupont only confirmed that. But what about Yelena Semenova? Her "distant" cousin had reacted with disdain at the mention of the woman's name and declared they didn't move in the same circles. Was Yelena a Red or did she, as she had told him, not care about anything political? He couldn't see her as a knife-wielding murderer but, then again, much of what he had experienced in the last month from battling artists to monstrous displays at the theatre seemed beyond the range of his mind's eye.

He closed his book and ordered a second glass of wine. Outside, a young couple leaned together under the umbrella of a café table, oblivious to the rain that had begun to fall again. He remembered the languorous love-making of the morning and suddenly realized he had never been happier in his life than this precise moment.

He sat as still as he could, not wanting this moment to pass. The waiter delivered the bill and, almost as if in a dream, he paid it and went back to the apartment to find Jacqui already asleep in their bed.

IT HAD BEEN OVERCAST when he went to bed but the clouds had parted before dawn and he awoke to bright sunshine and the sound of Jacqui singing to herself in the small kitchen. He didn't recognize the tune though it had a vaguely exotic sound and he supposed it might be from the new opera she was building costumes for.

Jacqui had to start work after two in the afternoon. The opera opened in two weeks but the costumes had to be ready at least a week before that so she would be working everyday except Sunday to meet that deadline. He had plans to go to the evening salon at Stein's house which started at nine and had hoped Jacqui would accompany him.

"I don't think I'll be off by then, and, even if I am, I'll be too tired to be any fun" she said. "Let's walk in the Luxembourg gardens this morning and then have lunch near the Opera. You can tell me about the salon at breakfast tomorrow."

It was his turn to cook in the morning and he had something special planned and would need to go Les Halles after lunch to pick up fresh salmon and the other necessary ingredients. He would spend the afternoon finding answers to some of his outstanding questions before visiting Stein to see if her inquiries had led anywhere. For now, there were the gardens.

The trees were in full leaf, the pale green of spring forming cathedral arches over the gravel paths. The lawns were still recovering form the weight of winter but the early blooms painted the ground around the many statues in shades or red, yellow and purple. They laughed at the courting dances of the varied species of birds that called the gardens home, the males, preening and jumping while the females largely ignored them.

"What do you see for us in ten years, Max?"

"Ten years!? I'll be an old man."

"Don't be silly. Forty's not old. Forty-two is old. But seriously."

"I don't know. I suppose we'll have a little house somewhere."

"And a dog."

"I could see that. And, maybe... a little girl that looks like you and a boy who looks like me." They had talked of children but had both decided it was too soon, that life was still too uncertain to make such plans.

"Or maybe, the other way around." She said, laughing. After a moment, she threw her arms around him and he leaned down to kiss her. "We'll just have to wait," she said. "And see what the future brings."

BACK AT THE OFFICE after a late and lingering lunch, Henri had still not reported back on the results of his and Gaston's investigations, though he had sent two brief handwritten notes by messenger. The first read: "Pursuing possibilities;" the second: "Clues abound." Max was reminded of the crime novels Henri was constantly suggesting he read as if they were some sort of instructive texts for the training of detectives. He had given Henri and Gaston their assignments and now had to trust they knew how to carry them out, though his anxiety over Alain's fate made it hard to resist taking the field himself.

A more formal, though almost as short, letter came on stationary of the American embassy.

Heard from contacts back home. Minter involved with
Italians, i.e. gangsters, in New York. Send information as
you gather it. Ginger.

He carried the note with him to Stein's salon, arriving a few
minutes before the scheduled start. He was ushered into the large
art-filled room where Stein was already ensconced in her chair like a
queen upon her throne. Several others had also arrived early though
Max only recognized Picasso. He still felt ambiguous about Jacqui's
modeling session and would have preferred to avoid him but he
needed to talk to Stein, and, now that he thought about it, had a
question for the painter as well.

After introductions were made and a natural lull in the
conversation—which was so esoteric Max had a hard time following
it let alone understanding it—he asked Picasso if he had a student
named Carlos Herrerra.

"Carlos? He came to my studio a few times. He wanted to talk
about my work with the Ballets Russe designing costumes and sets
for them. I've worked on three of their productions and hope to
work on another next year. I didn't mind, he came from Malaga
where I spent my childhood and it was enjoyable to revisit the
Spanish coast in my conversations with him. He has some talent but
I doubt he will ever amount to much. Not sufficiently dedicated to
the craft."

Picasso did not know the man well but thought "he is a typical
Spaniard, fierce in countenance but gentle at heart." It was not how
Max would have described Herrerra but Picasso seemed sincere,
almost wistful, when he said it.

Hemingway arrived moments after he had finished talking to
Picasso and greeted Max in his typical boisterous fashion, slapping
him on the shoulder before gripping his hand tightly.

"Where's that pretty young girl of yours?"

"She had to work today. She makes costumes for the Opera and got off late, too tired to come out tonight."

"Tired, eh? Hadley, my wife gave a similar excuse. Not work, other than the work of producing the next generation."

"When is your child expected?" Stein asked, sounding disapproving at the prospect.

"Hadley is four months along so he—I'm sure it will be a he, though I wouldn't mind a girl—should arrive in October."

"Are you returning to America or will your...son be born on French soil?"

"Hadley would like to go home but we agreed on Toronto. I'm still writing pieces for the Toronto Star and they agreed to take me on as a staffer to help cover the costs of the new baby."

"You can't abandon Paris," Stein seemed genuinely shocked.

"Make no mistake," Hemingway grinned at Max. "Toronto may call itself a city but it's no Paris, is it, Max?"

"I wouldn't know, I've never been there."

"Well, I won't hold that against you."

More people arrived until the room was crowded with artists and writers. He recognized some of them from the party at the Murphy's. Others were introduced in a flurry of names he could barely follow. Ezra Pound, the man Hemingway called Ez, was an American poet and quite striking in his appearance, tall and long-limbed with a great shock of hair crowning his head.

Others were faces detached from names and names detached from faces. Matisse, Bunting, Deschamps, Cowley, Tsara (as usual standing alone against one wall) and Sylvia Beach, Henri's bookseller friend and publisher of controversial books. She was one of the few women in the salon proper, the others having been escorted away by Alice Toklas to the kitchen. Max wondered if that would have been Jacqui's fate if she had attended.

Finally, near midnight, the crowd thinned a little and Max had the opportunity for a brief conversation with his latest, and most unusual, informant. Hemingway, who had been drinking steadily but didn't appear drunk, was nearby but deep in conversation with Pound.

He showed Stein Buchan's note. She raised her eyes at the letterhead.

"This may explain a lot. I've asked my contacts. As you suspected, Minter has come into money, a lot of money and the rumours are that he is involved in some sort of criminal behavior. I mean, other than the theft of a dead man's manuscript."

"Any idea what kind of behavior."

"Drugs, I suppose, based on the incident you described but the New York connection suggests something else, maybe smuggling."

"I can beat it out of him if you like." Hemingway clearly had one ear cocked on their conversation. "I only met him the one time but I didn't like him then and I like him less now."

"I may take you up on the offer," Max laughed, "but I think I'll try more conventional tactics first."

"Trust me. There's nothing more conventional than a punch in the mouth."

HE HAD AWOKEN TO THE sound of Jacqui throwing up. It was early, the sun had not yet risen, and Max was still groggy from the salon. When he left, it was after one in the morning though guests were still arriving. He had limited himself to three drinks but, combined with the effects of cigar smoke and little sleep, he struggled now to rouse himself. By the time he did, Jacqui had showered and dressed.

"Are you unwell?"

She smiled wanly and shook her head. "Late night, bad sandwich. Nothing more than that."

Max had his doubts but, given his own throbbing head, he didn't press the matter. The thought of preparing fish for breakfast appealed to neither of them and they agreed the salmon would keep until supper. There were plenty of cafés near their apartment, several of which catered to those recovering from the night before.

After a meal of steamed milk flavored with cinnamon and a platter of pastries, both sweet and savory, they both felt somewhat better though Jacqui announced that, as it was her only day off, she would return to bed with a book. Max considered joining her but decided a brisk walk in spring air would suit him better. When he looked in on Jacqui before he left, she was fast asleep with the book open across her chest. He scribbled a note, promising to return before lunch and headed out.

The sun was shining and the streets were busy, men and women in their finest heading to one of the many churches in the area while others were staggering home from whatever entertainment they had found the night before.

By the time he reached the Seine, the foot traffic had thinned, mostly flaneurs like himself, strolling slowly, seeing what there was to see, with no destination except the next vista. The Seine was busy as usual, filled with barges carrying goods to feed the city's insatiable hungers and pleasure crafts doing on water what he was doing on foot.

He crossed the river at Pont Royal and entered the gardens. More formal that the Luxembourg ones, the Tuileries consisted of vast lawns and stands of carefully pruned trees, all designed to show off the many statues that had accumulated over the three and a half centuries since it was created by Catherine de Medici, the Queen Mother of France. At its center was a large oval pool and Max took a seat at one of the benches around it and watched ducks taking off and landing while he considered his next moves.

Jacqui's recent behavior, the frequent tiredness, the shifting moods, her illness this morning confused him. He knew little of the ailments that women could experience but his conversation with Hemingway made him suspect that, like the writer's wife, Jacqui might be pregnant. But surely, she would know if she was and, just as surely, she would share the news with him. Openness was the foundation for their relationship and he couldn't imagine what might lead her to keep such a secret. No, he thought, it is as she said, overwork and bad food. It was, after all, overindulgence that had given him a bad stomach and an aching head this morning.

He continued walking through the gardens and then across the expansive forecourt of the Place de Concorde, the largest square in the city where King Louis XVI and more than a thousand others were guillotined during the reign of terror that followed the revolution. The thought made him shudder; if he and Henri couldn't prove Alain's innocence soon, his young friend might suffer the same fate. If Henri and Gaston didn't report soon, he would have to take a more active role.

With that thought in mind, he continued walking along the river until he reached Pont Alexandre III where he crossed back to the Left Bank. Les Invalides loomed to the right and he wondered if Hugo was working an early shift. He had not yet visited that hospital, to see if the mysterious visitor had graced its wards. He would ask Hugo about it when next he saw him.

When he returned home, Jacqui had prepared a simple meal of vegetable soup and quiche Loraine, filled with smoky bacon, ham and a hint of Gruyere cheese. She was quiet, though more thoughtful than unhappy, and, after a bit, announced she had arranged to have coffee with two of her Marseille friends who would be leaving that evening.

"I'll be home after seeing them off at Gare du Lyon, about six or so."

"I'll have supper ready for seven then."

He watched her from the window overlooking Rue Jacob as she made her way towards St. Germain de Prix. A strange feeling engulfed him and he had to lean against the window frame for support. It reminded him of the feeling he always had before the start of a battle, trepidation and a desire to be strong for those around him, to protect them from danger when he knew it was largely beyond his ability to do so.

MAX CHANGED INTO HIS dark suit for his visit to Pavlovna's house for the remembrance of Baron Denidov. The turnout was respectable, though not more than forty or so men and women crowded into the large parlour of the exiled aristocrat's house. Most were White Russians, still, Max was surprised to see both Joseph Asper and Ginger Buchan in attendance, though given the latter's interest in the anti-Bolshevik movement, his presence was understandable. Asper nodded a greeting before resuming a conversation with an attractive brunette, dressed in a black calf-length dress, a veiled hat partially masking her face.

Buchan waved him over and Max, after offering his condolences to Pavlovna and Countess Solikoff, Denidov's sister, joined him near the fireplace, which thankfully had not been lit. The day had been cool, but the room was warmed by the press of bodies.

"Good turnout," said Buchan. "Nice to be in a room of Russians without having to worry about Red spies."

"They wouldn't dare. If Federov didn't stop them at the door, Pavlovna would freeze them with a withering glance."

"You know Irina well. Any progress on your murder investigation. The boys in Washington have been asking."

Max felt no obligation to reveal anything to Buchan about Gladstone's death or Volodin's involvement in it. The last thing he needed were American agents interfering in his capture of the villain. He changed the subject by telling him about Lady Wentworth's visit to Mussolini in Rome and the possibility of fascist sympathizers among the royalty of Great Britain. Buchan had merely shrugged his shoulders. "We've seen their type before, nasty bastards for sure, but no immediate threat to the west, not like the Bolsheviks."

Max had his doubts but he was in no mood to talk politics with Ginger Buchan. He was here to offer his sympathies to his Russian acquaintances. After the second vodka toast to the memory of Baron Denidov, he had done his duty. He made his farewells and returned home to prepare dinner.

Chapter 18 Monday, May 21, 1923

He and Jacqui had finished breakfast and were enjoying a final cup of coffee. The illness and upset of the day before had disappeared and every thing seemed normal again. Max was dressing for the day when a messenger arrived at the door, a young man in an ill-fitting uniform, shifting from foot to foot as he waited to see if there would be a return message. He reminded Max of Alain, now sitting in jail awaiting trial for murder and a sense of urgency filled him as he scanned the note.

> Have evidence that may prove Alain's innocence. Should be able to confirm this morning. Come to my house as you need to speak to my guest before she leaves.
>
> Henri

"No reply," said Max, tipping the boy a few francs for his time. Henri's house was on the far side of Montmartre. He would need to take the Metro to Porte de Saint-Quen and walk from there. If he hurried, he could be there in forty minutes. He hoped to find Helen Miller still in residence.

She was, though only barely. Her bags were packed and on the front step. Henri was stalling her with one of his more amusing stories, gesticulating in time to the rhythm of the tale. Miller laughed, obviously humoring the old man who had been her host, while glancing frequently at her luggage. Max spotted Gaston, leaning against a light standard with his bicycle, ready to follow her whether she left on foot or by taxi.

"Miss Miller," said Max. slightly out of breath from his rapid walk from the station. "I'm glad I caught you. Do you have a few minutes to chat?"

"I don't know. Henri sent one of the neighbourhood boys for a taxi but..." She glanced at Henri.

"For sure, for sure. But it is Monday and taxis are hard to find in this part of town." Henri gave an elaborate shrug.

A taxi stand was only a few blocks away and Max wondered what instructions he had given his errand boy. "Hurry back" was probably not included.

"Let's go inside where it's more comfortable."

"Make yourself at home. There is coffee in the urn that should still be warm and some fresh baked rolls and jam in the icebox." Henri had already donned his hat and a multi-hued scarf. "I have a few tasks to complete while the morning is still young. I'll see you at Le Coq Bleu when it opens at ten."

Miller still hesitated in the door and Henri sauntered down the lane.

"The taxi will honk his horn when he arrives." Max gestured for her to re-enter the house and, when her back was turned, signalled Gaston to wait in case he was needed.

When they were seated with cups of surprisingly hot coffee in their hands, Max asked: "Did you know Gladstone was an agent for the American government here to spy on suspected Bolsheviks?"

She blushed slightly and looked away. "I wondered sometimes. He was so attentive, yet so diffident. At first, I thought he didn't like girls. It's more common than you might think, especially here in Paris, but he proved me wrong on that account, it was just me he didn't like."

"You haven't answered my question."

"No, I didn't know that particular fact but it doesn't surprise me. Now, anyway. I tested him. Made certain comments, you know, to see if he were receptive to... socialist ideas. He encouraged me, even quoted Debs and he knew a lot about the history of socialism."

"He led you along."

"Yes, I eventually figured out he wasn't serious. I thought it was a game he was playing, especially after I found out how well-to-do he and his family back in Chicago were."

"What about you? Are you a Bolshevik?"

"You make it sound like a dirty thing. It's not. What's going on in Russia is to be admired not feared. The tyranny of the Tsar and the wealthy has been overthrown. The Soviet leadership want to strive for the same values as France proclaims, liberty, equality, fraternity."

"What about the pursuit of happiness?"

Miller laughed bitterly. "Happiness for whom? Not the ordinary factory worker, not the shop girl, not anyone but the rich can afford to pursue happiness. It's vastly overrated in any case."

Max didn't think so. Everybody found happiness where they could. There were worse things people could and did pursue.

"Again, the question is a simple one."

"No, I think there is a better path forward. One that doesn't involve guns, bombs and guillotines. I admire what some of the Bolsheviks are doing. I was hoping to meet Trotsky when he came to Paris. I read his book, Our Revolution, and was moved by it. Now that the trip is cancelled, I'll go back to America. I've done everything I could do here to advance the cause but there is plenty of work to do there."

"Was that why you were threatened by the man claiming to be Gladstone's cousin. Because you admired Trotsky. His name is Volodin by the way, a well-known agent of the Soviet secret police."

"Again, I am not surprised. Yes, his threats did mention Trotsky by name. Vehemently enough that I thought he was with the White Russians. My instincts are not very well honed, are they?"

"Has he been in touch again?"

"Not here. I've been, how did you put it, as safe as houses. Henri has been a kind and generous host and a watchdog, as well. I'm going straight to the train station as soon as I leave here. Out to the coast to stay at a small pensione that Henri recommended until my ship sails from Le Havre for New York in a few days. But I have heard from a friend that this Volodin has been seen around my old digs, asking a few questions about me and about Walter."

"Was that friend Alec Minter?"

Her coffee cup made a faint rattle in its saucer as she put it down. Once again, she looked away.

"Alec Minter is not my friend. He's a greedy little man who will do anything to get what he wants—women, money, fame."

"Did you know he is trying to get Gladstone's manuscript published, likely under his own name."

"The bastard!" Her vehemence surprised Max. "Do you remember I told you that if Walter had lived something might have come of it?"

Max recalled their first meeting three weeks before. He had wondered then at the statement and at the tears that followed.

"Something had come of it, for me at least. I was in love with Walter, felt alive again after nearly a year of feeling dead. But a girl has her pride, doesn't she? He didn't care for me..."

She broke off then, her eyes glistening.

"Minter has come into a lot of money. Do you know where he got it?"

"How would I know? Nothing savory, I'm sure. He hangs with the ex-pat crowd but those aren't his only friends."

Max waited but Miller had nothing more to say on the subject. She took out a cigarette but before she could light it, a taxi horn blared from outside the door.

"That's me then."

Max helped load her luggage into the car and heard her instruct the driver to take her to Gare de Nord. He watched the car pull away and head ever so slowly towards its destination. In addition to telling the driver not to hurry back, Henri had told it not to hurry at all. Gaston mounted his bicycle and followed after.

HENRI WAS WAITING AT his usual spot at the zinc bar. He was frowning at Yesim but broke into a wide smile when he saw Max come in the bar. *He has news.*

Josette placed a plate of pastries in front of him while Yesim prepared a café au lait. The late breakfast was welcome and Max bit into a fresh croissant as he nodded for Henri to report.

"Eat first, work later is an excellent way to live. I'll save the best until Gaston arrives. After all, he did most of the leg work. However, I do have news on the stolen cognac."

"Cognac wasn't the only thing that was stolen."

"No, but it was the most important, and the most valuable, thing. It was, as you expected an inside job. The assistant manager's wife had recently had twins and the man had been refused a raise to help with the unexpected expense. He was, understandably, bitter."

"He could have looked for a better job."

"And, now, the poor man is. The manager was unhappy to let him go—he was a hard worker and, previously, honest to a fault—but the owner of the warehouse insisted.

"Regardless, I was able to trace the stolen goods and all have been recovered except for the cognac. I thought it was a lost cause, until I was making arrangements for Mme Miller to stay at a friend's house.

We chatted, I mentioned what I was doing now and he told me that a friend of a friend told him that the port was doing a brisk business sending French liquor to America. All below board, as they say.

With that lead, I was able to find which ship was to carry the illicit goods and, you will never guess—"

"It's the one Helen Miller is taking."

Henri laughed. "That's why you're the boss. Always one step ahead of the hired hands."

Miller had been truthful about Minter not being a friend but what about business partner?

Gaston had made his entrance while Henri was talking and now piped in. "The taxi stopped a few blocks from the train station and the lady got out and went to talk to a man on the steps of a small hotel. He was the one Henri described to me. Alec Minter. She didn't seem all that happy to see him especially when he tried to kiss her. He laughed and handed her an envelope which she put in her purse. He said something too but it was in English so..." He shrugged. "She got back in the cab and continued onto the station. I stayed until she boarded her train but nothing else happened."

Max nodded. Minter had arranged the theft, probably at the behest of his Italian friends in New York. According to Harvey, gangsters were satisfying America's thirst and fine French cognac would fetch a premium price. The cases would likely be included in Miller's luggage. Minter wasn't the only one who would do whatever it took for money—money that was almost certainly going to flow into the coffers of the Socialist Party of America. Max had no grudge against Miller and her party; the socialists were no better or worse than any of the rest. But he had a duty to his client to recover his stolen property. He would send a messenger to Buchan and let him deal with the port authorities and the two conspirators as he saw fit, provided the cognac was returned.

"The man of the hour has arrived," said Henri,

Gaston blushed, smiled and then blushed some more.

"I take it you have something that will get your cousin out of jail." Max glanced at Henri who couldn't have looked prouder than if Gaston were his own son.

Gaston nodded and looked at Henri.

"The neighbours clammed up when I asked them questions. Said I looked like a police informer."

"I can see that," said Yesim, from behind the bar, ducking when Henri mimed throwing his glass at him.

"But Gaston was another thing. Maybe it's that innocent expression he's so good at presenting."

The young man looked at Henri with eyes wide and lips slightly parted.

"That's the one! In any case, Gaston thought one of neighbours was being less than open and went back to speak to her on his own. Sure enough, in five minutes, she spilled the beans. She had been woken up by yelling from across the alleyway. She saw a man come down a fire escape, and another standing in the window yelling after him. Alain must have paused under a street lamp because she was able to give an adequate description."

"Is she willing to repeat that to the police?"

"Better than that," said Gaston. He removed a thick envelope from the inside pocket of his jacket and passed it to Max.

"Three signed testimonials will be more than enough to free Alain," said Henri.

"Three?"

"No-one else saw or heard the fight between Alain and Dupont. But then Gaston got the clever idea of tracking down people who might be in the streets early in the morning. Street cleaners, taxi drivers, delivery men. It took a while to track them down which is why we are so late in reporting.

"A garbage man was clearing out some bins when he heard some yelling from a second-floor apartment, some time after the first witness saw Alain leave. When I asked him which one, he pointed out Dupont's place. He didn't see the fight but he heard the yelling, which ended, he said, in a blood-curdling scream."

"Why didn't he go to the police?"

"He said it never occurred to him. It wasn't unusual to hear people fighting, usually married couples, and nothing suggested actual violence. Still, he was happy to sign a statement which we both witnessed."

"And the third?"

Henri gestured to Gaston.

"Henri said we should save the best for last. A taxi driver had dropped his last fare a block away when a man came running out of Dupont's building and tried to hail him. He was going to keep going but the fellow practically threw himself in front of the cab. He clambered in and gave an address in the 13th. The driver was still reluctant but a hundred franc note thrown on the seat persuaded him."

"Why is this important?"

"First, the garbage man remembered seeing a cab stop just after the yelling stopped, Second, the driver described the man as large, with a heavy beard and crooked teeth, speaking with a foreign accent. Third, when he glanced in the mirror at his passenger, he saw him cleaning blood off his hands with a large handkerchief. The driver said he was terrified and broke speed records in getting him to his destination."

Both Henri and Gaston looked extremely satisfied and even Yesim was expending one of his rare supply of smiles. And why not? The unlikely couple had done excellent detective work and deserved to see the results of their efforts.

"I think it's time the three of us delivered these to the Prefecture. I am sure Captain Fontaine will be thrilled to hear your report."

As it turned out, Fontaine wasn't in his office; he was giving evidence at Alain's hastily arranged initial hearing. Max would have paid money for the expression on Fontaine's face when LePêcheur interrupted his testimony with a quiet whisper in his ear and gestured toward Max standing at the back of the court with Henri and Gaston at his side.

"This had better to be good." Fontaine had begged the indulgence of the magistrate and dragged them into the outer hall. Max handed the envelope to the police captain and watched as his eyes narrowed and his mouth quivered beneath his mustache with each page he read.

"Who is this bearded foreigner?" Max knew that Fontaine had little use for foreigners in his city. Not his business, he often said. The statements would win Alain his freedom but was unlikely to lead to justice for Dupont or Gladstone.

"His name is Volodin, though he also goes by Rubenstein. He is an agent for the Soviet secret police. Dupont was either working for him or trying to sell him the stolen plans. They must have had a falling out and Volodin killed him"

"That's for a court of law to decide. Police, and especially private detectives, do not decide guilt or innocence. We only present the evidence and let the magistrates decide. But, in deference to our friendship, I will assign a constable to search for this man. Pepin is new, but reliable."

Max supressed a snort. This sudden deference to due process was a bit rich coming from Fontaine. As for their friendship, it was an off and on affair. Mostly off.

"This evidence shows that, whoever killed Dupont, it wasn't Alain Laurent."

"Yes, of course, I will have him released at once."

True to his word, Fontaine spoke to the magistrate who frowned and said something back that caused the back of Fontaine's neck to flush. Alain's manacles were unlocked and, still rubbing his wrists, he walked out of the court into the welcoming embrace of his cousin, Gaston.

"What's for lunch?" he asked. "I'm starving."

AFTER LUNCH, MAX RELEASED the others from their duties and invited them to join him at Chez Jake for supper at 8. Mondays were a quiet night at the club, with music provided by some of the staff and a few visiting players. He recovered the plans, as well as the various models the police had liberated from the locked wardrobe and took a taxi to the factory where Duvalier greeted him with a mixture of pleasure and sadness.

"I'm sorry to hear that Dupont was a thief and even sorrier to hear that his actions probably led to his death. He was a decent engineer and generally was well liked around the plant. I'll take up a collection to cover his funeral expenses and send any remainder to his sister in Lyon. I believe he supported her and her daughter; her husband was killed in the war."

"That's kind of you, given the circumstances."

"In the end, he did us no damage. Andre says the plans and prototypes are intact so I assume they were not passed on to our competitors."

"Yes. It appears he had been recruited by an agent of the new Soviet government. They had a falling out before their business was complete. Before Dupont could find another buyer, the agent killed Dupont."

"That's that then. I can stop worrying and get back to making automobiles. Can I write you a cheque?"

"I will submit a final written report with a final invoice to keep my bookkeeper happy. I should tell you that in the course of investigation we obtained reports on everyone who could have been involved in the theft. They all come out without a blemish, except your younger brother—"

"Has a gambling habit. Did you by any chance discover the nature of his system?"

"Only that it appears to work."

"Yes. Eventually the track owner will figure out he has a system and bar him for life. But there are plenty of other horse tracks in France."

Max smiled at Duvalier's indulgent tone. He thought of his brother Ben, whom he had had little contact with since he had joined the war. Sometimes, he thought he should return to Nova Scotia to see him, but no, his life was here now.

"I have a final question for you about Dupont. He had lunch a few times with Walter Gladstone, a young American who was murdered in Montsourris park? Did he ever speak of him? Did you meet him?"

Duvalier shook his head sadly. "This is the first I heard of it. Did Dupont commit that crime, too?"

"He was one of my prime suspects but now I don't think he was the murderer though he may have inadvertently led the killer to him."

Duvalier extended his hand and Max shook it. "I am relieved. I can bring myself to forgive a thief but not a killer. Thank you for your work, Max. You can be sure that if a friend or colleague needs a detective, I'll refer them to you." Duvalier sealed the promise with the traditional bise.

"I appreciate that. But, please, I don't do divorce work."

THE CELEBRATION AT Chez Jake was even bigger than Max expected. Yesim had closed the bar and he and Josette had come to celebrate Alain's release and Henri's success in his new job. Hugo, was there as well, with a slim brunette on his arm that he introduced as Chantal, a nurse at the hospital where he worked part-time.

The biggest surprise was the appearance of Jake Sullivan who had returned early from London, arriving on the afternoon train. As soon as he had heard of Max's plans to celebrate Alain's release, he brought in some extra staff "to do it up right." A trio, who had accompanied him from London to start a two-week engagement later in the week, was persuaded to put off their planned sightseeing to play the first set of the evening.

The kitchen outdid itself in preparing the three-course meal, starting with a saffron-infused mussel soup, followed by veal medallions in a cream sauce with a medley of spring vegetables and finished with chestnut cake in chocolate sauce. The wine selections brought up from the cellar by Smitty, who served both as bouncer and sommelier, were exquisite.

After the plates had been cleared and the house band had started the second set, Jake slid into the seat next to Max.

"I came home with big ideas, Max."

"How much are these ideas going to cost?"

"A better question is how much money are they going to make. And the answer to both is not much and a lot. Paris is hosting the Olympic Games next year; there will be athletes and spectators from all around the world. This being France and all, there will be a cultural component and I want us to hold a jazz festival as part of it."

"How do we do that?"

"We need to be there first and we need a track record, if you don't mind the pun. We'll need to hold a small festival this year, say early in September, five or six acts here and in a couple of other venues, one in Montparnasse and one outside at a nice park with a bandstand. I've got a list of contacts but I wanted to make sure you approved."

"You don't need my approval. This is your club, Jake."

"Sure, but it would still be a small-time operation if you hadn't stepped up and invested in it."

"I've gotten back every sou with interest, but... if you want my approval, I give it whole-heartedly and without reservation. If you need some money upfront, you know I'm good for it."

"Max you are the best partner a man ever had." He glanced over at Jacqui who was leaning against Henri and laughing at one of his jokes. "I bet the best one a woman ever had too."

"I don't know—"

"Well, I do and Jacqui does. So, keep up the good work."

"I'll try." All the cases were solved, except for the capture of the murderer of Walter Gladstone and the mystery of the missing Corporal Gidot. Tomorrow, he would find a way to track down Volodin. The man might have already left Paris but Max didn't think so. He had, as Pavlovna had said, gone to ground. But someone knew where he was. And soon so would he.

Chapter 19 Tuesday, May 22nd to Thursday, May 24th 1923

M ax went to the Grand Guignol a couple hours after lunch on Tuesday. No one would be there earlier than that, according to Hugo who continued to enjoy his shifts there. He needed all the money he could make, he had said, as he planned to ask Chantal to marry him before summer arrived.

He was looking for Yelena but found Carlos Herrerra instead. He was sitting outside the theatre on a bench with his arm around a young woman with dark hair and olive skin.

"Yelena Semenova is back stage," said Hererra, before Max could ask. "I'm sure she'll be thrilled to see you."

Max nodded. Herrera seemed different, calmer, almost peaceful, a far cry from his usually aggressive demeanor.

"This is my fiancée, Francesca Isabella de la Monte Cortes. It was why I returned to Spain. To persuade her to come to live with me permanently in Paris, as soon as we are married, of course. That will occur next month in our home town."

"Malaga?"

"You see, chica, Mr. Anderson is, indeed, a detective."

"Ah," she said, her French heavily accented but understandable. "You suspect my Carlos of killing a man. He told me so."

"I did briefly but no longer. Meeting you confirms I was correct to move on. How could a killer have such a charming fiancée?"

Herrera laughed. "In any case, Francesca was here in Paris on the night in question. We were dining together and spent the evening at Les Follies. I was quiet about it because...well..."

"You were not ready to announce your engagement. I understand entirely."

"Yes, exactly."

Max doubted that his fiancée was unaware of his infidelities but there was something in her expression that told him they had come to an end.

YELENA SEMENOVA WAS in the actors' lounge in the company of the same pair as the last time he had seen her. Without a word, they got up and left, closing the door behind them.

"I was expecting you," she said, gesturing him to take a seat. "Would you care for a drink? There is coffee in the samovar but it is not very good. I have some vodka though nothing to mix with it except water."

"I'm fine."

She shrugged and poured some of the clear liquor into an almost-clean tumbler. "Na Zdorovie!" She drained the glass and then poured another, setting it on her dressing room table.

"Do you know why I've come?"

"To ask me what I know about Nicky Volodin. I read about the murder of Jean Dupont. I knew he was one of Nicky's sleepers and it sounded like his style, a knife in the back before the sun rises."

"You seem to know a lot about Volodin's methods."

"I was one of his properties once. He recruited me when some of my relatives came to Paris."

"You spied on your own family."

"They are my cousins but not my family. I hated the way they looked down on everyone who was not of unsullied lineage, how they treated the men and women who worked the land, treated them as serfs even after they were granted their freedom. I was glad when the Bolsheviks took their lands and titles. I'm only sorry they escaped with their money.

"But Volodin wanted to finish the job. I disliked my relatives but I didn't want them to die."

"How did you escape his clutches?" Max doubted Volodin or his superiors would let an agent simply walk away.

"He is a man. Like most men, he sees what he wants to see. I went to bed with him. It was disgusting but I am a good actress. He was convinced I wanted him, he maybe even thought I loved him. Like every one in Russia these days, he had his secrets. I acquired certain documents. Seen a certain way, and the Cheka always looks at things a certain way, he would appear a traitor. Traitors do not live long in that world. My price for keeping them safe was the safety of myself and my family. If something happens to me, a lawyer will see that the papers reach the proper bureau in Moscow."

"Did Volodin kill Walter Gladstone?"

"I think so, though I don't know why. It was after we parted company. I thought maybe he did it to send me a message, that he could still hurt the ones I loved. Though, of course, I didn't love Walter. And I don't think he loved me either. In many ways, he was a closed book.

"Now I think it had nothing to do with me. I told you that I saw Walter in the park the night he was killed. He told me he was going to meet someone, that he had business to conduct. I told you I thought he was meeting Carlos but that was not true. On my way back to the puppeteers, I saw Volodin, though he didn't see me. He was in the glare of a lamp, deep in conversation with another man. I think it may have been this Dupont, based on the description I read in the paper. In any case, the other man went down the same path Walter had been on. After a few seconds, Volodin followed him."

Max showed her the picture of Dupont that he was still carrying in his jacket. She nodded.

"Why didn't you tell me before?"

"Volodin is a horrible man. I was, I still am, afraid of him. If I went to the police or told you, he might think it was worth the risk of killing me. But now that he has killed again, I think he no longer cares. Maybe he thinks he can find my lawyer. I think... I think you will help me, help me to silence Volodin or at least make sure he leaves Paris for good."

"Do you know where he is?"

"He had two boltholes. I can give you the address of both of them. He may be in neither but it is all I can do."

"What about other 'sleepers?' He was seen twice with a woman, tall, attractive, forty or older."

"Marta Chlebek." Yelena answered without hesitation. "A Polish communist who acts as a courier and sometime bedmate for Volodin. He was always careful to keep her away from the violent side of his business. She may still be in Paris but I doubt she had anything to do with these murders."

"How can you be sure?"

Yelena shrugged and turned away. She drank the second vodka in a single gulp and then wrote the two addresses on a slip of paper. After she gave it to him, she slumped into her chair, her elbows on the dressing table and her face in her hands.

MAX RETURNED TO HIS office and collected his Webley, shoving it into the holster under his arm. For good measure he dropped the Kolb .32 five-shot into his jacket pocket. By the time he got to the first address, located in a small boarding house not far from where Pavlovna lived, it was late, nearly six. A hundred francs gained him admittance to the room Volodin had rented by the month but there was no sign of him there, no clothes in the closet, no food in the small wooden cupboard. If he had been there recently, either the concierge hadn't seen him or wouldn't say.

The second address was in the deep south of the city in one of the banlieues that circled Paris. Nicknamed the Red Belt both for the brick that had been used to construct many of the cheap apartments there and for the politics of its denizens, it would take over an hour and a half to reach. Although it would still be daylight when he arrived, night would not be far off and it was not a place he wanted to be, alone and after dark. He would go early in the morning with Alain and Gaston in tow.

HUGO WAS ALSO AVAILABLE for their early morning assignation; Henri volunteered but Max offered an alternate, though equally essential, job. He was to wait by the phone in Le Coq Bleu, which was closer to Île de la Cité than Chez Jake. Max would find a phone to call him once he was certain Volodin was in residence. Henri would go to the Prefecture and then come with an officer to make the formal arrest. Max had called LePêcheur the previous afternoon and had been assured that both he and Pepin, the constable Fontaine had assigned to the case, would be available. Pepin had not bothered to be in touch but Max knew he could rely on the sergeant. It would take a half hour or more for the police to arrive and Max hoped to have Volodin under control by the time they did.

Max gave his Kolb to Alain but told him to keep it in his pocket unless his life was in danger. Hugo was armed with a switchblade and a pair of brass knuckles but Gaston refused to take any weapon, not even a weighted cane. Max questioned the wisdom of having the young man take part but Gaston assured him he would not be in any danger.

The address was for a small cottage on a quiet back street, surrounded by a low fence on three sides and a higher one at the back. The yellow painted stucco was in need of repair and small tufts of grass grew from breaks in the red tile roof. The yard was untidy but empty save for a badly-leaning shed in the back corner. The windows were curtained though light shone through a gap in one. A thin trail of smoke drifted from the chimney. Some one was there, though whether it was Volodin would require closer inspection.

He sent Alain to cover the rear of the building, where he could watch the back door through gaps in the wooden fence. Hugo was stationed down the street at the front door of a small hotel. A hundred francs had ensured access to the phone and Hugo would call Henri at Max's signal. Max was still considering where to station Gaston when he saw him creeping on his hands and knees toward the dimly lit window. There was nothing he could do now but wait and hope the boy would be safe.

Gaston lifted his head to the edge of the glass and did a quick scan of the room before ducking down again. He gave Max a thumbs up signal and retraced his steps, bent over and running on the return. Max, in turn, waved to Hugo who ducked into the hotel to make the call.

Max knew he should await the arrival of the police but they had done nothing to help with the investigation of Gladstone's murder and little more in the case of Dupont. He had found the killer; he had both the duty and the right to capture him. Drawing his Webley, he approached the front door and finding it unlocked, flung it open.

Two steps brought him to the entrance to the kitchen, where Volodin, dressed only in a loose pair of trousers, was standing at a counter, with a cup of steaming liquid in one hand and a fork in the other. The man was well muscled with a thick mat of hair covering his chest and shoulders.

"Put your hands on your head!" Max yelled, pointing the revolver at Volodin.

Without hesitation, Volodin hurled the cup at Max.

His aim was excellent and Max had to duck out of the way to avoid being hit in the head. Even so, he felt the sting of the hot coffee against his skin.

The cup was followed by the fork and then a plate full of scrambled eggs and sausages. Neither struck their target but by the time Max recovered his balance, Volodin had crossed the room, a long thin blade clutched in his right hand.

Before Max could bring his pistol to bear, Volodin slammed into him, thrusting the knife at his eye. Max twisted so the blade only flashed by his face, nicking his ear as it passed. The Russian followed with a vicious left hook and caught Max on the jaw and sent him tumbling to the floor.

Then, Volodin was past him, heading to the front door, with only Gaston between him and freedom. Max squeezed off a shot, thunderously loud in the small room and his vision was clouded by the acrid smoke from the barrel. He staggered to his feet; he had missed. Volodin had made his escape.

As he reached the open door, the sound of Russian curses assaulted his ears. Volodin was lying in the street, entangled in a weighted fishing net, which wrapped him tighter the more he struggled against it. Gaston had kicked the knife from his hand, and was standing over him, tugging on a pair of ropes to close the loop of the net. Alain came bursting through the house, the Kolb in his hand. Hugo ran up a few moments later.

"My dear cousin, you caught the big one that got away," said Alain, clapping the lad on the shoulder.

"I was working repairing nets yesterday when I got your message and I thought it might come in handy."

By the time LePêcheur arrived in a Black Maria, along with Henri, Pepin and two other swallows, Volodin had ceased cursing, refusing to answer questions or even look at his captors. Max suspected he was embarrassed to be caught in a fisherman's net, gape-mouthed like an enormous perch.

"Nice catch, Max. Perhaps I should add a net to my arsenal as befits my name," said LePêcheur. He handed Max his handkerchief to press against the small wound on his left ear.

"Gaston landed this one, but you can put him on ice."

"Henri tells me he's a member of the Soviet secret police."

Volodin started to protest his innocence. "These men attacked me, a complete stranger."

"Of course, of course, we'll get it all straightened out down at the Prefecture. If charges are laid, I assure you our courts are nothing if not fair."

"I think we have sufficient evidence to tie him to Dupont's murder. The murder weapon is over there." Max gestured to the knife lying in the street. "I think it was used to kill Gladstone, too,"

"The guillotine is impartial; one murder is as good as two."

Dropping all pretence, Volodin growled. "You will never bring me to trial."

LePecheur nodded sagely and directed the swallows to load him in the police wagon.

VOLODIN'S WORDS PROVED prophetic. When he went to deliver his files on the Gladstone and Dupont cases, he was greeted by Captain Fontaine himself. The man appeared calm but Max could see the tension in his shoulders.

"What have you gotten yourself involved in, Anderson? More important, what have you gotten me into?"

"What's happened?"

"Early this morning, a senior officer from the Gendarmeries came and took possession of my prisoner. It was... humiliating."

The Gendarmeries were the military police whose orders took precedence over anything the Prefecture of Police might be involved in. Captain Fontaine might be humiliated but there was nothing he could do about it.

"Will there be a trial?"

"If there is, neither you nor I will hear the outcome. But I can assure you, this Volodin will never commit a crime on French soil again."

That would be that. Max had done the best he could to find justice for Gladstone but, in the end, it was out of his hands. The murderer was dealt with but whether he would be executed, imprisoned or sent back to Moscow, he would never know. Perhaps it was better that way. Neither of the victims were who they said they were, nor, in fact, were most of the others he had met in the course of the investigation. Enigmas, all.

Leaving the Prefecture, he walked along the Seine toward the Louvre. It was cool and showery but the walk was pleasant and the heart of the city, beautiful. He had stopped to gaze at some of the hundreds of stone masks that decorated the inaptly named Pont Neuf, the oldest bridge crossing the Seine, when a familiar voice called his name.

Max hardly recognized Andre Bucard, the former leader of the Black Fist. His hair was unkempt and had turned grey in the year since he had seen him last. His usual erect form was stooped and he leaned heavily on an ornate cane.

"Monsieur Bucard, you look—"

"I look awful. No need to sugar coat it. Country life and retirement do not suit me. If you want my advice, never accept it. I've been ill and, worse yet, I've been idle. I came to the city to see my nephew but he is too important now to bother even to speak to me."

"I've always been happy to speak to you."

"You've always been happy to accuse me of murder. I missed that—always proving you wrong. You look... satisfied."

"Appearances can be deceiving but, for the most part, I feel I have everything I need in life."

"Oh, to be, what is it, twenty-eight or nine?

"I turn thirty on Sunday."

"I will be out of the city by then, but I hope you have a happy one. Here, let me give you an early present." Bucard held out the cane.

"I can't accept. Surely you need—"

Bucard straightened. "As you say, appearances can be deceiving. I'm not as spent as I would like some to believe. But I do not see myself needing this particular cane again." He touched a button on the head and showed Max a shaft of steel concealed within the stick. "Please take it."

"Are you sure?"

"Take it."

Max believed that on the third offer, it was only polite to accept a gift. He bowed slightly and accepted the hidden sword.

"Are you happy, Max?"

"I am. I have Jacqui and my friends. I have work worth doing and money to spend. What more can a man want?"

"The respect of your family."

Max's family was all in Paris now. He would never return to Canada. He was sure of that; everyone there had forgotten him.

"Sure you have no murders left unsolved to blame on me?" Bucard chuckled and Max joined him.

"The only thing left is to find a good Samaritan and return him to his home." Max had almost forgotten Gibot but the conversation with Bucard reminded him of the duty he had still to carry out.

Bucard turned to go but Max stopped him with a gentle touch. "Here is my card. Call me the next time you're in Paris and I'll buy you lunch."

Bucard tucked the card into his waistcoat. "I look forward to it."

Chapter 20 Sunday, May 27th 1923

Max woke late on Sunday morning. The curtains were drawn but he could sense the bright sunlight beyond them. Jacqui was busy in the kitchen, singing and preparing him a special birthday breakfast.

He had been busy in the two days since his chance encounter with Bucard, going from hospital to hospital in search of Corporal Jacques Gibot. He had found rumours of the secret visitor everywhere he went but it took a call from Hugo to come at once to Les Invalides that led him to find the man himself.

"I survived four years of war, saw combat many times and never sustained so much as a scratch," he had said. "So many of my comrades died, some right beside me. Many more sustained terrible injuries and, look at me." He opened his shirt to show unblemished skin. "I yearned to go home to be reunited with my parents, to take up my place in the shop and return to normal.

"But it's not normal, is it? Can it ever be normal? War fractures everything. For all the talk of glory and patriotism, it is the evilest act one man can commit against another."

"Soldiers must do their duty even if it means other men die."

"You don't believe that platitude and neither do I. To kill is a sin and to kill, not out of anger or injury, but to fulfill the ambitions of men who never set foot in a trench, it is an abomination. I took part in it, I volunteered as soon as the call came, but after..." Gibot's face twisted in pain but he shed no tears. "A friend from the village had suffered grievous, terrible wounds, both legs gone and his face a hideous jumble. I went to visit him and he died in my arms, but the last thing he said to me was: 'Thank you, no one else would come.' He had been abandoned by comrades and family, too horrified by what remained of him to do what was right.

"I determined that no soldier should die alone, without the comfort of knowing that someone cared. I visited the worst of the wards, told stories and jokes, sometimes we sang together, sometimes laughed, sometimes prayed. I always told them to visit me when they were well enough, knowing that none would ever leave the hospital."

"But you're wrong," Max said. "Your visit made all the difference. For some, it meant they could die in peace but for many more it gave them the strength to fight on. They recovered the will to live, returned to their homes and their families. One, Albert Braque, even came to see you and brought your parents the happy news that you were well. You've done your duty, Jacques, it is time to go home."

Now the tears came. Gibot had collapsed in his arms, his chest heaving and his arms shaking as he let down the burden it was never his to bear. When he settled, Max helped him take his few belongings to the station and watched him board the train to return home. He sent a brief telegram to Gibot's father to meet him at the train.

It had been a happy end to his thirtieth year and today he would embark on his thirty-first. He showered and shaved and dressed in his best clothes. The wound on his ear had largely healed and he discarded the bandage. Jacqui had laid out a sumptuous breakfast, A Canadian breakfast she declared as she spread it out before him.

A stack of mishappen pancakes was topped with a fried egg and surrounded by rashers of bacon, thick pork sausages and baked beans. A bowl of fresh berries covered in cream was set to one side, along with a large glass of orange juice, slices of toasted bread and a steaming mug of coffee.

"No one at the market had ever heard of maple syrup so I have substituted honey instead."

"It's amazing. But how did you know what to make?" As far as he could recall he had never described the special breakfasts his mother had served him when he was a boy, yet here it was.

"I have my ways," Jacqui said. "I have two surprises for you. The first I will give you now while it is only the two of us. The other must wait until the party tonight."

"I said I didn't want a party."

"Ha! I could easier stop the rain from falling and the grass from growing than to stop Henri and Yesim from celebrating your birthday."

Despite their shape the pancakes tasted exactly as he remembered, though the honey was only an adequate substitute for the sweet flavor of maple. He did his best, with Jacqui barely touching the food on her plate, but even he couldn't finish the enormous feast she had prepared.

"Tell me, what is this surprise?"

"You may have guessed."

I may have. Max kept his face still.

"I wanted to tell you before. I was sure you would have figured it out. Everyone else did and had to be sworn to secrecy."

"Everyone?"

"No, Henri and some of the woman at work. But mostly Henri. He was bursting."

"I'm bursting." He gestured at the remains of the meal.

"Well, I think we need a bigger apartment. Not right away but soon."

"Jacqui?"

"I... you... we are going to be parents."

He had known but he hadn't known. He had hoped but he was afraid. All of it must have shown on his face at once.

Jacqui put her hand to her mouth and her eyes glistened. "I had hoped you would—"

What ever she had hoped was cut off by Max's whoop of joy. He swept her up in his arms and twirled them both around the apartment until they were both dizzy, finishing by collapsing on the bed in a tangle of limbs.

"Yesterday," he said. "I thought I was happy, had all a man could want from his life. I was a fool. I had no idea what real happiness was. Thank you, thank you, my darling wife."

"Yes, I am your wife though you must never say so in public. My anarchist friends would be appalled."

JACQUI HAD MORE THAN a few surprises in mind as the day unfolded including walks in his two favorite parks, the Luxemburg Gardens and Parc Monceau, where they surprised local children by joining them on the carousel. Lunch was at the Café de la Paix near the Opera House. Jacqui only ordered a salad—"they tell me my appetite will return, soon, I hope"—but Max treated himself to the traditional onion soup, rich and dark and topped with smoky compté cheese, and a grilled Corsican sea bass with a confit of zucchini, tomato and basil.

The day finished with a visit to the grave of his friend and mentor, Havel Barzani. Jacqui wandered through the Montmartre cemetery while Max stood over the grave and told his friend all that happened in the months since his last visit. "I am happier than I ever thought I could be. The road to that happiness opened for me on the day we met."

The day ended, as promised, at Le Coq Bleu, decorated with streamers and candles and a gathering of his closest friends. Henri and Yesim had arranged an open buffet so that everyone could eat as much or as little as they liked. They were serving drinks behind the bar while Jake had brought a piano from Chez Jake and he played while Smitty sang songs in both English and French. All his operatives—Alain, Hugo, Gaston and Roget—were in attendance, each with a woman on his arm. LePêcheur was there to represent the Prefecture. Even Hemingway and his wife Hadley attended, bringing regrets and birthday greetings from Stein.

Presents were given and opened, books from Henri, of course and a splendid new dark blue fedora from Yesim, smaller but equally thoughtful tokens from the rest.

When Josette appeared with a birthday cake, ablaze with thirty candles, Jacqui raised her hand. "Wait, I have one more surprise for you. Meet the source of my breakfast advice."

A man stepped from the doorway to the kitchen.

"Hello, Max."

He hardly recognized the boy he had left behind now become a man.

"Ben? How?"

"It's a long story but it can wait until later. Tonight is your night."

"Ladies and gentlemen," Ben said in halting French. "Raise your glasses to Maxwell Michael Anderson, my brother."

The End

Don't miss out!

Visit the website below and you can sign up to receive emails whenever Hayden Trenholm publishes a new book. There's no charge and no obligation.

https://books2read.com/r/B-A-ZSKO-GPFOF

BOOKS 2 READ

Connecting independent readers to independent writers.

About the Author

Hayden Trenholm is an award-winning playwright, novelist and short story writer. His short fiction has appeared in many magazines, including Analog Science Fiction and Fact, and anthologies such as The Sum of Us and Strangers Among Us, and on CBC radio. His first novel, <u>A Circle of Birds</u>, won the 3-Day Novel Writing competition in 1993; it was recently translated and published in French. His trilogy, *The Steele Chronicles*, were each nominated for an Aurora Award. <u>Stealing Home</u>, the third book, was a finalist for the Sunburst Award. Hayden has won five Aurora Awards – three times for short fiction and twice for editing anthologies. He purchased Bundoran Press in 2012 and was its managing editor until the press closed in 2020. He lives with his wife and fellow writer, Liz Westbrook-Trenholm, in Ottawa.

Read more at https://www.haydentrenholm.com/.

About the Publisher

House of Straw is an Ottawa based publisher of mysteries and other genre books.

www.ingramcontent.com/pod-product-compliance
Lightning Source LLC
Chambersburg PA
CBHW022009010726
47494CB00003B/966